Acclaim for Janice Maynard

"Spicy, sweet success." —*Romantic Times*

"Sizzling heat and a creative story line." —Romance Reviews Today

"Readers will be caught up in the story from page one." —Love Romances

"The plot is carefully crafted, characters fully developed, and the level of writing is superb." —A Romance Review

"Janice Maynard did a great job with this story, and I'll definitely be looking for more of her work." —Fallen Angel Reviews

Raves for *Play with Me*

"For the reader looking for hot, explicit sensuality, with tons of happy endings and good character development, *Play with Me* delivers." —Two Lips Reviews

"Passion + Fun = *Play with Me!*" —Erin McCarthy

Praise for *Suite Fantasy*

"All three novellas feature likeable characters in sensuous scenarios. What sets Maynard's work apart from others in this genre is that she develops her characters and plot lines to the extent that the reader cares about what happens outside of the bedroom as well as within it." —*Romantic Times*

"Heated and passionate." —The Best Reviews

Improper
ETIQUETTE

Janice Maynard

A SIGNET ECLIPSE BOOK

SIGNET ECLIPSE
Published by New American Library, a division of
Penguin Group (USA) Inc., 375 Hudson Street,
New York, New York 10014, USA
Penguin Group (Canada), 90 Eglinton Avenue East, Suite 700, Toronto,
Ontario M4P 2Y3, Canada (a division of Pearson Penguin Canada Inc.)
Penguin Books Ltd., 80 Strand, London WC2R 0RL, England
Penguin Ireland, 25 St. Stephen's Green, Dublin 2,
Ireland (a division of Penguin Books Ltd.)
Penguin Group (Australia), 250 Camberwell Road, Camberwell, Victoria 3124,
Australia (a division of Pearson Australia Group Pty. Ltd.)
Penguin Books India Pvt. Ltd., 11 Community Centre, Panchsheel Park,
New Delhi - 110 017, India
Penguin Group (NZ), 67 Apollo Drive, Rosedale, North Shore 0745,
Auckland, New Zealand (a division of Pearson New Zealand Ltd.)
Penguin Books (South Africa) (Pty.) Ltd., 24 Sturdee Avenue,
Rosebank, Johannesburg 2196, South Africa

Penguin Books Ltd., Registered Offices: 80 Strand, London WC2R 0RL, England

First published by Signet Eclipse, an imprint of New American Library,
a division of Penguin Group (USA) Inc.

First Printing, July 2007
10   9   8   7   6   5   4   3   2   1

SIGNET ECLIPSE and logo are trademarks of Penguin Group (USA) Inc.

LIBRARY OF CONGRESS CATALOGING-IN-PUBLICATION DATA:
Maynard, Janice.
    Improper Etiquette / Janice Maynard.
        p. cm.
    ISBN: 978-0-451-22148-3
    I. Title.
PS3613.A958I47 2007
    813'.6—dc22   2006037518

Set in Berkeley
Designed by Spring Hoteling

Printed in the United States of America

For the Scamps and Vamps—you know who you are! Thanks, ladies (and gents), for the laughter, the daily fun, and the support for all our books. You guys are the best.

And a special hug to Judy F., Laurie, and Stacy . . . your friendship means a lot!

And to Emily—whose creative brain came up with the fun title. ☺

I must be candid, dear friends . . . we live in a man's world. But an intelligent and resourceful female can gently lead the male of the species in a desired direction. Men are simple creatures. Their needs are few . . . food, physical intimacy, and the opportunity to conquer. Keeping these realities in mind, I have put together a volume of advice that may well be invaluable for today's young woman searching for a mate. Follow my instructions (though they might make you blush), and soon you will be able to add that lovely appellation "Mrs." to the front of your name. Good luck, and happy hunting . . .

(Excerpted from *Miss Matilda's Guide to Love and Romance for the Proper Young Lady*—copyright 1949)

Improper
ETIQUETTE

Catering to His Needs

One

Good manners were good manners, plain and simple. Southern girls learned that from the cradle and ignored it at their peril. If the gentleman living next door had been eighty-five, deaf as a post, and crotchety, Francesca Fremont *still* would have taken him a plate of homemade dessert. But the fact that her new neighbor was well over six feet tall and fiercely gorgeous made the whole "welcome to town" overture much more fun and intriguing.

She smoothed plastic wrap over the mound of freshly baked cinnamon rolls and eyed the plate with satisfaction. It was part of her grandmother's wedding china, and she had even added a lacy paper doily that nicely accented the old-fashioned floral pattern.

Some people might balk at the idea of using heirloom dishes for such a purpose, but Francesca was a firm believer in the "use it or lose it" philosophy. Lovely things shouldn't be tucked away in drawers and cabinets. They deserved to be used and appreciated every day.

She set the plate on the table and dashed to her bedroom for a quick peek in the mirror. When she was baking, she tended to ignore her appearance, and today she wanted to look presentable. Not that her faded denim jeans and yellow tank top were going to win any fashion awards, but at least they weren't splotched with flour.

Her face was flushed from the heat in the kitchen. Her old window-unit air conditioners weren't very efficient, and when it was really hot, she sometimes opened all the windows in the house and relied on ceiling fans for circulation. She slicked a bit of gloss over her lips and ran a brush through her hair. That would have to do.

She retrieved the plate of goodies and set off across the yard. The piquant scent of honeysuckle hung on the early morning breeze. There wasn't a cloud in the sky, and the earth seemed verdant and teeming with life. The temperature was pleasant now, but by midafternoon the heat would be scorching.

Her property and her neighbor's had once upon a time been a small farm. Back in the 1930s, the old farmer had split the land right down the middle and given half to his son and new daughter-in-law.

Out at the road the entrances to the two long, winding driveways were at least a quarter of a mile apart, but the two homesteads actually sat near the middle of the original plot quite close together. They were separated by a large, mature screen of English boxwoods, but a narrow, well-worn rut in the dirt between two sections attested to the fact that the families had visited back and forth frequently.

Sadly, the young couple had been unable to have children. With no more descendants in line to inherit in the late eighties, the property began to change hands, and Francesca had been lucky enough to buy her portion several years back.

She slipped through the hedge and stopped abruptly. The neglected, run-down house, its design a mirror image of her own, was as dilapidated as ever, but its dismal appearance barely merited a glance. Her attention was firmly focused on the new homeowner, who at the moment was perched atop a rickety wooden ladder cleaning out his gutters.

He was bare from the waist up, and the muscles in his arms and chest flexed and rippled as he worked, making her knees weak. His iPod was tucked in his back pocket, and the jeans he had on looked like they had come straight from the department store. There was still a crease in the crisp, dark denim.

For some reason she doubted he was the kind of man who usually did his own home maintenance. Not that he wasn't capable. He was physically imposing, his masculine strength and power clearly evident. But she'd encountered him in town two days ago, and she was pretty sure that the man she'd seen at the bank was the real persona.

That day he'd been wearing a suit that probably cost more than her eight-year-old car, and it didn't take the New York plates on his Lexus and his clipped New England accent to convince her that he didn't belong in Camron, Tennessee. It was like seeing a shark in a freshwater creek. It just didn't add up.

Camron was only forty-five minutes from Knoxville, a university city with cultural opportunities and shopping and entertainment. But despite that proximity, her sleepy little town was decidedly rural. Everyone knew his or her neighbors, and newcomers were automatically suspect, particularly if they hailed from north of the Mason-Dixon line.

If this man planned to stick around, he'd have to develop a

thick skin. He was clearly out of his element. And as his closest neighbor, it was up to her to ensure that he felt welcome.

She cleared her throat. "Good morning."

He didn't acknowledge her presence, and she realized that with earplugs in place he couldn't hear her over his music. She sighed, feeling self-conscious. In spite of herself, her gaze drifted to his taut butt. It would be a yummy handful for a woman intent on carnal pursuits. She hadn't seen a nicer one in longer than she cared to remember.

Good gravy. She had to get a handle on her hormones. At the moment, she was reluctantly (and, please God, temporarily) celibate. Which made it difficult to view her neighbor with dispassionate courtesy.

She noted with appreciation his sculpted features and strong nose. His dark hair gleamed black as shiny coal in the morning sun, and his olive-toned skin was naturally tanned. Despite her Italian-sounding name, she'd inherited her Scottish ancestors' fair skin, blue eyes, and strawberry blond hair. She was envious of his ability to labor in the blazing sun with impunity.

The paragon of male beauty continued working, his broad, long-fingered hands covered in black muck. They were big hands, and they moved purposefully. She tried again, a little louder: "Good morning." When that produced no results, she yelled: *"Good morning!"*

As soon as the words left her mouth, she realized her mistake. He jerked in shock as her greeting finally pierced his music-induced deafness, and as he did, the ladder tipped backward. He grabbed for the edge of the roof and got a grip, but the ancient gutter pulled loose with an agonizing screech, and he tumbled several feet into the wildly out-of-control rosebushes below.

Francesca darted forward and then froze as a stream of profanity emanated from the still-quivering greenery. She knew from experience that the thorns were lethal, and she winced in sympathy as he struggled to his feet.

His scowl, when he finally stood up, was black enough to send a brave man scurrying, but her shaking legs didn't seem to be getting the message from her brain.

"I am *so* sorry," she whispered, her stomach in a knot. The skin of his beautiful torso and arms was covered with scratches that oozed blood. His jaw was granite, his piercing eyes shards of obsidian. She clutched the plate to her chest as though expecting to be protected from his wrath by carbs and sugar. She swallowed hard, her throat dry. "I didn't mean to startle you."

She saw his chest rise and fall as he inhaled and expelled a mighty breath. He started to rake the hair from his forehead and stopped abruptly, realizing that his hands were filthy. After a visible effort to control his temper, he spoke with remarkable control. "May I help you?"

She licked her lips, her heart pounding in her chest. "I'm your neighbor, Francesca Fremont. I brought you some sticky buns."

His lips quirked, and for a moment she thought she saw a lick of humor cross his stoic face. But it was gone in an instant, and his eyes narrowed. "Sticky buns?"

She nodded jerkily, like one of those silly bobblehead dolls on people's dashboards. "Yes. They're homemade. And still warm. I think," she amended hastily. In all the hullabaloo, she wasn't sure exactly how long she'd been standing there.

She held out the plate. "Welcome to Camron." It was a far briefer greeting than she had intended, but she'd totally lost her train of thought.

Still he made no move to take the food from her. Her arms began to get tired, and she felt ridiculously humiliated, even though he'd been the one to tumble in an undignified heap into the bushes.

When she was embarrassed, she tended to get mad. She frowned. "It's dessert, not a bomb." She was going for sarcasm, but he didn't appear to notice. In fact, he seemed to be ignoring her as much as possible.

He looked back up at the roof, where the gutter now hung drunkenly. He sighed, and it wasn't a pleasant sound, not at all. His arms hung by his sides. She had no trouble gathering from his expression that he was clearly anxious to get inside and clean up the blood and the grime. His impatience was a living, breathing entity.

She scuttled forward and laid the plate at his feet like a clumsy geisha. "They're good," she insisted, beginning to panic at his overly long silence. "And the calories shouldn't matter to you. You could stand to gain a few pounds. Not that you don't look good. You do, of course. Really good. Not that I'm look-ing . . . I just meant it in a general, healthy way."

Now he looked poleaxed, as though he'd come face-to-face with a rabid bobcat and didn't know quite what to do. She felt her face redden, heat creeping up her neck.

She wrapped her arms around her waist. "I'll go now. Let you get back to work. Sorry again."

She backed toward the hedge, and finally he spoke. At the bank two days before, she'd heard him murmur no more than a couple of terse sentences to the teller.

Now that they were this close, his voice slid over her raw nerves like a deep, rich bass sonata. "Wait."

She sensed his reluctance. Saw it on his face.

He sighed again. "I appreciate the gesture," he said with careful formality. "But I should tell you that I came here to be alone. I won't be socializing. I hope you understand."

She gazed at him blankly as the carefully worded rebuff sank in. Then her poor cheeks flamed even hotter. *Wow. Rejection via Emily Post.* His careful enunciation and courtesy almost took the sting out of the content. Almost, but not quite.

She lifted her chin. Most people were delighted to get a culinary gift from Francesca. Clearly he wasn't one of them. But damned if she was going to retrieve her offering. She'd give up one of her grandmother's precious plates permanently before she would ever set foot through that darned hedge again.

She turned to walk away, quite unable to think of a suitable response. Then she stopped. The devil should have a name. She managed to meet his impassive gaze, but it took guts. "Around here it's polite to reciprocate when someone introduces herself."

His jaw tightened a fraction more, and for the briefest second she could have sworn she saw pain in his eyes. "Brett Gilman," he said, the three syllables clipped and cold.

She frowned, trying to remember why that sounded familiar.

His scowl returned with a vengeance. "Feel free to Google me," he growled. "I'm sure you'll find out everything you need to know."

Brett watched his pretty neighbor escape through the hedge, and he let rip with another string of heartfelt oaths. Would it ever end? He'd come to the backwoods of Tennessee to get away from all the hell he'd endured for the past six months, and from the look on Francesca's face, even Tennessee wasn't far enough removed from New York to protect his secrets. The information age was a bitch.

He'd acted like a jerk, so she wouldn't be too surprised when she read about his sins on the Internet. His life was an open book, and the pages had been sullied, perhaps beyond repair.

He tried to shake off his gloomy thoughts and, instead of dwelling on the past, bent to pick up the plate. Though he sure as hell wasn't an expert, it looked like real bone china. He held the edges carefully, grimacing at his filthy hands, and went inside. The smell of cinnamon made his stomach clench in sharp hunger. He'd found to his dismay that except for Paul's Pizza Parlor, takeout was nonexistent in Camron. If he had a craving for pot stickers at one in the morning, he was out of luck. Other than a tiny diner, the Kentucky Fried Chicken franchise was about the only game in town when it came to restaurants.

Also conspicuous in their absence were Starbucks, any kind of public transportation, liquor stores, fitness centers, and major newspapers. He should count himself lucky that the cable company had finally (only six months ago, he'd been told) run the line out his road, or he'd be stuck with dial-up Internet, for god's sake.

He'd been born and bred in Philadelphia, attended Harvard University, and moved to New York City at the ripe old age of twenty-two. At thirty-nine, he felt almost like a native. He missed his adopted city already, but he had to admit that the charms of the country were growing on him, not the least of which was the sexy, attractive woman who had stopped by uninvited to bring him food from the gods.

He washed his hands, poured himself a glass of cold milk, and gobbled down three cinnamon rolls without blinking. They were almost better than sex. He couldn't cook worth a damn, and if he didn't figure out something soon, he'd be stuck eating peanut-butter sandwiches and tasteless frozen dinners indefinitely.

He carefully tucked the plastic wrap around the remaining cinnamon rolls and trudged back outside. The amount of work facing him was daunting, but he welcomed the physical labor. Every drop of sweat seemed cleansing somehow, obliterating even for one small moment in time the memories that kept him awake at night.

He'd purchased the property for an embarrassingly low price, but he'd vastly underestimated the repairs that needed to be made. Though the bungalow-style house was structurally sound, it hadn't received any TLC in years. The loquacious Realtor was eager to share the property's history and pointed out that since the last of the original owner's family died in the late eighties, no buyer afterward had stayed longer than a year or two.

Brett was waiting for a tale about ghosts or similar nonsense, but in reality, most had bought the property with the romantic idea of renovating it, and then when their enthusiasm faded and their pockets emptied, they moved on. It was a money pit.

Brett didn't care. He had money to burn, and nowhere he needed to be. He'd found out in a brutal wake-up call that his true friends could be counted on one hand. As an only child, he had no siblings to stand behind him, and his aging parents were too fragile to lend support, even if he'd asked. So here he was, tucked away in a little corner of the south, not exactly starting over, but perhaps hiding out. It was a hell of a thing for a man to admit.

He had no clue what the upcoming months would bring. He was emotionally and physically at the end of his rope, and if he couldn't find healing and hope here in the shadow of the ancient Great Smoky Mountains, then they probably didn't exist. At least, not for him.

He picked up a hammer and a handful of nails and reposi-tioned the ladder. He had a gutter to fix.

Francesca stared at the computer screen with her stomach churning and her heart crying out in sympathy for the man next door. Now she knew why his name had sounded familiar. MSNBC and CNN had made him a household word, every bit as much as the Enron principals. Brett Gilman had been in-dicted on a series of nasty white-collar charges, put through a very public and brutal trial, and ultimately exonerated of every offense. The only reason the legal proceedings hadn't dragged on any longer was that the culprit, at his wife's urging, had fi-nally made a full confession and put an end to the media circus. Financial restitution would be made a bit at a time, and Brett's partner and best friend was now facing five to ten years in a minimum-security prison.

No wonder her new neighbor's personality was as warm and fuzzy as an injured grizzly's. He'd literally been through hell and back. His company handled major real estate deals in Manhattan and the surrounding environs. The business had foundered on the rocks for a while, but was now stable again. So why was Brett Gilman, CEO, hiding out in Camron, Tennes-see? It didn't make sense.

She fixed herself scrambled eggs and toast for lunch, and after cleaning up the kitchen, she knelt in the corner to prowl through the medium-size cardboard box on the floor beside her refrigerator. It had been sitting there for long enough. She'd been to a yard sale a couple of weeks ago and had bought a mixed lot of old cookbooks.

She collected them, and although she would toss out dupli-cates or any that were too damaged, she usually found at least one or two that were interesting. Pushing disturbing thoughts of

Brett Gilman to the back of her mind, she began rifling through the dusty box and separating the wheat from the chaff.

The Joy of Cooking went into the "donate somewhere else" pile. She'd come across dozens of copies of that classic over the years. She was happy to find a first edition of a Julia Child volume she didn't have. And then her gaze landed on a small leather-bound book that didn't look like a cookbook at all. She turned it over curiously and flipped to the title page. *Miss Matilda's Guide to Love and Romance for the Proper Young Lady*—copyright 1949.

Well, this should be a hoot. It was almost sixty years old. She stretched out her legs and leaned back against the wall to read. Several of the suggestions made her giggle, but she stopped laughing when she hit number thirteen—*The way to a man's heart (or to his bed) is through his stomach.*

It wasn't twenty-first-century advice, to say the least, but something about it had the ring of truth. She skimmed a few pages, automatically storing away Miss Matilda's suggestions for later reflection. Would she be taking advantage of a vulnerable male by offering him food and maybe something more?

Then she laughed softly. Despite Brett's history, he looked like a man who could take care of himself. And besides, good etiquette demanded that she help out a neighbor in need. It was the same code that insisted she deliver a casserole to a grieving family or a full meal to a brand-new mom and dad. Certain things simply made sense. And with Miss Matilda egging her on (probably from beyond the grave), she felt it would only be taking the moral high ground to help Brett out.

If her good manners led to something far more titillating, well . . . Miss Matilda would be proud.

She tossed the unusable books and the dirty box in the garbage can outside and left the three keepers on the kitchen counter. After washing her hands, she flipped through the Julia Child cookbook and found a recipe for braised veal chops and twice-baked potatoes. It wasn't exactly a summer menu, but men seldom worried about niceties like that. They were hungry, and they wanted to eat solid, filling food. The more calories, the better.

Feeling an entirely unjustified sense of anticipation, she made a quick trip to the store, bringing home two bags of carefully selected ingredients. It took no time at all to prepare her special piecrust and fill it with sautéed peaches and cherries. When the pretty latticework top crust was in place, she popped the pie in the oven and went to work on the other menu items.

She really should have been concentrating on her new brochure, the one she hoped would bring in even more business. But she felt a sense of urgency. She wanted to get a meal to her neighbor before he left his house in search of tonight's dinner.

By four p.m. she had everything ready. The appealing food filled two large plastic containers. She wasn't about to risk another of her grandma's plates, and she didn't want her taciturn neighbor to get the impression that she was fishing for another encounter by leaving dishes that would have to be returned.

She carried the food across the lawn and hid momentarily in the shadow of the hedge. If she timed this correctly, he wouldn't get a glimpse of her. He didn't want to socialize, and she would respect his wishes . . . for now. She took a deep breath and sprinted for the front porch.

With shaking hands, she carefully set the containers on his doormat, rang the bell, and ran like hell.

As she got ready for bed later that night, her thoughts returned again and again to her grumpy neighbor. Despite his skin's healthy color, she'd noticed a pallor underneath, and though he was still extremely handsome, she could tell that he had lost weight. He didn't have the look of a naturally skinny man. The hollows at his collarbones told the tale, and the nurturer in her couldn't bear the thought that he might not be eating well. Did he even have a working refrigerator? The most recent time she'd been over there, the derelict appliances had been on their last legs.

She slid beneath the covers, her mind on his broad, lightly hair-dusted chest. She was thirty-two years old, and her love life was just about nonexistent. Surely that explained her fascination with a total stranger. It was hard to meet men in a small town. She'd known most of the guys her age since kindergarten.

The ones who were still unattached were either quietly gay, married and divorced already, or just not her type. And in a town the size of Camron, if you dated a guy for a while and it didn't end well, you were stuck seeing him in uncomfortable situations for a long time afterward. It wasn't really worth the effort.

In high school and college and later during culinary school, she'd dated on and off, but somehow that magical "spark" had eluded her. Her older sister accused her of being too picky. Maybe she was. But she wasn't willing to settle, and she would rather be single than tie herself to a man who wasn't her soul mate.

She was a closet romantic. After all, food was her passion, and food was, at its very core, sensual. The flavors, the textures, the aromas, the colors. Food inspired her, stoked her creative juices. Most of the time that was enough. But tonight she didn't even try to pretend to herself.

She was fascinated and in lust with her new neighbor, a man who had made it abundantly clear that he wanted to be left alone. Her body trembled with a gut-level response to his uncompromising masculinity. She yearned to be held and touched, wanted desperately to see a man look at her with passion and love.

Heck, for the moment, she would settle for passion. She was at her sexual peak, and her fit young body reminded her of that on a frequent basis. She slid her hand between her thighs and touched herself, separating the damp folds and finding the tiny spot that throbbed and quivered. Her fingers moved with gentle, sure motions, bringing her simmering hunger to a full boil.

She closed her eyes and pictured Brett's square jaw, his tight butt, his broad shoulders. Her breath came quickly, and she focused on the memory of his dark, compelling eyes. They had gazed at her with anger and frustration, but strangely enough, the emotion she remembered the most from their brief encounter was pain.

Brett Gilman was hurting, and no amount of baked goods would cure that. In her head she changed his scowl to a warm, welcoming, sexy grin. Ah, that was better. He was kissing her now, his lips firm and purposeful. His hands caressed her body confidently, stroking her sensitive flesh and cupping her aching breasts. They were both naked suddenly, and she felt his thick penis probe insistently between her legs. Her back arched off the bed and she moaned out her climax, even as his hips moved against hers with erotic intent.

Afterward, she felt tears prick the backs of her eyes. The chances of Miss Matilda's advice being on the money were slim to none. Brett Gilman was sophisticated and worldly and had no doubt eaten in any number of five-star restaurants. Francesca had no false modesty about her cooking. She was good.

But it was just food.

For a woman to end up in Brett's bed, there surely had to be something else. And in the erotic-arts department, Francesca was woefully unprepared. The whole situation sucked eggs bigtime. Why should she have to endure knowing that the most beautiful, interesting man she had ever laid eyes on was living right next door and wanted nothing to do with her?

Sometimes life just wasn't fair.

Brett jerked off in the shower that night. Though it was frustrating and ultimately unfulfilling, it was a relief even so. He'd almost begun to believe that his sex drive was dead. He'd been humiliated and scorned and falsely accused, and he had faced losing everything he had worked so hard to build, including his reputation.

Was it any wonder that he'd forgotten about sex in the interim? He'd even resorted to sleeping pills for a short period of time in order to survive, though the weakness had shamed him so much he gave them up after a couple of weeks. Both his mental and physical health had suffered, but he had emerged from his nightmarish ordeal stronger in the end. He'd been tested by fire, as it were, and had a new, though weary, perspective on life.

That was part of the reason he had come to Camron, a tiny spot on the map he'd picked entirely at random. He was strangely unsure of himself at the moment. He'd been given his life back. But he was no longer sure he wanted it. His second in command had run things admirably in his absence during the long, bleak months when Brett had been mapping out his defense with a cadre of lawyers. The hardworking, decent man had been visibly confused when Brett promoted him and then abandoned him.

If Brett could have explained, he would have. But he didn't

even understand it himself. All he knew was that he had a driving compulsion to hide out and lick his wounds. He had to find some measure of peace and closure, and he had to figure out what he wanted.

He washed his hair, running his fingers over his scalp and thinking of pretty Francesca. Poor little thing didn't deserve his boorish behavior. She was curvy and adorable and a damned good cook. He'd been stunned to find a second culinary offering, this time on his porch. He'd pigged out on the mouthwatering food and then sprawled on the sofa with a full belly and the sure knowledge that he had to make amends to his attractive neighbor.

He'd studied her more than he realized during their brief encounter, because he could re-create her memory in living detail. Her skin was pale as cream, and she had a tiny sprinkling of freckles across the bridge of her nose and at her throat. Her short, wavy hair was a pretty mix of gold and red, and her eyes were as blue as the Tennessee sky on a June morning.

She was neither tall nor short, but that was the only average thing about her. Her legs, covered by denim so well washed it was interestingly bare in places, were long and slender. She was not as thin as many of the women he knew in New York. She was curvy and cuddly, and her spectacular breasts were luscious and rounded and begging for a man's touch.

He stroked his dick again, feeling it return to life. God, did one small woman really have the power to jump-start his libido so quickly, or was it those damned cinnamon rolls? He'd cleaned the plate by midafternoon, and all evening, despite the enormous dinner he'd consumed, he'd brooded and wondered if he had a hope in hell of getting any more.

He'd always heard about the hospitality of southerners, but somehow Francesca's overture had taken him by surprise. His rational mind told him she was merely being nice and friendly, but he found himself wishing that her cinnamon rolls had been the prelude to flirtation.

He knew women pretty well, and, sadly for him, Francesca's innocent conversation had included not one iota of coy female come-on. To be truthful, after he'd been such an ass, she'd looked as if she might be thinking of putting her house on the market any day just to be free of him.

He wondered if her nipples were pink or brown. The jolt from that hypothetical question brought him to rock-hardness for the second time in twenty minutes. The water was running cold, and he didn't even care. He found a comfortable rhythm and pressure and closed his eyes, tilting his face toward the stream of water. He imagined her small fingers wrapping around his boner . . . or maybe it was her soft, glossy lips closing around his shaft. *Ah, shit.*

He wanted to spin out the fantasy, to milk every last nuance of memory, but his body betrayed him, perhaps making up for lost time. He shouted his release as he shot off, feeling dizzy and drained and light-headed and frustrated all over again.

Two

Francesca put the finishing touches on the last of her thirty-nine cream puff swans and eyed the large metal tray with satisfaction. The pastry birds joined thirty-nine individual chicken and broccoli quiches and thirty-nine fresh fruit compotes that would later be topped with a dollop of heavy cream. All of it had to be delivered to the fellowship hall of the Presbyterian church no later than eleven thirty for a bridal shower.

She washed and dried her hands and then stretched her arms toward the ceiling, feeling the kinks in her back pop and crack. She'd been up since dawn, and had worked straight through without a break for the last four hours. But it was worth it.

She felt very lucky to be earning a living doing a job that she loved. Camron was just far enough from Knoxville to make it impractical for the townspeople to use companies there.

Francesca's business filled a niche, and Fremont Catering stayed busy . . . so busy in fact, that she might soon have to seriously consider hiring extra help.

She changed into slim khaki slacks and the sleeveless white cotton blouse that was her summer uniform. Caterers were supposed to fade into the background. And although she didn't actually have to help serve this lunch, she felt obligated to stick around for a little while to make sure things went smoothly in the "dishing-up" phase.

Her doorbell rang while she was putting on her lipstick. The sound startled her, since unexpected visitors were few and far between. She glanced at her watch with a grimace, hoping it wasn't someone who intended to linger. She didn't have much time to spare.

When she opened the front door, her brain went totally blank. Christmas had come early to Camron. Brett Gilman without a scowl was even more handsome than the man she'd met yesterday. His lopsided grin and the empty plate he held spoke volumes about his improved mood.

A pair of khaki pants molded to his powerful thighs, and he wore a white polo shirt that stretched across his broad shoulders. Her goofy sense of humor got the better of her. She took the fragile dish from him. "Oh, good," she said with convincing seriousness. "You got the twin memo."

He looked startled for a half second, and then he chuckled, eyeing their almost identical clothing. "Apparently so." His mouth twisted in a wry grin. "I've brought your plate back, and it comes with an apology. You caught me at a bad moment yesterday, Francesca. I'm sorry I was such an ass."

Her heart bounced in her chest, but she managed to keep her expression calm and friendly. "No problem. We both know who caused the bad moment. Would you like to come in?" She had about twenty minutes at the max, but no way was she going to rebuff such a surprising about-face.

He followed her down to the hall to the kitchen and whistled in appreciation. As he drank the glass of iced tea she offered him, he looked around with interest. "This place looks great. Any chance you'd want to be in charge of *my* redecorating?"

She leaned a hip against the counter. "Sorry. I've got a job already. Believe it or not, my house was a lot like yours when I bought it. My grandmother passed away and left me a small legacy, so I had everything rewired, all the plumbing brought up to code, and the hardwood floors stripped and refinished. I did the painting myself a bit at a time. And, of course, I had the industrial appliances installed. I'm a caterer."

He grinned, flashing white teeth and a dangerous sexuality. "That would explain the almost-better-than-sex cinnamon rolls."

She laughed. "I don't know whether to be flattered for my cooking skills or insulted on behalf of my gender."

He set his glass in the deep porcelain sink. "I said *almost.* I'm sure I could be convinced otherwise."

Her pulse skipped a drunken beat as she realized that Brett, the hottie, was actually flirting with her. It had been a while, and certainly no man in recent memory had been as suave. Or as appealing. She smiled demurely. "I'll plead the Fifth." She glanced at her watch and frowned. "I hate to rush you off when you just got here, but I have a delivery to make."

He straightened and shoved his hands in his pockets. "I'd be happy to help you load the stuff."

She hesitated a fraction of a second, and his lopsided grin returned. "I may have fallen off a ladder yesterday, but I promise you I'm not usually so clumsy. I'll be infinitely careful with your goodies."

There it was again. A definite and intentional double entendre. The lick of heat in her stomach dried her throat and made her nipples tighten. This man was dangerous. She couldn't think of a response that wouldn't get her in trouble, so she merely turned and began removing food from the huge, double-door refrigerator.

She backed her van up to the rear of the house and got the AC running full blast. It was a short drive to the church, but she didn't want her swans to wilt in the summer heat.

Brett was as good as his word. He picked up the large, heavy trays as if they weighed nothing at all and slipped them carefully into the specially installed racks in the back of the van. When everything was loaded, she double-checked her list and slammed the doors. Then she locked the house and faced him.

His politely worded rebuff from yesterday morning rang in her ears. A woman would be insane to put herself through such rejection twice. Brett Gilman had made his feelings very clear.

Yet she couldn't quite dismiss the notion that he was regretting what he had said. It was there in his steady gaze. Regret. Remorse. Faint hope.

She nibbled her bottom lip, jingling her keys in her hand and desperately aware that she didn't have the luxury of time to figure this out.

Then she remembered the pain in his eyes yesterday, the aching vulnerability she was sure he hadn't meant to reveal. She sighed, realizing that her own pride could take a lick, if necessary. She was tough. Here was a man who had been through hell. He deserved a break, if anyone did.

She sighed. "Would you like to come over for dinner tonight?" She didn't dress up the invitation. He could take it or leave it.

He stared at the ground for a moment and then looked up,

his gaze a mix of emotions she couldn't quite decipher. "Yes," he said simply. "And thank you."

"For what?"

His eyes were dark and not at all flirtatious. "The sticky buns. Your friendship. A second chance."

She cleared her throat. "Well, then. Six thirty okay with you?"

He nodded solemnly. "I'll be here."

Brett ripped up another strip of nasty carpet and sneezed violently when the dust of decades assaulted his nose. Had he lost his mind entirely? All he had to do was pick up the phone, and anything that needed fixing in this ramshackle, weary old house could be taken care of with his checkbook or his Visa card.

Why was he breaking his back unnecessarily?

Because it felt damn good, that was why. Each little task he completed felt like victory. The dirty, honest work was solid, quantifiable. At the end of the day he could see measurable progress. And no one could take that away from him.

He paused suddenly, his arms covered in carpet fibers and dirt, realizing that he had lost something far more valuable than his reputation or his money. He'd lost his ability to trust. A sharp pain lanced through his chest as he thought about Peter's face in that courtroom.

Peter . . . his college roommate. A man he had known and trusted for almost twenty years. A man who'd asked him to be best man at his wedding, and later godfather to three wonderful babies. God, it still didn't make sense. He didn't want to believe it.

He wanted to go back in time and be able to forget that dreadful day when he realized his partner's perfidy. Nausea rose in his throat even now, and he had to escape the house and wander deep into the woods to try and evade the painful memory.

Peter's family was wealthy three generations back. He shouldn't have needed money. But gambling debts and a desire to keep his wife in the dark about them had started him down a slippery slope that had destroyed him in the end.

The two men hadn't spoken after the surreal day when Peter took the stand and confessed to stealing millions of dollars from the employee pension fund.

Brett had sat there in stunned silence. The knowledge that he was free to walk out of the courtroom had been a secondary consideration. The relief had barely registered against the blistering sense of betrayal.

Moodily, he kicked at a stump and watched a butterfly cavort drunkenly above and around an azalea bush. Before he left New York, he'd made sure that Peter's wife and kids were okay. At least, as much as they could be. The children were too little to understand what was going on. They only knew that Daddy was going away on a long trip.

He would never be able to forget Dana's eyes. She'd been shattered. She had stood by Peter, but at what cost?

Brett wondered what it would be like to have that kind of support. He'd remained single over the years, not because he had any deep fear of commitment, but simply because he'd never found the woman he could imagine facing across the breakfast table for the next three or four decades.

A vision of Francesca Fremont slipped, unbidden, into his mind, and he smiled in spite of his somber mood. Something about her lifted his spirits. She was like light and sunshine all wrapped up in one appealing package.

But what attracted him even more than her undeniably beautiful body was her confidence and her lack of artifice. He'd been incredibly rude to her the day before, and had regretted it instantly. Most women would have cut him dead after that, or at least made him crawl until they decided he had done penance enough.

Francesca had done neither. She had simply offered another gesture of uncomplicated friendship. A dinner invitation. Nothing more, nothing less. She'd been the bigger person, and he admired her for it, just as he admired her entrepreneurial spirit.

It was never easy to start and maintain a small business, but she had accomplished the task and appeared to be doing very well. Which was quite a feat in a town the size of Camron.

Was he being incredibly selfish to hope her dinner invitation might lead to something else? He was fairly sure that the sexual tension he'd noticed wasn't entirely one-sided. He felt like he'd been knocked in the head with a two-by-four. Running after a woman with his tongue hanging out wasn't his style at all but, by damn, he'd be willing to do it if it meant keeping the lovely Francesca in his life, at least for the moment. He liked her on so many levels already. So who knew how stupid he might turn out to be if sex came into the mix?

He gave himself a figurative smack and headed back to the house. He might as well work up a hearty appetite, because he was pretty sure that Francesca Fremont was the woman to satisfy all his cravings.

Francesca made a brief stop at the market on the way home. She'd eaten lunch in the church kitchen. As was usually the case, a couple of the guests hadn't shown up, which meant leftover servings. The mother of the bride, the bride herself, and the women actually giving the shower had been effusive in their praise.

Francesca had pocketed a nice fat check and the sure knowledge that other bookings would result from today's hard work.

She grabbed up a handful of perishable items and pondered what to cook for the evening meal. She normally shopped only twice a month. There were two decent grocery stores in town, and both managers were helpful about keeping the special ingredients she needed on hand, as long as she let them know in advance. Occasionally she drove into Knoxville to browse the specialty markets and the kitchen supply stores, but other than that, pretty much everything she needed was right here at home.

While she examined strawberries and arugula, she thought about feeding Brett. She wanted to make a good impression, but more than that, she wanted him to enjoy the meal. It gave her a great deal of pleasure to know that people savored her food, as opposed to choking it down and heading out to the next activity.

Back at home a little while later, she kicked off her sandals and poured a glass of lemonade. She carried it out to the screened-in back porch and plopped into a cushioned wicker chair. She'd also picked up the odd little etiquette book. She flipped to the page that had caught her attention the day before—*The way to a man's heart (or to his bed) is through his stomach.*

She squirmed in her chair. Was that what her dinner invitation was about? Was she trying to insinuate her way into Brett Gilman's bed?

She felt her face flush and chuckled nervously. She wasn't the kind of woman who pursued sex for the sake of sex. Growing up in Camron, Tennessee, she'd been subject to a rather rigid sexual code. And it had never really chafed until recently.

She might as well face facts. It was a pretty sure bet that she and her sexy neighbor had about zero in common. Whatever impulse had brought him here was bound to wear off soon, and he'd be heading back to where he belonged.

But for the moment he was here. And so was she. Was it wrong to contemplate having sex with him? Just thinking about it made her bones go weak. He was everything she admired in a man, and she'd known the moment she first saw him that she felt a strong, visceral attraction.

She had a good life. She didn't need a man to complete her. But glory hallelujah, she wouldn't mind having this man in her bed for a few weeks.

She reined in her fevered imagination and went back to Miss Matilda's chapter on food and men. Mesmerized, she read on. . . .

Exciting news for the future . . . As you may know, my dears, I pride myself on staying abreast of current ideas and developments that are of use to women in their pursuit of men. I am very excited about a revolutionary new product called Saran Wrap. Although it has only recently been approved for commercial applications (I'm proud to say that I was part of a consumer testing group), it will hopefully be available for household use in the near future. Saran Wrap is a thin, clear plastic that clings to itself without further adhesive and can be used to cover and protect items such as leftovers. Dull stuff, you say? Perhaps so, but imagine a more creative function. What if you were to answer the door when your gentleman friend calls and you were wearing only a Saran Wrap frock? Imagine his delight and immediate desire. You could even smear yourself with chocolate sauce prior to donning your transparent gown. The possibilities are endless!

But enough of that. I must get back to the here and now with some solid advice. Food can be a strong sexual trigger. Draw the man's attention to you as you eat. Let him see your teeth pierce the skin of the strawberry. Make sure he notices your tongue lapping up the whipped cream. Vegetables can be useful as well. Although it may be Freudian, slipping a whole carrot deep into your mouth is a surefire way to send a man's thoughts down the desired path. Keep your lips wet, if possible. If you enjoy wine, have a glass, by all means, but don't overindulge. A small amount may loosen your inhibitions. Too much can make you rash or impetuous. You want to maintain control of the situation at all times. Use a dash of cayenne pepper to season the meat, just a hint. It stimulates virility and raises the body temperature. Keep in mind that you are tending to two appetites at once. When a man's belly is satisfied, his other organs will rise to the occasion. If you do your job well, your partner will soon come to associate the pleasures of food and the pleasures of the bedroom with you and you alone. *Bon appetit.*

Francesca gulped a swig of lemonade and dropped the naughty little guide onto the table beside her. Her hands were shaking and she felt hot and shivery. Good grief. Who'd have believed that women of that generation knew so much about oral seduction? Or was that culinary seduction?

And Saran Wrap? Holy cow! She'd never again be able to look at a roll of the famous stuff without thinking of its fashion

applications. While the food advice had some intriguing possibilities, no way was she going to greet her hunky neighbor at
the front door wearing sheer plastic and a smile.

She stood up on quivering legs and wiped her damp palms
on the seat of her pants. She had to get hold of herself. At this
rate she'd be jumping the man when he came through the front
door.

She made it to the kitchen and stood there for a full two
minutes, staring blankly at the cabinets. Food. Cooking. She
had a dinner to prepare. Every lesson she'd ever learned had
leaked out of her head as if her brain were a sieve. Suddenly
Miss Matilda was the only instructor she remembered, and she
had a feeling that the divine Miss M was apt to get her into more
trouble than she could handle.

Brett worked at a steady pace all afternoon. He'd eaten three
peanut-butter sandwiches for lunch, but the whole time all he
could think about was those incredible platters of food Francesca had loaded into her van. His mouth watered and his
stomach growled.

He was ashamed to admit that he was almost as excited
about the food she'd be serving him tonight as he was about
the endless possibilities for après dinner. But sex won, hands
down.

He wouldn't press her. He'd make his interest clear, but he
wouldn't insult or offend her. She was a nice woman, and if she
wasn't interested in a physical tête-à-tête, he'd take his disappointment like a man.

Just before five, he put all his tools away and eyed the heap
of carpet he'd piled in a corner of the living room. Either he
needed to find someone who would haul the stuff to a dump, or
he'd have to rent a truck and do it himself. He'd probably wait

a bit, because there was bound to be a lot more debris before all was said and done.

The steaming shower and the late-day shave felt good. He slipped into dark dress pants and a cream button-down shirt with the sleeves rolled up. He'd already figured out that social life in Camron was casual, but he didn't want to show up at Francesca's house looking scruffy. If a woman was willing to cook for him, she deserved at least a bit of effort on his part.

He scrounged in the kitchen for a couple of his favorite bottles of wine. He hadn't discovered until he moved that this was a dry county. He wasn't a fan of hard liquor, but he did enjoy a good wine with dinner. Not that he'd actually had food that could qualify as dinner anytime lately. He refused to consider Lean Cuisine spaghetti as a real meal, even if he had eaten three boxes at one sitting. He'd still been hungry when he was finished.

He had, however, discovered something in the Tennessee grocery stores called Little Debbie snack cakes, and he was making a personal project of working his way through all the different varieties. Though he'd seen them before, he'd never had occasion to try them, and since the company was based in Tennessee, he decided it was high time.

He paused on his front porch and wished he had flowers to offer his new neighbor. And then it struck him. . . . Out by the fence he'd seen some pretty pink things that smelled nice. He headed for the backyard and picked a big handful. He wasn't sure what they were called. Francesca might think they were weeds. But what the heck . . . it was the thought that counted. Right?

As he traversed the short distance between the two houses, it occurred to him that he was nervous. It surprised him, because he was no stranger to the dating scene. But in New York he knew all the steps of the dance. A Broadway show, a late, intimate dinner at a trendy restaurant . . . a pleasant evening, and, with an adventuresome woman, skipping the cab and walking back to her place in the moonlight. All those were familiar activities.

But here in rural Tennessee with a woman who was as unpretentious as she was beautiful, he wasn't sure what he had to work with. There wasn't even a damned movie theater within thirty miles. It boggled the mind. Of course, there was a video store on every corner, so as long as you were willing to wait a bit for the blockbusters, you were okay.

He paused in the shadow of the hedge and straightened the collar of his shirt. He was determined to erase the impression he'd made the day before. Sullen and sulky was not sexy. And he sure as hell wasn't going to get into his reasons for moving here.

He lifted his face to the sky. Cicadas made their summer racket, and he smelled the aroma of freshly mowed grass from somewhere nearby. The sun was hanging low, but dusk was still more than two hours away, and the evening air was muggy and still.

At least the humidity made him feel at home. New York in the summer could be a sauna. For a brief moment he flashed to a picture of Francesca tucked up in bed with him in his Tribeca apartment. He wondered if she had ever been to the Big Apple, and if she had any desire to go.

With a shake of his head, he came back to the present. He was getting way ahead of himself. He glanced at his watch. *Damn.* He was early. Surely she wouldn't mind. She seemed like a woman who wasn't rattled by much.

He crossed to her front yard, went up the three shallow steps onto the porch, and rang the bell.

After a delay that seemed an eternity, the door opened slowly. Francesca stood there, wrapped in some kind of fuzzy ivory robe. Her feet were bare and her skin was damp. She had obviously stepped straight out of the shower.

His dick went rock-hard, and he was glad for the bottles of wine he held. He shifted them surreptitiously toward his belt. His tongue felt swollen in his mouth. "I'm sorry," he said. He'd been saying that a lot lately. "I didn't realize until I got over here how early I was. But then I thought I might help you get ready."

Her eyebrows flew up, and her cheeks flushed a delicate pink.

"The food, I mean," he stammered. "The last-minute stuff . . . you know. Buttering and heating . . ." *Good Lord.* He was digging himself deeper by the minute.

Her mouth gaped open, and all he could think about was tasting that soft pink tongue.

He took a deep breath. "I'll go," he said simply, "and come back later. Give you time to get dressed."

She snagged his arm, setting off little shocks everywhere she touched. "Don't be silly." Her voice sounded hoarse. "Come on in. You can relax on the back porch. And you brought wine . . . how nice of you."

Like a besotted puppy dog, he followed her back through the house into the kitchen. He set the wine on the counter and held out the flowers. "These are for you."

Her face softened, and a genuine smile lightened her features. "Sweet peas. I love them. But somehow I never take the time to go pick some. I really appreciate it. You're very thoughtful."

And he believed she meant it. No seventy-five-dollar roses. No overpriced restaurant. Just a man and a woman in a cozy kitchen, burning up with heat that had nothing to do with the stove.

Perhaps his gaze was a bit too predatory. She grasped the lapels of her robe and pulled them together at her throat. "I'll go get dressed, then," she said, the words breathless. Her husky alto grabbed him deep in the gut and ratcheted up his hunger about a bazillion percent.

"Wait." He hadn't meant to say a word. The protest slipped out unbidden. His libido seemed to be steering the conversation.

She looked confused. "The wineglasses are in that cabinet." She reached around him to open a drawer. Even with the remodeling she'd done, the room was still relatively small. She held up a fancy corkscrew. "And you'll need this."

He took it from her and put it beside the wine. "Don't go," he muttered. He slid his hands beneath her hair and cupped the sides of her neck. Her lips parted and her blue eyes widened in shock.

He bent his head, his mouth hovering over hers. "I've wanted to do this ever since I tasted your sticky buns," he muttered. And then he kissed her.

Three

Francesca's toes curled against the cool linoleum beneath her feet. Brett's mouth was warm and firm and surprisingly gentle. Barely even any tongue, just a hint that this amazingly delicious, erotic kiss might be the prelude to so much more. She murmured something incoherent and pressed closer.

He smelled wonderful, like summer nights and some kind of teasing spice that must surely be an aphrodisiac. It was the only explanation for the way her mouth was melding with his in soft, yearning little sighs.

She wanted desperately to wrap her arms around his neck, but she was afraid to let go of her robe. She was naked underneath, and if that fuzzy barrier between them disappeared, she just might hop up on the counter and beg him to have his naughty, Yankee way with her. So her hands remained chastely tucked between their two warm bodies, trying to maintain the pretense of maidenly modesty.

He released her slowly and stepped back. On his face she saw consternation and surprise and a healthy dose of male lust.

She cleared her throat, now staring no higher than the third button below his collar. "I'd better get dressed. Make yourself at home."

The words were prosaic, but the husky note in her voice might as well have been a billboard shouting her arousal to the world. She would have been even more embarrassed if she hadn't felt up close and personal the thick erection nudging her belly.

Oops. Don't go there again. She escaped with an awkward reverse shuffle and fled to her bedroom. She managed not to slam the door and sank onto her bed, trying to forget the fact that she had deliberately outfitted it with clean sheets just this afternoon. Sheets that had been dried on the clothesline outside. Sheets that smelled like fresh air and sunshine and delicious summer sensuality.

She stood on shaky legs and let her robe drop to the floor. In the mirror over her antique dresser, she eyed her nudity with a critical gaze. He was a man who moved in elevated circles. God knew, there might have been a model or a dancer somewhere in his past. Most assuredly a parade of beautiful women.

But she wasn't exactly roadkill. Her breasts were high and firm. Losing fifteen pounds wouldn't hurt, but if it meant giving up the joys of food, it simply wasn't worth it. She cupped her breasts and studied her reflection. She was not the kind of woman who seduced men, but she was damned sure willing to try something new.

She glanced at the clock and hissed in dismay. Playing Lady Godiva in her spinster bedroom while the man of her dreams lingered in the kitchen was not getting her anywhere. Dithering was wasting valuable time.

She had agonized all afternoon over what to wear. But the time for fashion questions was over. She dressed quickly, donning a short denim skirt and a pale pink spaghetti-strap top. The latter was lined, so she ditched her usual bra without a qualm.

She pulled on a pair of panties and slipped her feet into hot-pink flip-flops that were decorated with white daisies. A cursory brush of her hair, a flick of powder on her shiny nose, a spritz of perfume, and finally the necklace that had been her grandmother's . . . a tiny diamond star suspended on a delicate gold chain.

By the time she returned to the kitchen, she was breathless, but moderately in control of her overheated hormones. She made a quick check on the progress of her meal. She'd decided to play to her strengths and to take advantage of the abundant summer produce.

She'd prepared barbecued ribs with her own special sauce, corn on the cob, and a fresh green salad with mango dressing. Her small buttermilk biscuits were ready to pop in the oven at the last minute.

With Miss Matilda's sassy advice ringing in her ears, she reached in the fridge and pulled out a plate of fruit and veggie hors d'oeuvres. Then, with a deep breath to steady her rubbery knees, she joined Brett out on the porch.

He was leaning back in her wicker rocker, looking entirely comfortable and relaxed, exactly the opposite of her own emotional state. She put the platter on the small table at his knees and sat down on the matching love seat opposite him. The fabric covering the cushions was a wildly colorful tropical print. Brett looked like a dangerous jungle animal just waiting to pounce.

She smiled weakly. "Have an appetizer. You must be starving from all that work you're doing."

He leaned forward and snagged a handful of grapes. She picked up a strawberry and waited for an opportune moment. She asked him a question about possibly replacing the vinyl siding on his house, and when he looked at her to answer, she bit carefully into the biggest, fattest strawberry she could find at the local roadside stand down the way.

She had anticipated juice . . . even included it in her plans. What she hadn't expected was a plethora of juice, an abundance of juice, an unbelievable Niagara Falls of juice. It squirted down her chin, slid in twin sticky rivulets over her chest, and dripped onto her cleavage.

Brett stopped midsentence, perhaps shocked by her unladylike response to exploding fruit. She plucked at the stained fabric ineffectually. His wide-eyed gaze, understandably, zeroed in on her nipples, and her tiny, traitorous body parts responded . . . eagerly, proudly. If they'd been any more erect, she'd have signed them up for the Marine Corps band.

She shivered beneath his heated stare and stood abruptly. "I'll be right back. Sorry."

She escaped to her bedroom for the second time and dragged her ruined top over her head. She dared not look in the mirror. Quickly, she pulled a similar thin camisole from her closet, this one mint green, and slipped it on.

She was forced to look at her reflection for a brief moment as she tamed her rumpled hair. Her eyes were overbright, her cheeks flushed, her bare lips cherry red from where her teeth had bitten them.

Dear heaven. She was in big trouble.

Brett was in the same place she'd left him. He stood automatically and smiled faintly as she walked out onto the porch. "That was quick."

"I'm low-maintenance. Sit . . . sit."

He waited for her to be seated and followed suit. She drummed up a smile. "Guess I'll skip the strawberries and stick to something that isn't so messy."

"Messy can be good." He said it with a straight face, but his eyes twinkled with mischief.

She refused to let him bait her, and instead picked up a carrot. "Well, I must admit, I love the fresh berries we get this time of year. They're so plump and juicy and sweet. Almost like eating pure sunshine."

He bit into a berry, much more successfully than she had, and licked his lips. "I understand why you love to cook. I've never seen a woman so passionate about food."

She flushed. "I guess you can tell that by looking at me."

He frowned. "Don't be ridiculous. You know you're beautiful."

The shock must have shown on her face.

He wiped his mouth with a napkin. "You *are* beautiful," he insisted. "In a very real, genuine way."

She wrinkled her nose. "What you really mean is that I don't have an ounce of New York City polish."

His frown deepened. "Any woman can decorate her face or dress in a flattering way. What you have is far rarer. You're lovely, Francesca."

She was speechless. Either he was a better actor than Brad Pitt, or he was being sincere. Of course, he could simply be feeding her a line to get her into bed. Little did he know that she wouldn't put up much of a fight.

Talking about herself made her uncomfortable. Time to get the evening back on track. She swirled the carrot in the dip she had made from scratch, and casually slid the end into her mouth. She felt a bit ridiculous, but if the expression on Brett's face was any indication, the gentle sucking she was doing was having the desired effect.

Hot damn. Miss Matilda was right.

Brett spent the better part of two hours trying to decide if his sexy neighbor was deliberately driving him insane, or if her natural sensuality was so much a part of her, she didn't even realize what she was doing.

They ate in the small dining room just off the kitchen. She had clearly gone to a lot of trouble. She lit candles in a brass candelabra, although she left all the lights on. The real silver gleamed, and the china and crystal were classy and lovely, much like the woman who fed him so well.

He almost whimpered over the ribs. The meat practically fell from the bone, and she laughed when he ended up with his chin covered in sauce.

He watched, mesmerized, as Francesca bit into her ear of corn and licked at a drip of butter. He'd had a hard-on for pretty much ninety-five percent of the time he'd been in her house. And in spite of his sexual agitation, or maybe because of it, he ate until his stomach begged for mercy.

Afterward, he helped her clean and dry the pieces that were too delicate for the dishwasher. If he brushed up against her on purpose from time to time, he could hardly be blamed. That damned tiny skirt exposed long, toned legs that were just begging for a man's hands . . . to shape them, to stroke their length from ankle to knee, to slide deep into the sweet, forbidden shadows beneath her panties.

With a rapidly suppressed groan, he poured himself another glass of wine and went out onto the porch, this time claiming the love seat for himself.

Francesca turned out all the lights in the house and carried a small pillar candle out with her. "Citronella," she said. "The screen keeps most of the bugs out, but mosquitoes find their way in occasionally."

He'd hoped she might join him, but instead she opted for the chair he had occupied earlier. The shadows deepened. Dusk was only a memory, and the lush summer night enclosed them in a curtain of intimacy. The flickering flame of the pungent candle gave off only enough light for him to see her outline.

They sat in companionable silence, drinking their wine and listening to the croak of frogs down at the creek. Brett searched his mind and couldn't think of the last time he had been this relaxed . . . or this content.

And then, like an ass, for some unknown stupid reason he brought reality into the mix. "So I guess you know who I am. I've had press following me everywhere." He prayed she would say no . . . or that she would at least murmur a polite, face-saving lie.

He should have known better.

He heard her sigh. "Yes. Your name sounded very familiar, and then I looked you up . . . read a couple of articles. I'm very sorry, Brett. It must have been so awful for you, losing a friend like that."

He went still, stunned that she had picked up on the one worst, agonizing aspect of the whole damned business. "Yes," he said, his throat tight. "I didn't believe it at first. I thought he was doing the noble thing, trying to protect me. But instead, he was the one who trashed my life and threw twenty years of history in my face."

He heard the undisguised bitterness in his own voice and winced. God, nothing was more pathetic than a whiner. What woman wanted a man like that?

It was quiet for several long minutes. The darkness softened the edges of the pain and disillusionment he wore like a hair shirt, made it easier to receive her unspoken sympathy.

He heard her sigh. "Don't throw the baby out with the bathwater. What happened this year doesn't make those past two decades worthless."

"Doesn't it?" he asked, his voice hard. It was a question he had wrestled with many times in the last terrible months.

"People make mistakes, Brett. People disappoint us. Sometimes we keep loving them anyway. It's nothing to be ashamed of."

He absorbed her words, felt them punch into his chest and settle into his gut. And as he assimilated them, he felt a hard knot inside unfurl just a bit. He set his glass on the table and leaned forward, his elbows on his knees, his head in his hands.

He felt raw and exposed, and it sure as hell wasn't the direction he had expected or wanted the evening to take. He swallowed, his throat dry, and searched for a distraction. "So I guess if you've lived here all your life, you must have lots of family around."

She accepted his conversational gambit without protest. "Not exactly. At least not now. My dad died when I was in college. I have an older sister who is married and lives in Atlanta. She's a psychologist, and when the babies started coming along, my mom moved down there so her grandchildren wouldn't have to go to day care."

"You must miss them."

"Every day. But we're on the phone all the time, and I make the drive a couple of times a month to visit."

"Have you ever considered moving to Atlanta?"

"Not seriously. This is home, and I have plenty of friends, and my business, of course."

He pondered that information, realizing it was no surprise. She struck him as a woman entirely comfortable with who she was and what she wanted in life. A year ago he had been equally certain. Now he didn't know shit.

They talked for another half hour . . . nothing serious. Books and movies and politics. They disagreed on the first and the second and were pretty much in accord on the third. He was a hard-nosed businessman. She was a female and a romantic. Other than a love of good food and an appreciation for the Harry Potter books, they came from different planets. The lives they had lived up to this point were as different as earth and air.

So why did he feel like he had come home? Why was sitting on the porch of an old farmhouse, miles from anything remotely resembling a city, so damned comfortable? And why, at his age, did he feel like he'd been knocked flat on his ass by a sarcastic, quasi-demonic Cupid?

Francesca stood at one point to head inside and dish up their pie and ice cream. He snagged her wrist and rose to his feet. "Let's save it for tomorrow," he muttered. "I can't eat anything else, I swear."

After a long moment fraught with surprising tension, he found her lips with his. He kept the kiss gentle, although his body was screaming at him to seal the deal. Her mouth was soft and sweet beneath his, and when she responded, it was all he could do not to drag her down and ravish her on the spot. He was so hungry he felt like he might die if he couldn't have her this very second.

But it was too soon . . . and he didn't want her to think the surprising connection he felt was casual. It was anything but.

He released her reluctantly and raked a hand through his hair. "Dinner was wonderful," he said gruffly. "Thanks for inviting me."

He saw her lick her lips. "You're welcome," she said, her response little more than a murmur.

He sighed, feeling lost and uncertain and yet more at peace than he had in some time. "I'll talk to you soon." And then he opened the screen door and stepped outside, removing himself from temptation.

Francesca finished tidying up the kitchen, locked up the house, and turned out the lights. She read for a while and then closed the book with an irritated snap. She hadn't comprehended anything on the last ten pages.

What was she going to do about Brett? He was the most attractive man she had met in a long, long time, but she really knew very little about him. Would she be insane to wind up in his bed?

She turned out the light and blinked in the sudden darkness. For the first time in her life she wanted to throw caution to the wind.

She avoided her neighbor for the next few days, just to prove to herself that she hadn't completely gone around the bend. The following Saturday she had a list of chores a mile long, but she found time just before noon to fix some of her homemade chicken salad, make three sandwiches, and add some fruit.

As she gathered it all together, along with some cookies for dessert, her heart was pounding and her hands trembled. She had never been very assertive when it came to men and dating, but something about Brett brought out her inner tigress. She snorted at that unlikely mental image and stepped outside carefully, balancing her assortment of goodies with one hand and closing the door behind her. This whole thing was probably a very bad idea, but she couldn't seem to help herself.

She found Brett at the back of his house, again on a ladder, scraping off several layers of peeling paint from the cracked wood. She shielded her eyes from the sun with one hand and looked up at him. No iPod today. "You ready for some lunch?"

The noise he'd been making had masked the sound of her approach. He looked around and grinned, making her heartbeat stutter. "Hell, yes." He scooted down the ladder and greeted her with a quick casual kiss that stole her breath.

He brushed a finger over her lips. "I've missed you."

She couldn't think of an answer that wouldn't get her into trouble, so she followed him in silence around the corner. What did his easy, nonchalant intimacy imply?

While he cleaned up in the house's one bathroom, she peeked in the front bedroom. The space was bare except for an ancient twin bed with sagging springs. Brett had tossed a sleeping bag on top of the stained mattress.

She shuddered. Surely there weren't any creepy-crawlies lingering in the stuffing, but who knew? Seeing the Spartan conditions under which he was living made her uneasy. Why was he doing this? She'd bet her last dime that he was accustomed to six-hundred-thread-count imported Italian sheets. Was this supposed to be some kind of penance on his part?

He joined her in the kitchen as she was setting out their meal. A rickety wooden table and two spindly-legged chairs were the sum total of the room's furnishings. The white enamel sink had rusted through in spots, and the linoleum floor was cracked and peeling. It was a dismal space, but Brett seemed oblivious.

He dug in with gusto, polishing off two sandwiches and half the cookies in short order. He had put on a T-shirt, but it did little to detract from the impact of his broad shoulders and muscled chest.

They chatted about inconsequential matters until she stood up to leave. "I've got to get back to the house," she said lightly. "I'm working on a cookbook I hope to publish in the not-too-distant future. And I'm also computerizing all my current menus and recipes."

He wiped his mouth with a paper towel and tossed their trash in the garbage. "Impressive. Have you thought about hiring an assistant?"

"All the time," she said ruefully. "I've been saving up a nest egg. I want to take things to the next level, but it takes capital."

"You'll get there," he said with more confidence than she felt. "I have faith in you."

He followed her as far as the hedge and stopped her before she slipped through the leafy barrier. "How about a kiss, Francesca . . . for dessert?"

"You already had dessert," she reminded him primly, trying not to let him see how much his casual request rattled her.

"I'm still hungry." His eyes had darkened, and his cheekbones flushed with something that was more than the afternoon heat.

She told herself a nice girl wouldn't be so easy. "You're awfully chummy. We barely know each other."

He pulled her close, ignoring her halfhearted protest. "I'm working on my friendly southern hospitality. How am I doing?"

His mouth covered hers and his hands met at her spine, stroking, caressing. Her knees went weak and her own arms stole around his neck. She angled her head so he could deepen the kiss. It was insane how quickly their bodies ignited. Neither of them was a teenager. They were mature, responsible adults. Two people who didn't know nearly enough about each other to be contemplating what they were both clearly contemplating.

The firm erection pressed against her belly shouted Brett's interest loud and clear. And that interest was an enthusiastic copy of her own. She wanted what he wanted. *Yowza* . . .

But she backed away and broke the embrace. Not yet, but soon . . . She pacified her whimpering hormones with the desperate promise.

That afternoon her neighbor on the other side dropped by. Ada was a spry old lady of eighty-plus who looked at least a decade older. She had spent years as a younger woman working in the tobacco fields in the blazing summer sun, and her skin was leathery and wrinkled. But her eyes were sharp and bright.

She got bored occasionally with her soaps and her crosswords, and she would come over to watch Francesca cook. Usually Francesca enjoyed the company, but today she felt self-conscious. It was almost as if her hopes of seducing Brett were plastered across her forehead.

She listened absently to the older woman's chatter, until Ada mentioned a name that made Francesca's head pop up in shock. "He did what?"

Ada grinned. "The sheriff has a buddy at the FBI . . . he had that Gilman fellow investigated. A lot of weird stuff going on these days. Can't be too careful."

Francesca kept right on dicing carrots, feigning what she hoped was only a casual interest. "And?"

Ada shrugged. "He came out smelling like a rose. Other than that messy business with his partner, no black spots on his name. His bank records were clean, too."

"They accessed his bank accounts? My god, isn't that illegal?" She was vaguely horrified.

Ada rolled her eyes. "You been livin' under a rock? Nothing's private anymore if you got the right connections."

Francesca refused to ask about Brett's finances. But Ada wasn't finished. Her wizened face cracked into a big grin. "He's a regular white knight, Frannie. He gives a shitload of money to his favorite charities, and he started a mentorship program with his fancy-ass executives at a local high school."

Francesca barely noticed the old woman's language. Ada was far past the age where she felt compelled to watch her tongue. And her rambling monologue didn't really seem to require an answer.

Ada snitched a carrot slice and cocked her head. "You met the guy yet?"

Francesca felt herself blush and couldn't do a thing about it. "Yes. I took him some food when he moved in."

"And?" Ada's mischievous grin seemed to see past Francesca's carefully bland response.

Francesca shrugged. "He seems nice." She waited for lightning to strike, but luckily for her the skies were cloudless.

Ada chuckled. "You're a pretty gal. You could do worse."

"We barely know each other, and besides . . . he won't be here long. You know that. This is some kind of vacation, I guess."

Ada's eyebrows rose to her hairline. "No offense, Frannie, but Camron isn't exactly Pigeon Forge. People *leave* here to vacation. Besides, I hear he's been hounded by the press. I'd say he's hiding out."

"You're probably right, of course. He even made a point of asking me not to say anything to anyone about his being here. But I'm just one person. Anyone could spill the beans. I hope people respect his privacy."

Ada hopped spryly off the stool where she'd been perching like an inquisitive bird. "It's hard to keep secrets in a small town. You'd better keep an eye on him."

Francesca grinned. "My civic responsibility?"

Ada waved and wandered to the back door. "Beats the hell out of jury duty."

After Ada's informative visit, it seemed only neighborly to invite Brett to dinner again. This time the menu was sweet-and-sour chicken over rice. The meal was not the focus of their attention, despite Brett's vocal appreciation.

They were tuned in to each other . . . hungry . . . waiting.

Francesca had rationalized away most of her doubts. If the FBI said he was clean, who was she to argue? And if she told herself in advance this was a short-lived fling, how could she get hurt? She was a mature, thoughtful, sensible woman. Nothing impulsive at all about her decision.

Then Brett grinned at something she had said, and she knew she would probably have jumped him with or without a recommendation from the feds.

When they were finished eating, Francesca carried the dishes back to the kitchen. On her return, Brett took her wrist in a gentle grasp.

She allowed him to draw her near, but she tugged on her hand until he released it as she sat down. It was raining gently, and the damp breeze penetrated the screens and made her shiver.

Brett was very aware of her. They were so close their thighs touched. He could hear the soft, even tenor of her breathing.

His arm was stretched along the back of the seat, but he wasn't touching her, though he wanted to—more and more with each passing second.

He felt her shift sideways so that her face was turned toward him. He still couldn't see her expression. The candle was at least five feet away.

Her breath when she finally spoke brushed his neck and sent a hard shiver down his spine. It wasn't the only hard thing he was experiencing. By inhaling her scent, he was close to drooling like a dog in a Pavlovian experiment.

"Brett?"

"Hmmm?"

"Can I ask you something?"

He shifted a half inch away. It was either that or pounce on her. "Sure."

He sensed her hesitation, so he touched her hand lightly. Only he misjudged the distance in the semidark, and his palm settled on the bare flesh of her knee. They both gasped in unison. He jerked his arm back, breathing like a marathon runner on the home stretch.

He cleared his throat. "Sorry. Go on."

"Actually, I guess I'll explain something first, and then ask you the question."

He nodded. "Shoot."

"I love Camron . . . the people, the history, the land itself. It's a part of me."

"Do I hear a 'but'?"

She laughed softly. "Sort of. You see, it's hard for a female my age to meet single men in a place this small—for lots of reasons that I won't bore you with. But . . . I have the same needs as any other woman. You've moved in next door, and it's been clear from the get-go that you're temporary. You're doing some kind of penance in the wilderness, but your life is back in New York. I know it, and you know it."

"You seem to know me awfully well for someone who just met me."

"Is anything I've said not true?"

He ground his teeth. "No."

"Well, then . . ." She paused, and he could almost hear the wheels turning in her brain. "I'm very attracted to you, and I think the feeling is mutual. If you're willing, I'd like to explore an intimate relationship, as long as you're here, that is. You needn't worry that I have any expectations. This would simply be expedient . . . for both of us."

Two important portions of his body responded almost simultaneously. His prick went hard as granite . . . again. And his brain got seriously pissed. He could read between the lines. He wasn't butt-ugly. He was available. And he was temporary.

Good God. The woman wanted to use him, like renting a convertible on vacation . . . a flashy, fun, short-term entertainment vehicle.

He should get up and walk out.

But he was a man and not entirely stupid. He did leap to his feet and stride a few steps away. It was impossible to muster rational thought with her so close.

Her soft voice followed him, temptation swirling around him like an unseen cloud. "But only if you're interested. I'm not all that experienced. I may have misread your signals. And if so, I apologize."

How in the devil could she sound so damned cool? His forehead was sweating, and his hands were shaking. No experience, like hell. She had more moves than a Siren beckoning a sailor onto the rocks.

He raked his hands through his hair. "I'm interested," he said through clenched teeth. So interested, the teeth of his zipper were permanently imprinted on his dick.

Her response was a breathy little bedroom noise. "Oh . . . good."

He was paralyzed with lust and confusion and anger and hot anticipation for at least thirty seconds. And then he knew what he had to do.

He turned back to her, his eyes straining in the darkness. He deliberately infused his words with pseudo-boredom . . . sounding as though he couldn't care less whether she agreed. "I'm definitely interested," he repeated, with his best imitation of a slow southern drawl. "But I have a few conditions."

"Conditions?" Her voice ended in a little squeak, and she sounded alarmed.

Good. She deserved to be as off-kilter as he was. He sat down beside her again, smirking to himself when she scooted to her side of the seat. "Conditions," he said firmly. "For one thing, I'd like to move in with you. My house is a pigsty, and yours is all warm and cozy and comfortable."

She stuttered for a moment. "B-but Camron's a small, conservative town. People would talk."

He snorted. "About what? No one can even see your house tucked back here away from the road. No one will know anything unless you tell them." He wasn't serious about moving in, but he wanted to see how far he could push her. Clearly there was a motel out by the interstate where he could stay if he were so inclined. But for some reason it seemed important to needle her, to make her sweat.

"But I barely even know you."

That made him *really* mad. "So it's okay to screw me, but not live with me?" He didn't wait for an answer. "I think we've established that I'm not an ax murderer. Every tiny detail of my life is now public knowledge. I always use a condom. I'm disease-free, and I'm not into kinky, unless that's what you want, and in that case I'm sure I can compromise." He'd been kidding in the beginning, just to get a rise out of her, but now he kept up the ruse, not quite sure whether he was serious or not.

He sensed her waffling, could almost feel her begin to panic. He'd seen it a million times in the midst of a real estate deal. The buyer would find what he or she or they wanted. They'd be riding high on the sheer euphoria of realizing a dream, of stealing a sweet piece of property out from under someone else's nose. And yet at the last minute, when they sat down to sign papers and they took a good look at the costs, the cold, hard facts, they balked.

So Brett Gilman talked them down from the ledge. It was what he did.

He took her hand for real this time, linking their fingers and squeezing. "It's an inspired idea, Francesca. Right up there with picture phones and online banking. Don't back out now. And besides. I haven't even mentioned the other benefit to you."

Her voice quavered. "Benefit?"

His free hand stroked her leg as far as the hem of her skirt and stopped. "I can't cook worth a damn. I've been starving to death over there. Think how good it will make you feel to satisfy my hunger." He abandoned her leg and lifted a hand to cup her cheek. "You live to satisfy hunger, right?" His lips hovered over hers.

She pulled back a couple of inches, making him frown. She was indignant. "How is that a benefit to me? It sounds like you'd be getting all the perks. A clean house. Three meals a day."

His thumb stroked her chin. "I'll kill bugs for you," he promised. "And change lightbulbs. And don't forget the sex," he said huskily.

He could feel her trembling, and for one brief second he felt remorse for letting her believe he really expected to move in. But dammit, her no-strings-attached offer deserved some kind of retribution. He leaned closer. "Hot, sweaty, erotic, temporary sex."

But Francesca was no pushover. "No strings?" she snapped. "I believe you just tried to negotiate a meal plan and the guest room."

He nipped the curve of her ear with sharp teeth. "I don't like the guest room."

"You haven't even seen the guest room." Her voice was breathless.

"I want to sleep in *your* bed, Francesca. All night. Every night."

"Until you leave," she said stubbornly.

He ground his teeth again. At this rate he'd have to find a dentist, or at least a decent shrink. "I'm not planning on going anywhere at the moment," he said with as much calm as he could muster.

She fell silent again, and he practiced patience. It wasn't a skill he enjoyed, but he'd learned it in spades the last year.

She touched the top button of his shirt, just below his open collar. Her fingertip felt hot, even through a layer of fabric.

He cleared his throat. "So . . . do we have a deal?"

"No." She said it bluntly. "I think you're teasing me. Why, I don't know. But even if you were telling the truth, the answer is no. You have your own house and the means to improve it." Then she paused, and a tiny smile lifted the corners of her lips. He felt it deep in his gut.

She sighed, as if making an enormous concession. "But I suppose the occasional sleepover wouldn't hurt."

He couldn't suppress a grin. "You drive a hard bargain. I could use you on my team."

"Business?" She shuddered theatrically. "No, thanks."

He chuckled. "Then we're in agreement? Hot, sweaty sex with the occasional meal thrown in?"

The humor faded from her face, and her hands twisted in her lap. "I haven't been with a man in eighteen months." The mortification and vulnerability in her hesitant whisper grabbed his heart and squeezed it.

He sighed, consigning his male pride to the trash heap. He brushed his lips across her forehead and gathered her into his arms, silently rejoicing when she didn't protest. His hands roved over her back, from the bare skin at her shoulders, to the curve of her waist.

His chest rose and fell as he pondered the wisdom of what he was about to say. "I haven't had sex with anyone other than my hand in nine months. The last woman I was in a relationship with tossed me aside like day-old bread when the charges against me became public. Until I met you, I thought my sex drive was history."

Well, if he was aiming to have a go at trusting again, this was the equivalent of diving off a fifty-foot cliff. His stomach flip-flopped as he waited for her response.

She wrapped her arms around his neck so tightly he could barely breathe. Her soft, sexy little mouth found his and attacked it with a wet, determined kiss. When she let him catch his breath, he was light-headed.

She licked her way from his collarbone to his earlobe. "Brett Gilman," she said, her words muffled against his damp skin. "I would be honored to satisfy every one of your hungers. And I'm damned good at what I do."

Four

The husky certainty in her voice made every cell in his body harden. He lifted her across his lap and shoved up her skirt so she could straddle him. She was still kissing him, and it was damned hard to focus while her sweet, agile tongue was dueling with his.

He cupped her ass and groaned. Nothing beneath his palms but bare skin. He explored further and found the satiny thong that was the only thing between him and the end of a hellishly long period of celibacy. Two weeks ago his monkish lifestyle hadn't seemed like such a burden. Not when his whole life was in a shambles.

Now, with Francesca wrapped around him, her scent in his head and her warm, lush body his for the taking, he thought he might spontaneously combust. If he'd ever been as hungry for a woman, he couldn't remember it. He was aching, wanting, needing everything she had to offer, every last ounce of comfort and pleasure and sexual release. He was so over his head it wasn't funny.

He peeled her slender arms from around his neck and shook her gently, his breath rasping in his throat. "Wait," he said hoarsely, striving for reason.

He sensed rather than saw her pout. "I've been waiting," she said with pointed sarcasm, her voice petulant. "It's overrated."

He choked out a laugh. "This is our first time together. Give me a chance here, Francesca. I'd like to show you a bit of finesse."

"Screw finesse." She bit his bottom lip.

Sweet holy heaven. He tongued the spot where she had almost broken the skin and felt his arousal reach a new and nearly frightening level. The reins of his control came close to snapping. He didn't want to hurt her. She was small and delicate. He was big, and so aroused his entire body was trembling.

"Jerk me off," he said roughly. "Please. If you don't, I won't last ten seconds inside you."

For a long, agonizing moment he thought she might refuse. But she slid off his lap and onto the floor without ceremony. Her hands found his zipper and dealt with it in record time. When she lifted him free of his boxers, the night air on his aching prick seemed painfully stimulating. But not nearly as much as the feel of her soft fingers wrapped around his shaft. It was torture and ecstasy in one mind-blowing cocktail. He was so sensitive, he hurt.

She squeezed once . . . twice. Then her grip gentled, and she began a rhythm that was sure to send him crashing over the wall. But seconds later she released him. He would have howled out a protest, but his voice was trapped in his throat. He moaned and shivered, held captive by his raging hunger. He would die right there on her porch if he didn't get some relief in the next sixty seconds.

He went rigid with shock when her mouth closed around the head of his penis. Wet heat engulfed him as she eased down his shaft. His hands fisted in her hair. *God.* He couldn't bear it. He felt the rake of her teeth and he tried to pull out, but she licked and sucked at his erection as though she meant to devour him.

His vision went black, and he climaxed violently, no longer aware of where he was or even if he had a name. He tumbled into the abyss.

Francesca rested her cheek against his knee, feeling stunned and breathless. She'd never been a big fan of oral sex in either configuration, but eating Brett Gilman, feeling him pulse and flex in her mouth, was the most erotic act she'd ever experienced.

She wiped her lips with the back of her hand, not sure what to do next. He lay sprawled against the cushions, his body limp, his chest heaving with gasping breaths as he recovered. But amazingly, his cock wasn't limp at all. It sprang from the nest of wiry hair at his groin, stiff and proud.

She'd had trouble getting her mouth around him. He was thick and long, and just thinking about what came next, no pun intended, made her belly quiver and her pulse race. She wondered if she would survive.

She felt his hand ruffle her hair deliberately, his fingers pressing gently against her scalp. "Get up here, woman."

His demand brooked no opposition. Not that she had any intention of objecting. As she stood up, he waved a hand. "Ditch the skirt."

She unfastened the side zipper and stepped out of it. He took her hand as she tried to resume her earlier position. "Stand on the cushions," he said roughly. "Put your feet beside my hips. Bend your knees a little."

She obeyed mindlessly, feeling the slide of his palms on her thighs. She rested her hands on top of his head. The position felt awkward, but she was willing to be convinced. Beneath her, Brett sat up straight, putting his mouth right at the front of her tiny panties. He gave the hot pink satin a firm lick.

Her knees threatened to buckle, and she gulped. He gripped her hips in a firm hold and went to work. She waited for him to remove her underwear, but he wasn't interested in wasting any time. He was too busy kissing and wetting and playing with the scrap of fabric that barely covered her damp curls.

He moved it back and forth with his tongue, probing at her entrance through a tantalizing layer of cloth. Finally, when she was whimpering and writhing against his mouth, he dragged the fabric aside with his teeth and exposed her aching clitoris.

The first touch of his tongue directly on her supersensitive flesh was like an electric shock. She cried out, but he showed no mercy, sucking delicately until her entire existence centered at that one incredible spot. She tensed, poised on the brink of some fantastic discovery.

She couldn't speak; she couldn't move away. All she could do was stand submissively in his grasp and let him dissolve every one of her reservations and inhibitions in the most carnal, earth-shattering, blinding orgasm she had ever experienced.

He caught her up in his arms as she peaked, and then stood as she collapsed in a boneless heap in his embrace. She swayed drunkenly when he put her on her feet long enough for him to move the candle out of harm's way and drag a cushion on top of the table.

He took her face between his hands, his searing gaze demanding that she focus. "Condoms?" he said through clenched teeth. "Please tell me you have some."

She blinked, trying to process his words. "The pill," she muttered. "I'm on the pill."

"Thank God."

With gentle hands he turned her around and bent her forward over the table with her knees on the floor. She gripped the corners of the wood, feeling the soft padding beneath her belly, and realizing that it wouldn't have mattered one whit if he'd pressed her down on the rough, bare furniture without ceremony.

His hands lifted her hips, and he pulled the thin band of her thong to one side. She felt the head of his prick nudge between her thighs. She shivered hard and widened her stance. He was even more impressive from this angle. He entered her slowly. She felt stretched, filled, invaded. She caught her breath in an almost instinctive protest, but he went deeper still, making her vision blur.

There was nothing crude or rough about his claiming. Even so, the feeling of being possessed was alarming. And incredibly arousing. Her body accommodated him, throbbing in response to the steady pressure and gripping his rigid shaft. He muttered and groaned and finally buried the last inch deep inside her aching flesh. She could feel his balls brushing her ass.

He muttered something and touched the back of her neck. "Are you okay?"

She wasn't sure how to answer. She might never be okay again. "Yeah," she whispered.

He started to move and they both moaned. The slide of flesh on flesh was excruciatingly pleasurable, at least from her perspective. She had to assume he felt the same, because he cursed soft and low as he found a rhythm that threatened to induce insanity.

She felt a second climax bearing down and tried to hold back. She wanted it to last forever. His fingers clenched her hips, and she sensed him trying to slow things down. But it was too late. He drove into her with one final, out-of-control motion and they both came with mingled cries that echoed in the night air.

Brett wondered if Francesca was some kind of sexual goddess planted here in this sleepy little town to drag him under her powerful spell and make him forget all about New York and his other life. It wouldn't take much effort on her part. He lifted his weight onto his elbows and kissed the little indentation at the base of her spine.

She wiggled her hips. "That tickles."

He responded by lightly biting one cheek of her beautiful, round ass. The gentle teasing on his part was not so smart. He felt his prick begin to lift out of its exhausted torpor, and he shook his head in amazement. John Thomas was making up for lost time.

But she deserved something more for their next go-round. He stood up and helped her to her feet. "I'm guessing you have a nice, soft bed where we can continue this. Maybe after a shower?"

Without speaking, she blew out the candle, took his hand, and led him into the house. As they passed through the kitchen he caught a whiff of cinnamon and apples and warm bread. Francesca Fremont was doing a damn good job of feeding his hungers . . . every last one of them.

In the bathroom he reached for the light switch just as she cried out, "Don't."

But he had already flooded the room with sudden, harsh illumination. Her eyes were huge in her flushed face. Her hands hovered at her waist, clenched together. She looked ready to bolt.

His stomach fell to his knees. "Regrets, Francesca?" His voice was even, but he felt like a raw kid waiting for a kind word from the class princess.

She shook her head, glancing around the claustrophobic space as though searching for an escape route.

He needed to know where he stood. He folded his arms across his chest. "I asked you a question, Francesca. Do me the courtesy of answering."

She met his gaze slowly, reluctance etched in her posture. "I'm not sure."

It hurt more than he could have imagined. "I see." He saw the two of them clearly for the first time. His pants were unfastened, his shirttail flapping. She was nude from the waist down except for a crooked pair of sexy undies. For god's sake . . . he hadn't even touched her bare breasts. He tried to look at the last couple of hours from her point of view, and he began to understand her discomfiture.

He sighed, raking both hands through his rumpled hair. It stood on end where she had grabbed handfuls while he made her come apart in his arms. That one flash of memory made his semierect prick stir in eager anticipation.

He pounded a fist lightly against the wall, reaching for every one of his negotiating skills. "Talk to me, Francesca. The freaked-out look in your eyes is scaring the hell out of me."

That coaxed a tiny smile. She wrinkled her nose. "My God, Brett. You must think I'm easy. I haven't even known you two weeks."

He wanted to smile, but he dared not. Not yet, anyway. He shoved his hands in his pockets. "Tell me, Francesca. How many opportunities have there been for you to have sex with a man in the last couple of years?"

"Well, I—"

"Think hard. I want to know specifically."

She shrugged and leaned back against the wall. After a long moment she sighed. "Probably half a dozen."

"And did you have sex with any of those men?"

She shook her head slowly. "No."

"Weren't you horny?"

"Brett!"

"I want to know, Francesca. Were you content being celibate?"

Her eyes narrowed. "No. No, I wasn't."

"And yet you didn't sleep with a man when you had the chance." He paused a moment. "Why?"

Her eyelashes flickered, and he saw a pink flush steal from her throat to her cheeks. "I didn't feel any kind of a connection. It would have been nothing but a momentary physical release. And I don't believe in that. At least, not for me."

He felt his heart lift. "So you lied earlier."

That put a lick of heat in her gaze. "About what?" she asked, clearly incensed.

He took a step closer, crowding her just a tiny bit. "You tried to make me believe that you wanted me to screw you because I was passably attractive, close by, available, and transient."

"So?"

"So . . . I think you feel something between us." He swallowed hard. "And God knows I do," he said quietly, risking courage despite the odds.

Her lower lip trembled. "How can we? There's no such thing as love at first sight."

"Probably not. But nevertheless . . . you can't deny that something sparked between us from the beginning. I can't explain it. But I know it's real."

"It doesn't change anything," she said stubbornly, her face

reflecting the tug-of-war she was feeling between hope and common sense.

He took her shoulders in his hands and pressed a kiss to the top of her head. "You've changed *me*," he said gruffly. "I looked at you that first day, and as mad as I was with my butt full of rose thorns, I knew there was something special about you. Call it chemistry or fate or whatever you like, but it's real, Francesca. And I want you so badly at this very moment, I'm having a damned hard time carrying on a rational conversation."

A tiny smile curved her lips, and the shadows in her lovely blue eyes lifted. "Talk is cheap, hotshot. Let's see how you handle a woman when she's actually naked." Without waiting for an answer, she stripped off her undies and top and ran out of the room.

After less than a moment's shock, he shed his own clothes with clumsy haste. His boxers got hung up on his erection, and he ripped them away with an oath. Then, his heartbeat drumming away like a freight train, he went after her.

He found her sitting buck naked on the tall butcher-block island in the center of the kitchen, holding a small piece of apple pie in her hand. No plate. He stopped in the doorway, his body hard all over. He stared at her lithe, toned beauty, and he wanted to drop to his knees and say a prayer of gratitude.

But that would have to wait. Nothing was going to prevent him from claiming what was his. Nothing.

He was almost afraid to touch her. And then she upped the ante.

Francesca sprawled on her back gracefully, her legs hanging over the edge, and placed the pie over her navel. She stared up at the ceiling, her mouth in a pout. "It hurt my feelings that you ate only one piece of pie this evening. I worked hard to make it . . . just for you."

He walked forward slowly. "My apologies. I seem to have worked up an appetite in the interim." He placed a hand on her knee and watched her shiver.

She turned her head, her blue eyes dark and mysterious. "I didn't want to dirty any more dishes," she whispered.

He bent his head and licked the crust. It was shiny and perfect, but not as tasty as Francesca.

"No problem," he muttered.

She ran her fingers through his hair. "That's more like it. Help yourself."

He opened his mouth and took a big bite, his teeth scraping her belly. He moaned in pleasure. It was sweet and tart at the same time, the apples just the right firmness. He kissed her, letting her lick the crumbs from his lips. "Perfect," he murmured.

She pulled his head down. "More."

He complied willingly. Eating the dessert from such an erotic plate made him dizzy. After two more mouthfuls, he grabbed a bottle of wine from the counter, jerked out the cork, and swallowed a mouthful.

Then, as inspiration struck, he finished off the pie and filled her navel with sweet, cool merlot. He sucked it out and laughed when she squirmed.

That seemed to go so well, he was forced to dribble a stream over her pretty pink sex. He braced his hands beside her hips and licked her hard. She moaned and lifted into his caress and came with an almost silent cry.

He nuzzled her belly, drunk with arousal. "*Now* can we go clean up?" He picked her up, and she curled an arm around his neck with a yawn. "If you insist."

He set her on her feet in the tub and let her adjust the water temperature. She flicked the button on the faucet and drenched them both. Then she turned to face him and reached above her to grasp the showerhead. She tilted her neck to one side, allowing the water to cascade in sheets from her neck to her breasts. Stray drops hovered at the tips of her nipples as though reluctant to let go.

He touched her reverently, cupping the weight of her tits in his hands and squeezing gently. How could he have fucked her so mindlessly the first time and ignored these lush, lovely curves?

He heard her breath catch when he bent his head and sucked a pert nipple into his mouth. He teased it with his teeth, plucking at its twin with his free hand, loving how each one tightened and firmed at his touch.

She tasted better than anything he had devoured for dinner. He would eat frozen spaghetti forever if it meant having the privilege and the right to feast at just this spot for an eternity.

He stepped back and ran a fingertip from her collarbone to her navel. Her hair was a mass of dark red-gold waves. Her eyelashes were spiky, and her skin glowed wet and slick. He was so hard, his boner could pound nails.

He closed his eyes for a brief second and reminded himself of all the reasons he needed to cherish this amazing woman. "Hand me the shampoo," he muttered.

She abandoned her provocative pose and complied. He squirted a small dollop of white gel into his hand and rubbed his palms together. "Turn around."

She presented her back to him, and his stomach clenched in sharp hunger that had nothing to do with calories. From her narrow shoulders to the feminine flare of her hips, she was poetry in the flesh.

With shaking hands he massaged the shampoo into her scalp. She leaned back against him—instinctively, it seemed—and his cock nestled in the crack of her ass.

It was everything he could do to follow through with his

task. Finally, he rested his forehead against the back of her head, sliding his arms around her and capturing her breasts. He shivered, feeling the sense of homecoming. It was stronger than before. Stronger than lust. Stronger than doubts. Strong enough to rein in his hunger and offer tenderness in its stead.

He whispered in her ear, "Close your eyes." He nudged her forward and let the spray hit her directly. When the last strand of hair was soap-free, he turned her and found her mouth.

They kissed ravenously, smashing their lips and teeth together as though trying to climb into each other's skin. Her breasts were crushed against his chest. His prick throbbed against her belly.

With a groan of defeat, he lifted her in his arms and positioned her legs at his waist. When he thrust deeply into her slick core, she sobbed his name.

He pressed her into the wall of the shower, bracing his feet in the slick tub and pounding away at her as though she were a rag doll. He felt the red tide bear down on him again. *Too soon. God, too soon.*

Her fingernails scored his shoulders. She bit his ear. He could hear her frantic pleas echoing in his head.

He wanted to give her tenderness and gentleness and hearts and flowers. But even with what had gone before, his body drove him relentlessly, demanding that he press toward the ultimate prize, no matter what.

With a mighty roar, he flooded her sex with his come, feeling each spasm go deeper and deeper. And then his world went black for a moment, his muscles rigid with incredible pleasure, before he tumbled back to earth.

Francesca's eyes stung. She blamed it on the soap. She was not a sentimental girl in the first flush of youth. She knew the score. And yes . . . Brett was right. Obviously there was something between them. Something strong, unexpected, and beautiful. But that reality didn't negate the facts of their situation.

She and Brett were from different worlds.

She shoved the unwelcome thought to the back of her mind and locked it away. She wouldn't ruin the present with dismal thoughts of the future. A future without Brett.

He looked dazed, and she sympathized. Her body ached in areas she'd never felt before. The old country saying, "rode hard and put away wet," came to mind. Her legs felt like Jell-O, and only sheer will enabled her to coax her partner in crime out of the shower.

She dried him off, smiling gently as his eyelids drifted shut. The man had come three times already, and though she was no expert, she suspected he might need a bit of time to recover.

She gave her own wet body a cursory toweling as well, and tugged him stumbling along behind her to her bedroom. She threw back the covers and they fell onto the soft mattress with simultaneous groans of satisfaction.

His big arms snaked around her and dragged her up against his broad chest. He spooned her and pressed a soft kiss behind her ear. "G'night," he mumbled.

Before she could answer, he was asleep. She lay there in the darkness, absorbing the alien presence of a man in her bed. It was queen-size. There was room. But his presence was so much more than physical.

He had shouldered his way into her house, her body, and very possibly her life. It was alarming and unsettling and way too much to contemplate. With a delicate yawn, she rested her cheek against his forearm and closed her eyes.

Sixty-five minutes. That was how long it took him to recover. She knew, because she glanced at the digital clock when she felt two of his fingers part her intimate folds and stroke her swollen flesh.

She sucked in a sharp breath when he hit a pleasure spot, and she rolled to her back. His thumb worked at her clit as his fingers massaged her vaginal walls. He had her panting and begging for mercy in an embarrassingly short amount of time.

Her first climax lifted her hips off the bed. He didn't allow her to savor it. She was still racked by waves of pleasure when she felt his erection settle between her thighs and demand entrance.

Slowly this time. Pressing her into the mattress and stealing her breath. She wrapped her legs around his waist, and the new angle sent him deeper still.

He nuzzled her ear. "Francesca . . ."

"Hmmm?" She wasn't all that interested in pillow talk. She squeezed her inner muscles and grinned when she heard him curse.

But he was a gifted man. He actually managed to hold on to his original thought. He kissed her hard. "Behave, witch. I'm trying to be romantic."

"Go for it," she panted, digging her heels into the small of his back.

"You make love even better than you cook."

The simple, earnest compliment caught at an unexpectedly vulnerable spot deep in her psyche. She was renowned for her culinary skill. Up until now, she'd thought she was somewhat lackluster in the bedroom. She swallowed, her throat tight. "Why, thank you, Mr. Gilman. I may include that in my references. With your permission . . . of course."

He chuckled, moving his hips just enough to keep things simmering. "And one more thing."

"Geez. Cut to the chase. I'm dying under here."

He reached between them and pinched a nipple. "Smart-ass. Now I want to know, Francesca . . . was that carrot thing the other night on purpose?"

She grinned in the darkness. "I don't know what you mean."

"You damned well do."

She could tell that his desire to talk was rapidly waning. She raked her fingernails down his spine. "The carrot was good . . . but not nearly as tasty as you."

Evidently, reminding a man of a recent blow job was the sexual equivalent of striking a match to dry straw. He shuddered violently and started screwing her with long, tormenting strokes. All the way out . . . back in to the hilt. Slowly at first and then faster and faster until they were both sweaty and hoarse and crazy with lust.

It was like riding the wildest roller coaster on the planet. No time to catch your breath. No time to prepare for the next exhilarating plunge. She clung to him mindlessly, unable to do anything but feel and feel and feel.

He possessed her inside and out, mind and body and soul. She was ready to lay her heart at his feet, if he'd been interested.

But what he wanted was her body. And he took it . . . urgently, masterfully, as though it were his right. She gave him everything she had, her muscles quivering with exhaustion. Then she held him tight as he climaxed, and she didn't even regret not taking that last hill with him.

It was enough to hear his shout of completion and to know that for tonight, at least . . . Brett Gilman's hunger was satisfied.

Five

Francesca awoke to an insistent pounding at her front door. The old house didn't have a doorbell. She glanced at Brett, lying so peacefully beside her. He was dead to the world.

She pulled on her robe, knotted the sash firmly at her waist, and tiptoed from the room, closing the door behind her. She glanced at the clock in the hallway. Eight thirty. A bit early, especially for a Sunday morning.

She opened the door and stepped back instinctively as a microphone was thrust in her face.

There were three of them—intruders, not microphones—one thin, heavily made-up woman with hard eyes and a lined face, and two cameramen with cigarettes dangling from their mouths. They all wore plastic-coated IDs with the word "Press" and the name of a particularly nasty grocery-store-rack tabloid.

She lifted her chin, hiding her unease, and waited for them to speak.

The woman pushed closer. "We've traced a credit card purchase to this community. We're looking for information about Brett Gilman."

Her heart thumped unpleasantly in her chest, but she managed to maintain a pleasant smile. "Sorry. Can't help you. He was probably just passing through. We're a tight-knit community. I think we'd know if a stranger came to town." She paused, wondering if it was wise to encourage them. "Why are you looking for him?"

The woman glanced back at the cameramen to make sure they were getting everything. Then she smiled, but it was the kind of expression that made the hair on the back of Francesca's neck stand up. "We had a tip that he was stealing from his own company."

Francesca frowned and leaned forward, speaking directly into the microphone. "I understood that he was cleared of all charges. Someone else was at fault."

The weasel-woman's eyes narrowed. "We think the friend was covering for him. That Gilman let his buddy take the rap to save his ass."

Fury boiled in Francesca, searing hot. But she kept her expression and her words even. She lifted an eyebrow. "I can't imagine anyone willing to go to prison if he was innocent. But whatever . . . I can't help you."

She stepped back to close the door, but the woman wedged her bony foot into the opening. "Somebody in this dump of a town is going to get rich. It might as well be you. I'm authorized to offer a hundred grand for photos and concrete information as to his whereabouts."

"A hundred grand?" She blurted it out, stunned by their determination to bring torment to an innocent man. She was afraid she might be sick. She couldn't speak anymore. Her chest hurt, her throat ached, and tears stung her eyes.

"Francesca."

She jerked and whirled around, kicking the woman's foot away and slamming the door with desperate haste. Did they see him? Brett was standing in the doorway to the hall, his face paper white. He had pulled on his pants, but they were unfastened at the waist, and his feet and chest were bare.

She wasn't sure how much he had heard. She went to him and buried her face in his shoulder. He held her carefully. It took a full minute for her to realize that his entire body was rigid.

She pulled back, staring at his stony expression. "I'm sorry you had to hear that, Brett. Those people are the lowest of the low. But don't worry. Most of my neighbors around here are good folks. Even if somebody spills the beans, you won't be a story for long, surely. A political scandal or a Hollywood divorce . . . something big will happen soon and you won't be newsworthy anymore."

His eyes were opaque, his face a mask. "A hundred grand, Francesca? What was your answer going to be? I almost expected you to invite them in for tea. . . ."

She gaped at him. "You can't be serious. I told them you were innocent."

His jaw thrust out in an expression she'd never seen from him. "But you waited to hear the offer," he said, the accusation clear. "And you repeated it. I heard you. Were you giving it some thought? Maybe considering that capital you needed? If you truly cared about my privacy you would have slammed the door in their faces a hell of a lot sooner. I have to go."

He set her aside and strode to the bedroom. She followed him, shocked at the change in a man who had been sexy and playful and happy just a few hours before. Was this what he had looked like during the trial? This blank-faced shell of a man?

He was dressing rapidly. She grabbed his arm. "Don't leave.

It's Sunday. I can stay here all day, and no one will have a clue where you are. They'll give up, Brett. Don't do something rash."

His expression was hard, but for a brief moment she could swear she saw an aching regret and deep emotion. "I won't wait around to see if the money persuades you," he said quietly. "Even great sex isn't worth a hundred grand." And ten minutes later, despite her increasingly frantic protests, he was gone.

Francesca knew from the first moment she met him that Brett's presence in Camron was temporary. But she'd had no clue that he'd be gone so quickly, and her heart felt ripped from her chest.

She had no phone number, no e-mail, no address. He had vanished from her world as surely and completely as if he'd been a figment of her imagination.

Were it not for the lingering soreness in her legs and the faint smell of his aftershave on her sheets, she might have thought she was losing her mind.

And it killed her to know he believed her capable of ratting him out to the gutter press. But the more she thought about it, the more she understood his stunning reaction. If a man he had called his best friend for two decades was capable of betraying him, why should he automatically trust a woman he had known only a short time?

The whole thing was a disaster, and she couldn't even blame him for his lack of faith in her. His nightmare was too fresh. He hadn't been thinking clearly.

But in the end, Brett's motivations and reasons didn't change the final result. He was gone.

June was a busy time for her business. Weddings and graduations. Life transitions all around.

It was a hell of a moment to realize that she had fallen in love for the first time in her life. She was thirty-two years old. She should have known better. But she'd been lying to herself even since the day she carried cinnamon rolls through the hedge.

It occurred to her, finally, that the damage had been done that first day in the bank. Though they had not spoken or even seen each other face-to-face, she had looked at Brett Gilman, felt the impact of his presence in her town, in her life, and she had known. He was the man she had been waiting for all her life.

It was pathetic and futile and depressing. And the sad fact was, she got no sympathy from anyone. No one was even aware she knew the man, much less that she had fallen into his arms with an eager disregard for any future consequences. She'd leaped headfirst into a dizzying well of pleasure, and it had been indescribably wonderful.

But it was over.

No matter how many times she told herself, her stupid heart didn't seem to get the message.

He'd been gone two weeks when she decided she *had* to talk to someone. On the pretext of needing a taste tester for a new cookie recipe, she called Ada and invited her to come over for coffee and dessert.

Francesca blinked and choked back a laugh when Ada, elderly in name only, sauntered in the door. She was wearing magenta capri pants and a hot-pink T-shirt with gold lettering that said, *Old Lovers Are the Best.*

She hopped up on a stool with no apparent difficulty and raised an eyebrow. "Well, Frannie . . . where are these mysterious new cookies? I'm willing to be your guinea pig as long as they don't have tofu in them or any of that organic crap."

Francesca poured Ada a cup of coffee and laced it with tons of sugar and cream. Ada claimed that the additives kept the caffeine from giving her insomnia.

"Coming right up," Francesca murmured. She placed three still-warm little pastry puffs on a china plate and handed them over. "See what you think. They're lemon rounds filled with mascarpone."

Ava bit into one and her eyes rolled back in her head. "Damn, girlfriend . . . I don't know why the hell you're not married by now."

Francesca grinned wryly, realizing that Ada had given her the perfect opening. "Despite my best intentions, I seem to run men off," she said lightly, trying one of her own goodies and smiling wistfully as the taste exploded on her tongue. She had mastered baking. Romance was another story. She swallowed and licked her lips. "I must be doing something wrong. With men, that is."

Ada was sharp as a tack. Her eyes narrowed, almost disappearing in the deep wrinkles surrounding them. "Any one man in particular?"

Francesca shrugged. "Your tabloid hunk has already cut and run. Seems he thought I was going to sell him out." It took her entirely by surprise when hot tears burned the back of her throat. She thought she had gotten a handle on her messy emotions.

For a brief second, Ada's face softened with love and affection, but then her spine snapped straight and she glared. "Then he's an idiot," she declared roundly, her unwavering support clearly voiced.

Francesca sighed. "We hadn't known each other very long, even though . . ."

"Even though what? Even though you'd been shaggin'?"

Francesca choked. "Shagging?"

Ada nodded, her grin sly. "I got a DVD player. I've seen *Austin Powers*. So out with it, honey . . . was he good? I hear those real sophisticated types like it kinky. Is that what went wrong? Did you get all uptight and prissy? Men like wild women in bed. I read in one of Dr. Ruth's books that there are at least a dozen positions that will blow a man's mind if you do them right."

Francesca felt herself turning red, even as control of the conversation rapidly slipped away from her. She cleared her throat. "Sex wasn't a problem. And I knew he wasn't here to stay. I just hadn't expected it to be over so soon."

Ada tucked another lemon puff in her mouth and spoke around it. "Well, it seems to me you'd better be making a trip to New York Citeeee and knocking some sense into that inconsiderate jerk . . . if you still want him, that is."

Francesca leaped to her feet and started washing dishes. The familiar ritual helped steady her nerves. "But that's just it, Ada. I can't. I told him I was only interested in casual, recreational, temporary sex."

"Well that's a load of hoo-ha." Ada picked up a dish towel. "Why the hell would you say that?"

"I didn't think we had a future, and I—"

"You were horny."

"Ada!" She hissed a protest, reluctantly aware that her grizzled neighbor had hit the nose on the head. Francesca *had* been horny, and she had convinced herself that a pleasant sexual interlude was just what she needed.

Now her own idiocy was coming back to haunt her. She didn't want Brett Gilman for a hot and heavy fling . . . she wanted him for the long haul.

Ada wagged a bony finger in her face. "Then go tell him

you've changed your mind. People do it all the time. Politicians . . . actors . . . you'd be in good company."

"It's not that easy. I wouldn't have a clue where to find him."

"Grow some balls, girl. MapQuest his ass. You know the name of his business. How hard can it be?"

"I can't just show up at his office."

"Why the hell not? Sandra Bullock would."

"Sandra Bullock?" Somehow she had missed a line or two of this conversation.

"You know . . . in all those sappy romantic comedies. I just watch 'em for the hot guys, but still, ya got to admire the plucky little scrapper. She never says die."

"That's fiction, Ada. And besides, I'd just as soon not be shot down in a public place."

"Candy-ass."

"Nosy old broad."

They exchanged insults amicably and grinned at each other as they went back to their tasks.

Ada stepped off her stool and bumped Francesca with a sharp hip. "But if he makes the first move?"

Francesca sighed. "I'll be waiting."

Two mornings later she started her period. She had taken her birth control pills faithfully. There was no reason to think she might have been pregnant. But evidently her subconscious had been working overtime, busily weaving delicious fantasies about the future for no good reason. Fanciful scenarios where she gave birth to Brett's beautiful baby and they all three lived happily ever after in a co-op overlooking Central Park.

She staggered back to bed and pulled the covers over her head. Cramps set in with a vengeance, and the thought of breakfast made her physically sick. It was a familiar pattern.

She would sleep for a while and keep her stomach empty and soon she would be back on her feet, good as new.

Denial was a good thing. Denial was her friend. Unfortunately, denial wasn't able to erase the list of chores on her to-do pad. She had menus to plan and shopping lists to prepare. It would be enough to keep her mind occupied today . . . barely.

Even when her body returned to normal later that week, her appetite was nonexistent. She decided that now was as good a time as any to lose those fifteen pounds. She wasn't interested in food, so why force it? Surely the splitting headache would disappear eventually . . . when her body got the message that she was too miserable to eat.

Midafternoon on Saturday she finished up in the kitchen and was just contemplating a nap and some ibuprofen when she heard a loud knocking at the front of the house. Her heart sank. *Dear God, please, not those awful people again.*

She opened the door cautiously, and her stomach pitched and rolled. Brett stood there with a tentative smile on his face.

He held a cluster of sweet peas in his hand. "Hello, Francesca."

Her vision went fuzzy, her knees buckled, and that was the last thing she remembered.

Brett dropped the flowers and grabbed her just before she hit the floor. Her face was so white, every one of her freckles looked painted on.

He kicked the door shut and carried her into the bedroom, depositing her carefully on top of the quilt. He chafed her cold hands. "Come on, baby. Wake up." When she didn't respond, he went into the bathroom and returned with a wet rag. His hands were shaking, and he was cursing his own stupidity in not calling first.

He wiped her forehead and cheeks and neck. She was wearing those faded jeans he loved and a cropped white T-shirt with aqua lettering that said, *Good cooks know how to heat things up*. He did his best not to stare at the strip of skin exposed just above her waistline.

"Francesca, sweetheart. Wake up. I'm sorry I startled you. Come on, angel." He continued to talk to her in a low, careful voice, and finally her pretty eyelashes fluttered and opened and she came back to the present, albeit looking a bit confused.

She lifted a hand to her head, rubbing her temple as though it ached. "What happened?"

He expelled the breath he'd been holding. "Jesus, Francesca. You scared the hell out of me. You fainted. Is it that shocking to see me again?"

She struggled to sit up. Her teeth worried her bottom lip. "I've been dieting. I suppose I should have eaten lunch." She paused, staring down at her fingers that were twisting a corner of the sheet. "I wasn't expecting you."

"Obviously." He was torn between guilt and uneasiness. She didn't look too happy that he was here. Of course, it might have helped if he had at least talked to her in the last three weeks.

He sighed, leaning back against the headboard. "I should have called you, I know. But I was trying to get my life in order. You didn't see me at my best, and I wanted you to be proud of me."

She scooted up beside him, but left a good twelve inches between their shoulders. "I don't understand."

He saw that a bit of color had returned to her cheeks. "I'm sorry I accused you, even for a minute. I was so angry that they had found me, and I couldn't imagine how they knew I was at your house."

"It wasn't me," she interrupted urgently. "I swear."

He nodded slowly. "I know that. And honestly, it doesn't matter how or why they showed up. I'm not going to hide out anymore. That was a dumb idea to begin with. I have a business to run, and people who depend on me."

"Oh." Her usually open face was shuttered, and he couldn't read the expression in her eyes. The blue had darkened to a murky navy.

When she didn't say anything else, he stumbled on. "First off, I took out a restraining order against the newspaper, and I threatened to sue if they took things any further. My lawyers were very convincing. I don't think we'll have any more problems."

She nodded slightly. "Good."

"And I went to see Peter. . . ."

Her face lightened and she smiled. "Oh, Brett. I'm so glad. That must have been very hard."

He swallowed, his throat tight as he remembered the brief, heart-wrenching encounter. The raw gratitude on his friend's face had shamed him. He sighed, feeling the ache of regret. "He'll be up for parole in four years. It will seem like a lifetime to Dana and the kids, but they'll make it. She loves him, and those babies mean the world to them both. I think their marriage will survive."

"You're taking care of them financially, aren't you?"

He stilled, feeling uncomfortable. "How did you know that?"

Her smile was genuine and warm. "Because you're a good man. And I *am* proud of you."

He took her hand. "I'm happy to hear it. That makes what I have to say next a bit easier."

It was her turn to look uneasy, and his heartbeat skipped and stuttered in dismay. Had he misread the situation? He gripped her fingers. "Here's the thing, Francesca. I have to go back to New York, but I don't want to leave you. Not when we've barely had a chance to get to know each other. I need you. There's something real and special between us. You can't deny it. So I thought you might consider coming to stay with me for a while . . . see if you like it there. . . ."

He couldn't look at her face. He stared down at their hands. "If you don't want to leave Camron, I'll fly down as often as I can to visit you, of course. But consider this: I have the money and the contacts to get your catering business set up in New York. You could consider it a loan, if you want. I know this is your home, but with your family in Atlanta, maybe it wouldn't be so much of a wrench to leave Camron. There are great direct flights from New York to Atlanta every day, and you could go down to visit as often as you like."

Still no response. He was starting to sweat. "New York is a great city. It would be so much fun for me to show you the sights. I swear you'll love it."

After a split second of silence, she spoke quietly. "And what about my house, my property? And your house, your property?" The flat question had an accusatory note that made him wince.

"I've already thought about that," he said quickly. "I'm deeding mine to you. As a thank-you for saving my life. Because you did. We'll bring the land back together like it was a hundred years ago . . . one big, wonderful place . . . We can fix up the other house or bulldoze it, whatever you want. I love Camron. I love the mountains. This could be where we come for long, lazy summer vacations, or maybe at Thanksgiving. You can invite all your friends and relatives and we'll watch you cook to your heart's content."

He stopped finally, having run out of things to say. Either

she was interested or she wasn't. He had one final bargaining chip, but he was saving it, if necessary, for a last-ditch effort.

Now her slender fingers picked at a loose thread on the quilt. "And what if it doesn't work?" she asked quietly. "What if we break up, lose interest, fizzle out?"

Well, hell. There went the last chip. He would just have to suck it up and be a man. He hadn't expected it to be quite so terrifying. She turned to face him, and her eyes were huge pools of blue. She was still pale, and somewhere deep in her guarded gaze was something that made him tense with an unexplained sense of dread. She didn't look like a woman ready to say yes.

He smiled and hoped it didn't look as much like a grimace as it felt. "It will work because I love you, Francesca. And I was wrong. Love at first sight does exist. I'm living proof. You knocked me off my feet."

"Literally," she teased, her mouth curving in a faint smile. She scooted closer and he pulled her firmly against his chest, feeling everything in his universe settle into place.

"So," he said calmly. "Do you have a response to my incredibly brave and sincere declaration?"

He thought he heard her smother a laugh. He tugged them both to their knees, face-to-face. He gave her his best intimidating scowl. "Give it up, woman. I'm swaying in the wind."

She smiled, and he felt it all the way to his toes. "I love you very much, Brett Gilman." And then she kissed him, and he wondered how in the hell he'd managed to stay away for so long.

He explored her mouth lazily, enjoying her soft, panting sighs, her low, sexy murmurs. He stripped the T-shirt over her head. She wasn't wearing a bra. He brushed the undersides of her breasts and used his thumbs to rasp across her nipples.

Her talented hands had already unfastened his zipper, and when her fingers closed around his prick, he shivered in delight as memories meshed with the present. He dragged them both off the bed and onto their feet. "It'll be faster if we undress ourselves," he muttered. She was laughing at him, and he didn't even care.

She beat him in the nudity race, but in all fairness, he was wearing more clothes. She knelt on the bed, waiting, a sensual welcome in her pose.

He joined her and tried to push her onto her back, but she turned the tables.

"My turn on top," she said with a husky command.

He gripped her hips as she moved astride him, and then he lost his train of thought as her full, beautifully shaped breasts bounced mesmerizingly just above him.

He pulled her down and sucked one perfect nipple deep into his mouth. She tasted like sin on a plate. He switched breasts, and her fingernails raked his collarbones, leaving scratches that he barely even noticed.

She leaned down even farther and kissed him. His hands went to her ass, shaping and plumping it and tracing the crack between her cheeks.

They weren't even fucking yet, and he was ready to explode. Suddenly his erotic sex kitten lifted to her knees, took his hard prick in her hand, and guided it to her wet, welcoming entrance. She lowered herself with deliberate, sinuous motions until he was firmly seated deep against her womb.

Her head fell back, and his hands came up to her rib cage. His hips flexed and she whimpered. And then she gave him the ride of his life.

Francesca lay panting against her lover's chest, feeling the weight of her secret threaten to choke her. Was there ever a good time for this kind of news?

On the other hand, a man's guard was definitely down postcoitus. Maybe he wouldn't flip out if she said it out loud.

Or maybe he would walk away. The man was thirty-nine years old. If he'd wanted to be a daddy, he'd had plenty of opportunities.

At the moment, he was asleep, his long lashes dark against his tanned cheeks. Razor stubble darkened his chin. He probably had to shave twice a day to keep it smooth.

She slipped carefully from his embrace, feeling the dribble of wetness on her thighs. She was exhilarated and terrified at the same time. He loved her. She loved him. It seemed like a miracle. But she wanted more.

When she returned to the bedroom, his dark gaze was fixed on the doorway. He had positioned the pillows behind his shoulders, and his arms were tucked behind his head. The sheet rested just below his waist, and his bare chest was enough to make her swoon.

He was hard everywhere she was soft. Muscular and strong. But even more impressive than his physical strength was his emotional toughness. He'd survived a betrayal and an ordeal that could have destroyed him. And in the end, he'd been able to forgive.

She had paused to put on her robe, and now she leaned in the doorway, enjoying the sight of him stretched out on her bed.

He patted the sheet beside him. "It's lonely in here. Come, my love."

The words gave her a shiver. She went to him, dropping the robe at the last second, feeling unaccountably shy. He flipped back the sheet until she got settled. She snuggled against his side.

The lump in her throat was getting bigger, and her pulse

was racing like an Indy 500 pace car. She laid a hand on his chest. "It's sweet of you to offer, Brett, but moving my business isn't really practical. It works here because I fill a need. Caterers in the city are a dime a dozen, and besides, New Yorkers want far more sophisticated and trendy fare than I prepare."

He turned on his side and propped up on an elbow. The scowl on his face was that of a man not used to being thwarted. "We'll make it work," he said stubbornly.

He put his hand on her abdomen, and she had the strangest notion he was staking his claim. She shook her head. "I enjoy my job, but I can't see doing it in New York. I think I might be interested in taking on a new challenge." She nearly chickened out, but she heard Ada's voice in her head suddenly: *Grow some balls, girl.*

His scowl was replaced by a look of confusion. "Like what?"

Her heartbeat was so loud now it threatened to deafen her. She was tempted to flee to the kitchen, to fix him an early dinner . . . anything to postpone the inevitable.

But the Fremonts were tough people. Their ancestors had come over the mountains in wagons, had farmed rugged rocky soil, had held on to a sturdy individuality. She licked her lips and did her best to smile. "I think I'd be a good mom. You know . . . one of those cookie-baking, homemade-baby-food-making, PTA kind of moms."

The scowl *and* the confusion were gone, but so was every last expression or nuance on his face. His features were a blank slate. Even his eyes were unreadable. "A mom?" he asked carefully.

She nodded slowly, doing her best to channel Sandra Bullock. "I'm proposing to you, Brett. Not that we would get married and start popping out little rugrats anytime soon. But I thought you should know where I stand. I can't just pick up my whole life and move to New York on a whim. I need to know that you see a future for us."

He had paled, and fear ate like a corrosive acid at her stomach.

She winced. "Apparently you've never thought about being a father." She felt sick.

He shook his head. "Of course I've thought about it. I'm godfather to Peter's kids. Each time I held one of those tiny, beautiful babies during a christening ceremony, I was a bit envious. Not that the timing was right for me. But yeah, in the abstract, I've thought about it."

He paused, and puzzlement furrowed his brow. "But what about your catering? And the cookbook you wanted to write?"

She grinned happily. "I'm assuming you entertain quite a bit. I could make myself useful on that front. And I could still do a cookbook if I wanted."

The dawning amazement and happiness on his face eased the ache in her chest.

"I'm sorry, Brett. I know I'm springing this on you, and I'm sure a wife and a family weren't in your plans so suddenly . . . but I promised myself I'd be honest with you if you came back."

He caressed the flat plane of her belly, his eyes filled with tender wonder. He laughed roughly. "Nothing about this last year has been in my plans. But without all the turmoil, I wouldn't have met you." His brows narrowed. "But are you sure? You've lived here all your life."

She nodded shyly, still feeling scared and wonderful and hopeful and overwhelmed. "Very."

He leaned over and kissed her. The love and acceptance in his lips and on his face made her go all teary.

He licked the tears away and flipped back the sheet so he could study her body from head to toe.

A lock of hair fell across his forehead. He looked young and happy and content. "You'll be one heck of a beautiful pregnant woman. Do you think you'll have cravings?" he wondered aloud. "A woman who loves food like you do will surely crave something."

She mustered a frown. "I'm sure I will. And I was hoping you'd get me what I want."

He sat up instantly, his shoulders square with determination. "You name it, sweetheart. I'll go to the store any time of the day or night. What do you think you'll crave?"

She captured his hand and brought it to her breast, shivering at the touch of his fingers against her skin. "You," she said simply. "I crave you. And as long as you love me and our children, I'll be completely satisfied."

He moved back down beside her, folding her into an embrace that spoke volumes. "That's good to know, my love." He stroked carefully between her thighs, teasing her until she gasped. He nuzzled her belly. "Now, can we discuss *my* cravings?"

And somewhere, Miss Matilda smiled. . . .

Tag, You're It!

One

If Lily Langford were as exotic as her name, it would be easy to seduce the man across the street. But despite her glamorous moniker, she was ordinary. Not in a bad way. She was happy with her average intelligence (B student all the way) and her middle-of-the-road looks. Mostly.

Some days she might wish for bigger boobs or longer legs, but usually she was content with what the good Lord had doled out. Dark brown hair, straight as a board. Brown eyes. Good teeth. Skin that tanned at the first hint of spring. It might not be the premier package, but she really had no complaints.

But perhaps if she were just a tiny bit more . . . noticeable . . . Benjamin Reynolds might be able to tear himself away from his laptop long enough to realize that she was available. Hungry. Head over heels in lust.

Benjamin lived in the modest two-story house across the street from her sturdy brick ranch. Their homes sat near a cul-de-sac in a sleepy Boston suburb. On the day she moved in eighteen months ago, gorgeous Ben had appeared at her door in time to help unload the contents of her U-Haul.

Her tight budget meant moving herself. She'd had plenty of help on the Mississippi end of the trip, but here in Massachusetts she was on her own. She'd bought her little house furnished, and even though the previous owners had played fast and loose with the exact definition of that term, she was grateful that all she had had to bring with her were boxes.

Lots of boxes. Heavy boxes. A mountain of boxes. All of which the handsome tousled-haired blond Adonis had unloaded with knee-weakening ease. Her knees, that was, not his. He hadn't seemed at all favorably affected by her road-weary feminine self clad in ancient jeans and a sweaty T-shirt.

Except for Benjamin Reynolds, the neighborhood had been strangely deserted that day. Kids at school, moms and dads at work. Ben had emerged from his front door just as she was opening the back of the trailer. He'd been munching on a breakfast bar (at three in the afternoon), and his attire suggested he'd been about to go for a run.

But with a killer smile and gentle courtesy, he'd changed his plans and spent the next three hours helping her schlep all her junk into the house. He'd even whipped out his cell phone and ordered pizza at six when they'd both been starting to flag.

That first day she'd been bowled over by his deep blue eyes and his tall, rangy physique. But his friendliness had been just that. It wasn't flirting or the prelude to a sexy relationship. Benjamin Reynolds had simply been helping a new neighbor get settled.

After that, it was several weeks before she saw him again. Long weeks during which she put her house in order, handled all the million and one details that had to be dealt with when relocating, and started her new job.

She'd barely had time to breathe, much less fantasize about a man she'd met only once. But she was a pretty darned good multitasker, and even in the midst of her frantic days, she'd been drawn again and again to thoughts of the yummy male across the street.

She'd casually trolled for info about her mystery man when she saw other neighbors out and about in the evenings. He was some kind of genius mathematician inventor, and word on the street was that he spent every night holed up in his basement laboratory like some kind of modern-day, *GQ* version of Dr. Frankenstein.

Lily didn't spend an inordinate amount of time wondering about Ben's availability. As the lowest-ranking pediatric nurse on the community hospital's rotation, she'd been stuck with the night shift. She liked her assignment for a couple of reasons. For one thing, she enjoyed the quiet and the chance to interact with her little patients, to stroke their hair or to coax them into sleep. When you were five years old and hurting, the world could be a scary place.

She'd found the job opening online, and after a long, hard look at her predictable life and the recent demise of a lackluster relationship, she'd decided she needed to cut a few apron strings and start over in a new place.

The second reason she hadn't quibbled over taking the unpopular night shift was that it meant her schedule mirrored Ben's. At night, when his big brain was doing things she couldn't even imagine, she was at work as well. And when she pulled up in her driveway shortly after seven in the morning and wasted no time tumbling into bed, it was comforting somehow to know that she wasn't entirely alone. Ben, too, called it a night and slept when she did, just across the street.

Now, if she could figure out a way to sleep *in* his bed, she'd be even happier.

Over the past year and a half they'd developed a pleasant camaraderie. Often they even went running together, although she would much rather have explored another, more intimate form of indoor exercise.

Ben was a quiet man. He could converse on any number of topics, but in general he preferred silence. Probably because the wheels in his brain were always turning. She was lost, however, when he turned that intense, focused gaze directly on her. Sweet lordy, that man's laser-beam regard made her stomach tighten with all sorts of delicious little nervous impulses.

What was it about the guy that made her want to strip off all his clothes and beg him to concentrate his intellect and his talent on making love to Lily Langford? When had his understated friendship ceased to be enough?

Day one, probably. She'd never met a man who made such a big impression in such a small amount of time. Every hormone in her body had shown up for calisthenics, and Ben was oblivious. She'd done an embarrassing number of things to grab his attention—everything from loosening the wires on the distributor cap of her car to purposely muddling her tax return to importing spiders into her kitchen for him to kill.

And Ben was great. He solved every one of her problems with ease. But he never took the hint. He never once indicated he might be amenable to inventing a new Kama Sutra position or even a variation of the tried-and-true favorites.

Perhaps she wasn't being obvious enough. After all, the man's head was so full of weighty thoughts, there was probably no room for something as pedestrian as mere lust. He was a guest lecturer at MIT, for Pete's sake. And Lily could barely master the remote that came with her new TV.

But all that intellectual labor surely needed to be balanced with some good old-fashioned horniness. A man had needs, even if he sublimated them with fierce concentration. Unfortunately, his sexual urges weren't the only things he ignored. Ben tended to completely shut out the world around him when he was immersed in work.

Only last week the fire department trucks had roared up in front of his house just after noon, yanking Lily out of a peaceful slumber. Panicked, she had flung a robe over her shorty pajamas and raced across the street barefooted, terrified that her hunky brainiac was lying dead or maimed in his lab.

Nothing so dramatic. Ben had awakened early and decided to make himself a grilled-cheese sandwich. He'd left the unattended oven on broil when a new idea suddenly dragged him back to his notes. The kitchen was filled with roiling black smoke, and the stove was a mess when the professionals arrived.

That wasn't the only time his famed mental prowess failed him in more mundane situations. One day Lily and Ben had been chatting in his kitchen when he took a swig of milk straight from the carton. He'd gagged over the sink, spitting out the curdled milk, and then gazed, incredulous, at the lapsed sell-by date printed on the plastic.

His look of indignant dismay had caused Lily to dissolve into a fit of giggles, but the truth was, the man needed a keeper. Someone to run his house and his life and leave him free to do what he did best.

Lily yearned to take care of him. She was a nurturer at heart. It was why she had gone into nursing, and why she now wanted to get a lot closer to Benjamin Reynolds. Well, that and his amazing abs and pecs and other, less visible body parts.

She'd gone in search of him one evening, found the door

unlocked (no surprise there), and tracked him down in his exercise room. The sweat glistening on his hard body and the steady precision with which he lifted and lowered a truly impressive set of weights explained why his physical attributes were in as good or better shape than his off-the-charts IQ.

Wow. Now firmly back in the present, she fanned her face with an unopened bill and peered through her curtains. She was in danger of overheating, and it was December. With a sigh of self-disgust, she dropped into a chair and began flipping through her mail. Her many attempts at snagging Ben's attention had failed miserably. She might as well admit defeat.

The medium-size cardboard box on her kitchen table perked her up a tiny bit. She'd done some online Christmas shopping, and now she looked forward to wrapping the gifts and tucking them under her tree, ready for the trip home to Mississippi. Even though it meant leaving Ben behind, she was excited about her upcoming week's vacation.

Starting a new job meant she'd had to wait for vacation time, and this would be her first chance to return to the bosom of her family since she'd been in Massachusetts. Her parents had visited her last summer, but it just wasn't the same. Homesickness swamped her suddenly, and she wondered if flying so far from the nest had been a mistake.

She loved her job, and she had hoped Benjamin Reynolds might be part of her future, but apparently she'd been building rosy castles in the air about something that didn't exist.

She sniffed and wiped her nose and tore into the box to distract herself from depressing thoughts. Most of the contents were exactly what she had ordered. A *Sound of Music* DVD for her mom . . . a Civil War history book for her dad. One of her baby sister's favorite boy-band CDs. At the last minute, she had added an Emily Dickinson poetry collection for herself.

It wasn't there.

Instead, at the bottom of the box she found a tattered slender volume with an odd title inscribed in faded gold leaf on the navy cover. *Miss Matilda's Guide to Love and Romance for the Proper Young Lady.* She checked the copyright page—1949. *Holy cow . . .* The book was a first edition and almost sixty years old. It might be valuable to a collector, but it sure as heck wasn't the poetry she had ordered.

She flipped the fragile pages stained with brown age spots. Something on page sixty-two caught her attention, and her eyes widened as she read Miss Matilda's advice.

Men are hunters and conquerors by nature. Modern man is at a bit of a disadvantage, because his opportunities to be dominant are somewhat curtailed. It is important for you, the female, to provide situations where he can exert his masculinity. Testosterone fuels the male libido. Testosterone peaks during the chase. Although it might seem manipulative, it is imperative that you situate yourself in his path time and again until he becomes aware of your charms, but then you must back off and give him the chance to pursue the prize. All of this must be done casually, so that the male thinks he has come up with a battle plan on his own.

It is very important for you to maintain other interests and activities. Nothing is sadder or more pathetic than a clingy woman who has no identity of her own. I recently made a visit to Detroit and was introduced to a marvelous new product for women called Tupperware. Chances are you've seen a newspaper article about the innovative "sealed" bowls. With a bit of effort you can begin or add to your collection of these amazing plastic containers. You can even invite a few female friends to your home, serve them snacks, and demonstrate the product. Later, while in conversation with the man you hope to win, make sure to mention your endeavor. He will be impressed by your initiative, and may even be jealous of the time and energy you are expending elsewhere.

The man you seek will most likely feel the need to draw your interest back to him if he perceives that you are slipping away. Pursuit and capture raise the male's lust to new levels, and as long as you preserve his illusions, you will soon have him eating out of your hand. Sexual activity in the aftermath of his triumph will be everything you have dreamed of and more.

Lily's jaw dropped nearly to her chest. Had she been going about this all wrong? True, the old-fashioned advice sounded politically incorrect. That whole war-of-the-sexes thing was supposed to have fallen by the wayside now that society recognized equality between men and women. And Tupperware? *Good grief.* She had cabinets full of it, and she had neither the time nor the inclination to throw a party.

But, hey . . . the other ideas were worth a shot. She peeked out the window one last time and saw Ben emerge from his house in running clothes. Most days lately she had joined him. She looked down at her sneaker-clad feet. She was ready. It was sort of a routine.

And then she glanced back at the book. *Well, heck . . .* If there was the slightest chance Miss Matilda was right, Lily was willing to give it a chance.

*   *   *

Ben glanced at his watch and picked up his pace. He tried to shave ten seconds off his time every day, and today he might make it twenty. The skies overhead were leaden, and the late-afternoon breeze was cold and damp. He tucked his chin deeper into his scarf. It was irritating that he found himself worrying—no, make that wondering—why Lily had decided not to come with him.

He was perfectly happy making this five-mile run on his own. But he'd become accustomed in recent months to having the luscious Lily at his side as he pounded the pavement, working up a sweat and trying his damnedest to remember all the reasons why he had to keep his focus.

The project he was in the midst of had international ramifications. His parents had taught him from the cradle that his unusual intellect was a gift that came with a high price. He owed it to the world to search out new solutions for eradicating world hunger, for developing security technology, for enabling his fellow man to live and work and learn in a safe, productive environment.

At the age of twelve he had contributed to a weapons design still being used by the navy today. The Pentagon had him on retainer by the time he was twenty, primarily to search out flaws in their newest computer systems. At twenty-five he was a finalist for the Nobel prize.

Without a doubt he was contributing to the global community. But at what cost? He was thirty years old, and he'd never had a relationship with a woman that lasted more than a couple of weeks. Sexual hunger was a constant, almost living entity in his life.

When it became unbearable, he sought out a one-night stand. Carefully, of course, and using good judgment about protection. But the encounters left him feeling guilty and confused and ultimately unsatisfied.

In the last couple of years he had tried to give up sex entirely. Immersing himself in work was not a problem. He was single-minded when he was involved in something that interested him. His body didn't like it. But at least he didn't have to deal with those awkward mornings after, or feel that disturbing sense of loss over not being able to connect with a woman.

He'd told himself that celibacy was probably best, at least for the foreseeable future. Nothing was more important than his work. And he had believed both of those things . . . until Lily Langford moved in across the street and turned his world upside down.

Lily was the most naturally sexy woman he had ever encountered. Her slim, athletic body vibrated with health and energy. Even in the scrubs she wore to work she looked good. The royal blue ones with the teddy-bear print were his favorite. Lily exuded warmth and charm and a gut-level, enticing sensuality that made his recalcitrant dick hard and his supposedly superior mind mush.

That in itself was a miracle. Even the need for sexual release had always been tempered by his will, his utter focus. Nothing had ever been able to distract him when he was working.

Nothing until Lily. And to tell the truth, the woman was a mess. She might not be blond, but she was a ditz. He wondered sometimes how she managed at the hospital. At home, some crisis was always coming up. He'd bailed her out a dozen times, and it was almost second nature to him now. After all, it was what he had been trained to do.

See a problem and solve it.

But fixing Lily's messes was only the tip of the iceberg. He had far more serious matters to grapple with. He was seriously, head-over-ass in lust. And his famous, never-dented-by-any-distraction concentration was beginning to look like the mental equivalent of Swiss cheese. He couldn't afford it, not in a professional sense.

And Lily sure as hell wasn't a one-night-stand possibility. She was that double-edged sword so lethal to the male of the species—a warm, appealing, sexy woman who lured a man into thinking that hot, sweaty sex might be worth a wedding ring and some *I-dos*. And Ben simply wasn't marriage material. He'd spent his life being more or less ignored by his overachieving parents. They were proud of his genetically accumulated intelligence, but they hadn't a clue what it meant to be nurturing and loving.

He'd been groomed for the think-tank lifestyle, and no way in hell would he ever have kids. He couldn't even fix a damn grilled-cheese sandwich without burning down the house. How could he be responsible for a tiny, fragile life? It just wasn't in the cards for him.

And as depressing as that thought was, it was even more depressing to think that an honorable man would stay away from the luscious Lily. She had home and hearth written in her lovely brown eyes, and only a scumbag would use her for sex and then discard her.

But somehow he couldn't visualize that last scenario. If he finally had the chance to bury himself deep between those toned, fabulous thighs, he wasn't sure he'd ever be willing or able to leave. It might be winter now, but he had a mind that latched onto details and filed them away.

Never in a million years could he forget the sight of Lily Langford in a fiery red maillot bending over the hood of her car as she washed the dirt away while wiping his mind clean of conscious thought. He'd been reduced to a pair of aching testicles and a prick so hard he had trouble breathing normally. Six months later he still remembered that swimsuit and those legs.

He wiped sweat from his forehead before it had a chance to freeze. His lungs were burning and his eyes were stinging. A light, icy rain started to fall, and suddenly that "home and hearth" thing sounded damned appealing.

Which brought him back to Lily. Why hadn't she met him outside today? It was ridiculous for a grown man to admit he'd had his feelings hurt. He might as well tattoo the word "pussy" on his forehead. Why the hell should he care if Lily joined him in his habitual exercise?

It wasn't as though he had any claim on her. They were casual friends and neighbors. Nothing more.

He rounded the corner onto their street, and his gaze zeroed in on the sight of her car in her driveway, right where it had been when he left. So, she didn't have an errand to run. She hadn't been called in to work unexpectedly. What if she was ill? It was flu season, and she was around sick kids all night.

The squiggle of unease in his belly tightened into a knot of anxiety. The thought of soft, lovely Lily alone and hurting in her drafty house made something in his chest ache. Not his heart, surely. He was pretty sure that organ had been bionically replaced with a CPU at birth.

Unbidden, his legs carried him to her front door. He hovered there on her narrow stoop, trying to bend his neck and keep his head beneath the overhang. But in that position, the nasty, bone-chilling rain found the gap between his sweatshirt and his skin and slithered in, making him miserable and mocking his uncertainty.

Finally he rang the bell. He heard movement inside, and suddenly there she was, framed in the doorway, giving him a slight smile and a quizzical look.

She tucked a strand of hair behind her ear. "Ben . . . what's up? Shouldn't you get home and shower before you catch your death of cold?"

Clearly she recognized the fact that he had been out for his usual exercise. Without her. Irritation replaced his uncertainty. "I wondered why you didn't come running today." If the quasi-question sounded terse and accusatory, he couldn't help it.

She frowned slightly. "Um, well . . . the weather looked as if it might turn nasty, and I had some Christmas cards to address."

"Christmas cards." He said it flatly, trying to decipher her expression. *Bloody fucking Hallmark.* His mood went from surly to blistering, and he wanted to pound his fist against something. *Shit.*

So what? Did it matter that he ranked so low on her list of priorities? They weren't a couple. Their lives connected only on the most superficial of levels. He knew all the reasons why his reaction was illogical. And he was *never* illogical. But he sure as hell couldn't explain his overreaction.

He tried changing his grimace to a smile, but judging from Lily's expression, he hadn't succeeded. He cleared his throat. "Okay, then. I thought you might be sick. Just wanted to check."

Suddenly he realized that the wonderful smells emanating from her house weren't Lily herself. His brain clicked into gear, identifying the mouthwatering fragrances of garlic and tomato sauce and . . . chocolate?

Lily often invited him to share a meal when she cooked. Just last week he'd joined her in her tiny kitchen for some kind of marinated pork chops and a side of old-fashioned, marshmallow-topped sweet potatoes. His stomach growled on cue.

Lily was oblivious to the path his thoughts had taken. She smiled, and he sensed she was getting ready to shut the door. "Nope," she said with a cheerful smile. "Not sick at all. I'm healthy as a horse. But it's nice of you to be concerned."

His irritation roared back to the forefront, aided and abetted by righteous indignation. His Lily was cooking something that smelled a lot like homemade lasagna, and she wasn't going to invite him to share it. Had she found another man to bump knees with under her table?

The thought was disconcerting to say the least, and he felt as if he should stake his claim and make a move. He eased his toe into the door opening and crowded her personal space, grinning inwardly with an evil smirk when she moved deeper into the house. He lifted a hand and touched her cheek. "I'm glad you're not sick."

Her expression had changed from calm curiosity to definite wariness. He saw her swallow before she spoke. "I'd better get back to my cards."

Screw the cards. He almost said it out loud, but he snatched the words back just in time. Instead of speaking, he stepped closer and proved beyond the shadow of a doubt that he *could* indeed be illogical. Jealousy rode him hard, and all his caveman instincts rose to the fore. Lily was his . . . no other man was going to steal her away while Ben had breath left in his body. It was time he showed his hand. He kissed her.

Her lips were soft and warm and tasted like honey. He kept the movement of his mouth on hers gentle, though God knew it was difficult, especially when he felt her respond. He had one hand curled around her neck to pull her close, and his free hand was itching to slide beneath her shirt and find a breast.

But he wasn't entirely lost to reason. He exerted his famous will and let the hand settle innocently at her waist. Or maybe not so innocently. She had gone up on tiptoe to better align their faces, and her shirt rode up, exposing a band of smooth, warm skin to his questing fingers.

He couldn't help himself. He caressed the indentation of her waist and rubbed a thumb over her denim-covered hip bone. Lily made an odd little noise, and suddenly the kiss went from gentle to greedy in a nanosecond.

Sweet Jesus. It was hotter than nuclear fusion. His heart pounded. His pulse raced. The muscles in his arms tightened with the tension it took not to shove her up against the nearest wall.

The fact that she wasn't smacking his face stunned him. Had Lily been interested all along? Had she only been waiting for a sign from him? Had he wasted precious time when he could have been in her arms . . . in her bed?

He forced himself to break free and step back. The quicksand at his feet was dangerously close. He was acting completely out of character, and it was enough to scare the shit out of him. He dared not risk adding to his impulsive, not-thought-out actions. But even then he waited a split second for the meal invitation that never came. Lily was looking down at her feet as she straightened her clothing.

So that was it . . . maybe she did have a date.

He moved back out into the cold, lonely rain. "Good-bye, Lily." He could have been persuaded to stay.

Her smile seemed wistful. She lifted a hand in a halfhearted wave. "Good-bye, Ben." And then she shut the door in his face.

Two

Lily slumped back against the closed door and put her hands to her face. *Wow.* She'd grown up experiencing the blistering heat of southern Mississippi summers. They hadn't prepared her for kissing Benjamin Reynolds.

The unexpected experience shocked and intrigued her. Her overloaded mental synapses had scrambled to assimilate every wonderful nuance of being in his arms. His firm, forceful lips. The taste of him, so male, so exciting. The feel of his fingers against the bare skin of her neck, her waist. He'd been close enough at one point for her to feel the thrust of his erection against her belly.

And she had wanted him. Painfully, urgently, no-waiting-on-aisle-seven-do-it-now.

If Ben hadn't pulled back, what might have happened? She'd have liked to think she would have recognized it was too soon to jump into bed. But maybe not. Her hormones were importunate rascals.

What really amazed her was that old Miss Matilda was apparently right on the money. She thought about it. Lily had skipped one afternoon run with Ben, and suddenly he was on her doorstep looking forlorn and hungry and kissing her like there was no tomorrow.

It had practically killed her to send him back out into the rain. He'd looked so sad and hurt beneath all that macho exterior. Any other day she would have offered him lasagna and warm garlic bread and a free pass to her bedroom, not necessarily in that order.

But with the advice maven's sixty-year-old words ringing in her ears, she'd held firm to her new plan. Lily's be-nice-to-him-and-he'll-fall-at-your-feet approach hadn't been working, so it was time for tough love. Miss Matilda seemed to understand the male psyche. And Lily wasn't too proud to admit she needed help.

If Benjamin needed the thrill of the chase to get his juices flowing, testosterone-laced or otherwise, then by golly, Lily Langford would run far and fast until he caught her.

Ben gobbled down two bowls of cold cereal and came as close to sulking as an enlightened man could in the privacy of his own home. Lily had blown him off. After a world-class kiss.

Christmas cards? That excuse was only a notch above the old "I have to wash my hair" line. He deserved better. Hadn't he been an excellent friend and neighbor? Hadn't he fixed leaky faucets and replaced broken windowpanes and performed delicate automotive repairs with precision and finesse? Surely that warranted one goddamned plate of whatever was cooking in her kitchen.

He tossed his bowl and spoon in the sink, nearly shattering the heavy crockery. Lily Langford could rot from pneumonia in her tidy little house, for all he cared. It would be a cold day in hell before he ever ventured back across the street and checked on *her* well-being and safety.

He'd ignore her and concentrate on his work, as he should have been doing all along. His research was important and should take precedence over . . .

He froze suddenly, his gaze glued to the scene being played out in full view of his plate-glass living room window. The drapes were pulled back to let in as much weak wintry light as possible. The rain had stopped an hour ago, and the sun was trying to make an appearance.

As he watched in stunned, angry disbelief, pretty Lily, clad in a heavy wool coat, turned to lock her front door and was escorted down the walk by an attractive man. He had a solicitous hand at her elbow, as though to make sure her feet didn't slip on any slick spots.

Lily's gentleman caller held open the door of a late-model Honda and tucked her inside. Moments later the car disappeared around the corner.

Ben rubbed a hand against his chest and felt the oddest mix of emotions. At this time of day he usually answered e-mails from friends and colleagues and then headed to his lab for a good night's work.

He'd fallen into the working-overnight habit years ago, when he realized it meant far fewer interruptions. While the majority of the world was sleeping, he was able to concentrate on whatever thorny problem needed his attention.

He was paid well for what he did, but truth be told, he would do it for free. He loved the exhilaration of digging and digging and digging and finally discovering a long-awaited solution. He got off on examining a faulty design that fifty people before him had studied and yet Ben was the one at last able to pinpoint the weak spot that needed fixing.

The work was personally fulfilling. The results were professionally important. And then an idea came to him. A Mensa-worthy idea. He could solve the problem of Lily. All he needed to do was apply the same principles that guided his careful research. Then he would be able to make his way through the muddle of confused emotions and physical responses that were keeping him on edge.

This was momentous. He felt as pumped as when he *knew* he was just inches away from discovery. He'd make the Lily project a priority. It wouldn't hurt to take a couple of days (or in his case, nights) off. He usually worked seven days a week, and that wasn't even healthy.

His jubilation was cut short when he remembered Lily wasn't home. He was momentarily pissed, and then he realized he needed time to plan. He grabbed a notebook and the sharpened pencils that he preferred when he was in the early stages of new work, and he got started.

Two hours later his enthusiasm had waned. Women weren't like matrices and mainframes. They didn't always follow scientific principles. He was accustomed to dealing with digits and finite entities. Numbers reacted predictably. Even in the field of theoretical mathematics, there were certain immutable properties.

Lily was entirely beyond his scope of experience. He never knew what she was thinking. She had responded to his kiss. That much was clear. But less than an hour later she had gone on a date with another man.

He hovered near the front of the house until he saw the mystery Honda return. It was dark, and he wasn't able to see the driver. Lily slipped from the backseat, gave a quick wave, and with her coat collar turned up around her ears, scurried up the path.

He waited fifteen minutes and headed across the street to launch his offensive. He knocked hard on her door and waited for her to answer. He could have used the doorbell, but at the moment he needed a more physical outlet.

Lily was clearly surprised to see him. "Ben?" Then she smiled. "Still no flu."

He didn't feel like smiling. "May I come in?"

A look he couldn't decipher crossed her face, but she stepped back and allowed him inside. The house smelled warm and welcoming . . . a mix of Lily's light perfume, a lingering hint of garlic, and the wonderful scent of fresh-cut evergreens.

She had decorated every available surface with holiday doodads. A bare spot in her living room indicated where her tree would stand.

He shoved his hands in his pockets and leaned against the wall. His plan of attack had really gotten only this far. Now he was winging it. He stared at her, taking appreciative note of the red cashmere sweater that clung gently to her modest curves. A silly Santa pin perched on the slope of one breast. Lucky Santa.

Her slim black skirt reminded him that he had touched that hip and waist very recently, and he yearned to do it again. That and so much more. He surveyed her tiny foyer as though he hadn't seen it dozens of times. But that diversion kept his gaze off her face and enabled him to speak casually. "Hot date tonight?"

When he sneaked a glance to catch her response, confusion etched her features for a split second, and then her eyes narrowed. "No offense, Ben, but how is that any of your business?"

He straightened his spine, facing her. "I thought we were friends," he said mildly, trying to figure out what he had done wrong. And he *had* done something wrong. He just couldn't figure out what it was.

"Platonic friends," she said evenly, the expression in her chocolate brown eyes guarded.

His chin jutted. "I kissed you this afternoon."

Her nose went up in the air. "Briefly, and only once in eighteen months. I don't think that gives you the right to have an intimate knowledge of my calendar."

Intimate. That word hit him right in the nuts. "I was concerned," he said, his voice stiff. "I thought you didn't know very many people yet. That's what you told me."

Now exasperation marked her posture—hands on hips and eyes sparking her displeasure. "I told you that a year ago, Ben. Surely you don't think I live like a nun."

The sense of loss caught him hard, stealing the breath from his lungs. He'd come to regard the luscious Lily as his own special friend. "I see." He didn't quite know what to do now. Did this mean she had a boyfriend? And was he obligated to back off?

He studied her from head to toe, feeling his body react predictably to the visual stimulation. God, she was beautiful. And funny. And smart, even if a tad flaky. No way was he going to back off. Lily was his. Perhaps not officially. Perhaps not forever. But here and now and for the short term.

He glowered at her. "I'm surprised you went out on a work night."

She rolled her eyes. "Oh, for Pete's sake. I'm not in high school, and for your information we met up with his wife."

Ben blinked. "Kinky."

She blushed, and suddenly his good humor returned.

"May I have the details . . . as a platonic friend?"

She sighed. "Their child was a patient of mine. Little Jeremy was in a pageant at their church tonight, and he wanted me to come. His dad picked me up, because Jeremy and his mom had to be at the church early to practice. They were all three in the car when they brought me home."

Better, much better. The knot in his stomach eased. "Good," he said gruffly.

Her eyebrows went up. "Good? What the heck does that mean?"

He stepped closer to temptation. "Good, as in he won't care if I do this."

He slid his arms around her, monitoring her reaction. A tiny, breathy sigh escaped her lips when he plastered their bodies together, chest to thigh. He might have sighed as well, but all the oxygen in his lungs seemed to have evaporated.

He tipped her head back against his shoulder, his lips hovering over hers. Her eyes had gone so dark they seemed all pupil. When she licked her lips, he actually felt his dick sit up and beg.

The second before their lips touched, she stuck out her hand and held him at arm's length. "Wait."

"What for?" he muttered, pulling her back and nibbling the soft skin just below her jaw.

"I want to know why you're doing this."

He shrugged, confused by the question, but not about to be deflected from his goal. "Because you're sexy and cute and I can't keep my hands off of you."

She went stiff in his arms. "You haven't had a problem keeping them off me for the last eighteen months."

Even a much less sensitive man would have realized that his luscious Lily was not in the mood. He smoothed her hair and brushed his lips across her forehead. "I was an idiot, and slow to boot."

Now she was glaring at him. "You're a genius. That excuse won't fly."

He kissed her in spite of her ill humor. "Please, Lily," he groaned. "Have pity on me. I need you so much I'm dying inch by inch."

He captured her mouth in a desperate kiss and wanted to weep with gratitude when her lips responded. She went soft in his arms, and she didn't even protest when he backed her up against the wall. His hands were under her skirt, and he cursed softly when he found panty hose.

He rubbed her mound through the nylon and groaned when Lily lifted her hips into his touch. He deepened the kiss, letting her feel his tongue, stroking deep into her mouth. She whimpered when he gently fondled her breasts, exploring their shape and weight.

His breathing was ragged. Condom. Did he have a condom? He hadn't come over here to screw her, but if he didn't get inside her in the next two minutes, he might go up in flames. Any previous sexual hunger he'd experienced was the merest pang compared to how he felt at the moment.

Lily Langford was turning him inside out.

A moment later she was doing something else entirely. She was struggling to get free.

He dropped his arms suddenly, feeling embarrassed and totally confused. A minute ago she had been rubbing up against him like a starving sex kitten, or so he had thought.

He backed away, aghast that he might have misread her signals. "Lily, I . . ." He was dumbstruck.

She smoothed her hair and her clothing with hands that weren't all that steady. And she wasn't looking at him.

His stomach fell to his knees. "God, Lily. I'm sorry. I didn't intend to attack you like that."

Her smile was a brave effort. "I have to get ready for work," she said softly.

He glanced at his watch. It was ten fifteen. He ran a hand across the back of his neck. "Of course you do."

She smiled again, this time more convincingly. "We can talk about this later if you want."

"I *do* want," he said stubbornly. He remembered his vow to take time off. "Let me drive you to work," he said, struck with the brilliance of that idea. "It might start raining again, and if the temperature drops it will be nasty."

She unfastened the Santa pin from her sweater and dropped it in a dish on the small table at her side. "I'll be fine. You go get started on whatever big project's on the schedule for tonight."

He frowned. He knew what he *needed* to be on the list for tonight, and sadly, that wasn't going to happen. "I want to drive you to work," he said stubbornly.

She was still clearly hesitant, and he cocked his head. "Why, Lily? What's the big deal about me giving you a ride? I assure you I'm an excellent driver, and I've never had a ticket."

Now her teeth were mutilating her bottom lip. She wrinkled her nose and cocked her head in clear apology for what she was about to say. "I'm afraid you won't remember to pick me up."

His jaw dropped and he felt his neck heat. In her shoes he would probably think the same thing. But dammit, this was different. Lily was important. Lily was special. Didn't she understand that?

His jaw clenched. "I won't forget," he said gruffly. "You can trust me. I swear."

She still didn't look entirely convinced, but she nodded

slowly. "Okay. That would be nice." She glanced at her watch. "I'll be ready at ten forty-five."

The hospital where she worked was very close. It would be a short drive, unfortunately. He started for the living room. "I'll wait."

Lily touched his arm. "Go on home, Ben. Really. I won't leave without you."

Their eyes met, hers oddly blank, his probably filled with the hunger he wasn't able to hide. "Right." He slid a quick kiss across her cheek, and then opened the door and headed across the street.

Lily looked at her watch again and hissed in dismay. She dashed into her bedroom, stripped off her nice clothes, and pulled out the first pair of scrubs hanging in her closet. They were a gaudy red-and-green holiday print, but the kids loved them.

She put on her socks and walking shoes and pulled her hair into a ponytail. She had five minutes left to make her dinner. She usually ate around three a.m., and a sandwich was the quickest and easiest way to brown-bag it. But she was out of bread, so instead she scooped some lasagna into a small Tupperware bowl, grinning as she thought of Miss Matilda, and tossed a plastic bottle of Diet Coke into the bag.

By the time Ben knocked on the door she was ready . . . flushed and frazzled, but ready. He held her coat as she slipped an arm into each sleeve. When it was on, he wrapped his arms around her in a tight hug.

His lips brushed her ear. "You look so sexy in your work clothes."

She chuckled weakly. "You're nuts, Mr. Reynolds. Come on. I like to get there a few minutes early."

She preceded him out to the car, and once he had tucked

her in and shut her door, she watched him run around to his own side. He slid in, turned the heat on full blast, and put the car in gear.

Lily had never had any problem talking to Ben, but now, given their earlier activities, she couldn't think of a thing to say that didn't sound suggestive or just plain stupid. She cleared her throat. "It will be nice not to have to find a parking place."

He half turned his head, his expression hard to read in the dim light of the car. "I could do this every night, Lily."

The intimacy in his voice made her shiver. "I wasn't hinting," she said softly. "You have too many important things to deal with to worry about me."

He pulled up across the street from the hospital and eased the car into a parking space. When he shut off the engine, the silence was deafening. She could hear his breathing and her own.

He unfastened his seat belt and turned sideways, his knee bumping the gearshift. "Nothing is more important than you, Lily."

What did a girl say to a statement like that? Maybe Miss Matilda's advice had worked a bit *too* well. Lily wasn't prepared for such a blunt, forceful statement.

She stared out the window, ignoring his words, because she didn't trust them. She unbuttoned her coat. The car's heater was superefficient, and she was burning up. She refused to think it might be Ben's proximity causing her discomfort.

He touched her cheek. "I don't have many people in my life who are close. You've become special to me, Lily. I enjoy our friendship."

She eased closer to the window, causing his hand to fall away. "Friends don't kiss like we did."

This time he took both of her hands in his. "Lovers do."

His voice was rough and low. His thumbs rubbed the backs of her hands.

She was trembling from head to toe, and uneasily aware that she was running out of time. "It bothers me that you've decided so abruptly you want to make love to me." The honesty was painful to verbalize, but necessary.

Ben raised her hands to his lips and kissed them. The warm, wet rasp of this tongue against her fingers made hunger coil in her belly. He met her gaze straight on. "There's nothing abrupt about it," he said quietly. "I knew the day we met that any man would be lucky to share your bed. You're warm and real and so damned sexy you make me ache."

She bit her lip. "You've acted like a brother."

"Because I thought I didn't have the time for a relationship."

"And now?" She was torn between hope and caution.

He released her and sat back in his seat. His body language wasn't reassuring. He drummed his fingers on the steering wheel. "My work has been my life. Literally. But I'm not willing to go on like that."

"You haven't had relationships before?"

"I've had sex. I haven't had relationships."

She inhaled, feeling her conscience prick. "I have a confession to make."

He lifted an eyebrow. "Oh?"

She winced, awash in guilt and embarrassment. "All those times you helped me, I was just pretending to be in trouble, because I was trying to get your attention."

His long fingers wrapped around the steering wheel. "I see."

"Except . . . " she amended hastily, "not when the dishwasher flooded. That was real. And the squirrels in the attic."

This time he was the one staring out the windshield. Lily

sighed inwardly. Miss Matilda probably wouldn't approve of this at all. But Lily couldn't help herself. Where she came from, lying was the ultimate form of bad manners. And her own personal code of etiquette and ethics demanded she come clean before she and Ben went any further.

The silence piled up, and she felt her confidence wane. She unfastened her seat belt. "Thanks for the ride." Clearly she had offended him.

As she unlocked the car door, she heard an echoing click as Ben relocked her side from the control panel on his door. He gave her a look that curled her toes. "Not so fast."

He took her arm and pulled her closer, ignoring the awkwardness of the maneuver she was forced to make.

He deliberately cupped her breast through cloth that was covered with reindeer and giant wrapped presents.

Lily felt her nipples tighten and peak. Streaks of fire shot from her breasts to her womb. "What are you doing?" she whispered.

"Copping a feel," he muttered, tugging up her top and bending his head to place his mouth where she ached.

Then he went still. "You're not wearing a bra," he said with hoarse incredulity. His lips closed over one nipple, and she groaned. It was hard to speak with her body gripped in the thrall of madness.

She swallowed hard. "The fabric isn't thin, and I don't have much on top anyway."

"You've got plenty," he growled, switching sides and making her whimper with frustration when her hip bumped the gearshift.

She panted, hanging on to her common sense with one last thread of self-control. "Got to go . . ." she gasped.

He abandoned her well-kissed breasts and zeroed in on her

mouth. His lips had an IQ about as high as his brain. They knew every little torturous nip and slide that made her thighs clench in helpless need.

She'd thought the earlier kiss had prepared her for this go-round. Nope. Fireworks went off. Symphonies played. Sirens wailed . . . *Wait a minute.* She struggled back to the present.

Ben's hands had burrowed somehow beneath the elastic waistband of her pants and were squeezing her butt. Until now she had not realized that her ass was an erogenous zone. "Stop," she demanded.

She had to say it again, because the first time really held no conviction at all. "Stop, Ben."

He shuddered and rested his forehead against hers. "Do I have to?"

She chuckled weakly. "I need this job. Last time I checked, the city wasn't handing out free electricity."

He released her and allowed her to wriggle back to her own side. "I could keep you warm," he said mildly.

But when she opened the door and the overhead light came on, his eyes were anything but casual. They burned with a masculine determination that made her skin break out in gooseflesh. And she was plenty warm.

She slid her legs out and stood up, wondering if they would support her. Ben leaned across the seat, looking up at her. "This isn't over."

She didn't respond. Couldn't respond. Her mind was a total blank, which was probably not an optimum situation for a hospital employee.

She stepped backward onto the curb. "Thanks for the ride."

He nodded, his gaze turbulent. "I'll be here at seven."

"If you get tied up, I can take the bus."

"I'll be here," he said stubbornly.

She glanced across the street and took a deep breath. "Good-bye, Ben."

And then somehow she went in to work and managed to pretend her nice, normal life hadn't just been knocked on its ass.

Three

Ben was nowhere to be found when Lily stepped out the front door of the hospital at 7:05 a.m. She looked around, shoving back the disappointment that made her eyes sting with tears. . . .

She *knew* Benjamin Reynolds. He wasn't like other guys. His brain was a freaking calculator. He couldn't be expected to retain every little unimportant detail of daily life when he was doing work that could literally change the world. It would be selfish of her to expect him to.

But he promised. She ignored the tiny little voice inside her head. She was a big girl. A mature medical professional. And this wasn't a tragedy.

The icy early morning breeze found every crevice in her outerwear and slid beneath to make her skin cold and miserable. She shivered and grumbled, wondering if the receptionist back in the nice, warm hospital lobby had a bus schedule.

The happy, fizzy feeling of expectation she had carried with her for the last eight hours lay in ashes at her feet. He couldn't help it. She'd watched him work before. You might try detonating a bomb in the next room, and he wouldn't even flinch.

Tucking her chin to her chest, she headed back inside to see what she could find out about transportation.

The shriek of tires squealing on pavement jerked her head up. That new ambulance driver was a bit of a show-off.

But the navy car speeding in her direction was not medically necessary. Unless you considered the fact that the sight of it magically healed a crack in her heart.

He jumped out practically before the car came to a stop. His hair stuck out in seven directions, and his eyes were wild. "It was a wreck," he blurted out, breathing heavily. "Two cars in front of me. They blocked off the road and had to land the medevac helicopter. I couldn't back up. It was pandemonium. I—"

She lifted her hand to his cheek, feeling the whiskery stubble. The panic in his eyes was receding slowly. "It's okay," she said softly. "It's okay." She went up on tiptoe and kissed his lips. "Let's go home."

They were silent in the car. He held her left hand gripped in his right, and Christmas carols played faintly from the radio.

All around them people were heading for work, for school. Lily felt special somehow to be going in the opposite direction, tired, ready for eight hours of sleep, but content and very, very happy.

Ben parked the car in his own driveway and walked her across the street. They stood on her front steps, watching with indulgent grins as the lady down the street tried to lasso a seven-year-old boy who clearly didn't want to go to school.

Ben bent his head, his breath warm on her cheek. "Are you going to bed?"

That last word hung between them . . . tantalizing . . . deliciously evocative.

She stretched her back to ease out the kinks. "Yeah." A yawn took her by surprise and she laughed. "And you?"

He nodded silently.

Ask him to come in. The words echoed in her head. But she stayed mute, her tongue silenced by uncertainty.

With an inarticulate murmur, she opened her door and went inside.

Ben discovered to his dismay that even though he was exhausted, sleep didn't come easily for a guy with a perpetual boner. He'd spent the entire night while Lily was at work arranging his bedroom for a possible visitor. He put fresh sheets on the bed. He actually cleaned his bathroom with surgical efficiency and might possibly have stumbled upon at least one new type of mold.

He rummaged in a box in the garage and found some candles. With flowers not available, he dragged out a set of shears and cut sprigs of holly, heavy with crimson berries. He unearthed the crystal vase his grandmother had given him for college graduation (go figure) and filled it with a clumsy arrangement.

Then he looked at the room with a critical eye.

Would Lily feel at home here? His solid navy comforter was hardly the stuff of romantic boudoirs. And the beige carpet and walls were uninspired, to say the least.

But when he envisioned Lily's lithe body spread-eagled on the mattress, he lost all interest in decorating.

Just before dawn, the world outside his window had been dark and bleak. Now, courtesy of heavy shades, his bedroom was plenty dim enough to be conducive to sleep, but he was wide awake.

What would it take to convince Lily he was serious about becoming lovers? And was it fair of him to go down that path knowing he had no intention of ever marrying and fathering children?

Maybe he was creating problems where none existed. Not every woman expected to hear wedding bells when she got horizontal with a guy.

But Lily hailed from a pretty conventional part of the country. And she loved children. He'd stake his reputation that she had wife and mother embedded in her genetic code. He wouldn't lie to her, but he also couldn't disappoint her. Which left him in a devil of a position.

He wanted. He needed. But he didn't have much to offer in return.

Lily brushed her teeth and climbed into bed. She smiled, thinking of Ben just across the street doing the same thing. There was a hitch of jittery excitement sliding through her veins. Today was Saturday. She didn't have to be back at work until eleven p.m. Monday night. That left a lot of time for getting into trouble.

She turned out the light, expecting to fall asleep immediately, as she usually did. Her job was physically and emotionally demanding, and insomnia was seldom a problem. But nothing about the last twenty-four hours had been normal. And the memory of Benjamin Reynolds's big, talented hands mapping her body with determined skill was not conducive to peaceful slumber.

After thirty minutes, she gave up and flicked on the lamp. Miss Matilda's guide lay innocently on the bedside table. With a sigh of surrender, Lily picked it up and turned to the chapter that had proved so amazingly successful.

Unfortunately, she hadn't read far enough. . . .

Although your chase-him-till-he-catches-you plan may work out well, keep in mind that you have merely secured his attention sexually. If you have greater goals in mind for him, i.e., marriage and fatherhood, you have your work cut out for you. Conventional wisdom suggests postponing sexual intercourse until the union is officially and legally sanctioned. You may, of course, follow that plan, but if you are of a certain age, you might not wish to wait to enjoy the pleasures of the flesh. You walk a tricky line. Deciding whether a man really loves you or is simply relating to you sexually is one of the great fears we women face. If you press too hard too fast, you may drive him away. But if you are a creative, generous lover, you may bind him to you permanently with the sensual cords that are difficult if not impossible to break. Make him yearn. Make him sweat. And in the end, you may achieve the realization of each and every sweet dream.

Lily closed the book and leaned against the headboard, lost in thought. The old gal was darned savvy. She'd pretty much nailed the problem. Lily was in love with Ben. She'd known it for some time, but had managed to shove it to the back of her subconscious. As long as Ben had been relating to her with brotherly affection, nothing more was going to happen. So why torture herself by admitting that she was crazy about the guy?

But now that he had popped the lid off an enticing and provocative can of worms, her much-vaunted common sense was running for the hills. Benjamin Reynolds wanted to have sex with her, she thought bluntly. Repeated it once out loud . . . there . . . she had no starry-eyed illusions. Even if she wanted something more, Ben wasn't on the same page.

Heck, it had taken him forever to notice her as a woman with sexual potential. If she was smart, she would take what the Fates had tossed in her lap and be content.

And as for Miss Matilda's suggestions . . . well, Lily was out of luck. Make him yearn? Make him sweat? *Ha!* That sounded like fodder for a *Cosmo* article. Lily was convinced that all those dos and don'ts and advice columns weren't much help for a woman whose life and whose job weren't glamorous in the least. Common sense she had in spades, but sensual allure? She must have been absent the day they passed out those feminine wiles.

She closed the book and pulled the covers to her chin, hunkering down beneath the blankets to keep warm. She was more confused than ever. Was she supposed to chase him, let him chase her, meet in the middle?

Her poor tired brain shut down and dragged her deep into an uneasy slumber.

Ben woke up horny and irritable. He'd had a total of four hours of sleep . . . maybe . . . and for the first time in his life, his waking thoughts weren't about projects and work. All he could think about was getting Lily naked. Quickly. He showered and dressed, pondering his options.

The list he'd made for the Lily Project was frustratingly short. He was stymied. Lily had responded to his kiss last night, so did that mean he should assume she was interested? He made the bed, just in case.

When it was time to go running, he dressed in his T-shirt and sweats and glanced at his watch. Would she join him?

But she was not outside to meet him, as was their usual ritual. He even resorted to snapping some dead branches off the bushes in front of his house, just to make sure she had time to see he was out there. Finally, feeling like a fool, he headed off down the street.

Lily woke up feeling disoriented and oddly aroused. She was pretty sure she'd had some intensely erotic dreams, but darn it, she couldn't remember a single one. She had housework she needed to do today, but her heart wasn't in it. Was it too soon to invite Ben over for dinner? Had she left him hanging in the wind long enough?

She whipped up a batch of her mom's snickerdoodles, and put a pork roast in the oven. With some new potatoes and a salad, it would make a nice meal. Unfortunately, she couldn't think of a way to serve it that shouted, *Take me. I'm ready for down-and-dirty sex*.

She was switching loads and folding clothes when her doorbell rang. Her heart skipped a beat, and she walked slowly down the hall, lecturing her riotous hormones. *Act casual. Don't be too needy*.

When she opened the door, every last coherent thought fled her brain. Ben was sweaty, and the wind had tumbled his hair, but he had "stud muffin" written all over him. She swallowed the lump in her throat and leaned against the door frame.

"Hey, there," she said with admirable restraint. For a nickel, she'd be all over him.

He shoved his hair from his forehead, his expression hard to read. "Still not in the mood to exercise? Or was it more Christmas cards?"

From another man, that would have sounded like sarcasm, but she'd never once heard Ben make a cutting remark. He was amiable to a fault. At this exact moment she decided she might have been mistaken about his basic personality.

He was crowding her personal space. His arms were folded

across his chest. His eyes were almost navy, and the expression on his face was a mix of sullen and brooding. He'd gone from pleasant neighbor to dangerous bad boy in a sexy overnight metamorphosis. And she liked it.

The heat that popped and crackled between them was scary and delicious. She wet her lips with her tongue. "The Christmas cards are done. I suppose I was feeling lazy. It's hard to get excited about running in the dead of winter. At least for me."

"You could have called me." He was pissed. That much she got. He moved forward, forcing her to step back into the house.

"Would you like to come in?" There was plenty of sarcasm in *her* voice, but he seemed oblivious.

He locked the door behind him, his eyes never leaving her face. "I'm going to kiss you, Lily. Unless you tell me not to."

The whole time he was talking, he was stalking her, backing her up step by step until she was pressed against the wall. She had never been so turned on in her life. Her heart was slamming against her ribs and her breathing was rapid. She lifted her chin. "Who's stopping you?"

His blue eyes flared into life and he pounced. His mouth possessed hers. There was no other word for it. He devoured her as if he hadn't kissed a woman in years. The restless hunger in his lips had her fingers clenching handfuls of his shirt and her mouth opening to his tongue, even as her legs tangled with his.

He lurched backward and dragged in a lungful of air. "Invite me to dinner," he demanded.

She blinked, trying to focus her eyes. Her legs felt like overcooked pasta. "How rude."

He looked her over from head to toe with a heated glance that threatened to melt the clothes from her trembling body.

"If that's what it takes. Guys don't give a flying fuck about etiquette, my dear. Not when they want a woman the way I want you."

She lifted her chin. "And what if I don't invite you? To dinner, that is . . ."

One corner of his lips lifted in a half smile that should have been illegal. "Then I'll just have to persuade you to change your mind."

For a half second she was tempted by the implied threat. Imagining a scenario where Ben *persuaded* her only made her hotter. But she wasn't willing to let him get the upper hand. At least not yet. "Fine. Come to dinner." *Please. And stay for breakfast.*

His cheekbones flushed as though he had heard her unspoken addendum. But he merely grunted some sort of caveman acknowledgment of her deliberately nonchalant invitation, and then headed for the door.

The shock put some starch back in her spine. "Wait," she cried. "Where are you going?"

He half turned, picking up a handful of his own shirt and bending his head to smell it. "Home. For a shower."

"You can use mine." Her hand flew up to cover her mouth, but it was too late to retract her inflammatory offer. He looked as shocked as she felt.

But he recovered more quickly. He moved so fast she wondered if his mighty brain had mastered time travel. Now he was touching her tight nipples where they poked through her T-shirt. His fingernail lightly scraped one and then the other, and she shuddered, closing her eyes and letting her head fall back against the wall. He tormented the aching buds deliberately, circling and flicking and finally even tugging.

Her panties were damp, and she was shivering from head

to toe. Her voice was trapped somewhere beneath the lump in her throat.

Ben's lips grazed her neck, and she felt the sharp edge of his teeth.

He muttered against her skin, "Only if you share it with me."

She turned her head enough to find his mouth. She latched onto his lips with a sigh of pleasure, trying to memorize the taste of him. His big hands cradled her head, his thumbs doing little massaging circles beneath her ears. He kissed her eyes, her cheeks, and then her nose.

He was breathing like a marathon runner, and he muttered something she didn't catch. "What?" Her voice was slurred and faint.

He chuckled roughly. "I said, Are we in agreement?"

She gazed at him blankly. "Agreement?"

"About the shower."

His clarification was having a hard time penetrating the urgent arousal that insisted she not stop kissing him. "Mmmm."

He took her face between his hands and shook her gently. "Hello. Earth to Lily. Are we taking a shower together, my love?"

Those last two words cut through her sexual fog. *Wow*. But she cautioned herself. *No need to get too excited, Lily. Men say all sorts of things in the throes of passion*. Nevertheless, she couldn't help the jolt of pleasure she experienced from those two simple words. Lord, women were easy.

She pushed against his massive chest and gained a few inches of breathing room. "I already took a shower," she said primly.

He lifted a hank of her hair and sifted it through his fingers. "You might have missed a few spots," he said, his deep voice mesmerizing her with its hushed sensuality. "I could check for you."

Her knees gave out, and he scooped her into his arms with gratifying ease. "Lily?"

His face was so close, she could see the little nick where he had cut himself shaving. She kissed his chin deliberately, circling one arm around his neck. "Down the hall on the left," she whispered.

Ben was hard-pressed to keep from stumbling and dropping his precious cargo. All his blood had rushed south, and he was dizzy as hell. He was sweaty and grungy, and this was not at all how he had envisioned his first time with Lily playing out. He gave a fleeting thought to the careful preparations he had made in his own bedroom, and then said a mental "what the hell."

A moment like this was too fragile to dick around with. Lily was in his arms and willing, and that was all that mattered.

With his last ounce of precious brain cell function, he paused and grimaced. "I sure as hell don't want to have another visit from the fire department. Is there anything in the kitchen that needs your attention?"

She shook her head slowly. "Nothing will be ready for a half hour or so."

"Long enough," he muttered. "At least for this first go-round." He prayed he had enough staying power to perform at maximum efficiency, but it had been a hell of a long time, and he was on a hair trigger.

The bathroom was small. No, make that tiny. He barely registered the circa-1950s yellow-black-and-white tile. He was too busy doing a quick mental assessment of square footage and angles. This would be a challenge.

He deposited Lily gently on her feet and nuzzled the top of her head. "Are you sure about this, Lily? I don't want to rush you."

She made a sound that sounded suspiciously like a muffled

laugh, but she didn't respond otherwise. She was too busy ripping his T-shirt up and off over his head. He would have helped
her, but she seemed like a woman on a mission, and she had
his arms tangled, so he stood patiently, waiting to be freed. She
abandoned her task for a split second to turn on the water, and
then resumed her torment.

He was sporting a massive erection, which she now eagerly
explored through the thin fabric of his athletic pants. When her
fingers cupped and pressed, he groaned. He held her head as
she knelt and untied his sneakers.

God help him, even feeling her nimble finger on his ankle-
bones was arousing. He was a goner.

She peeled off his socks and helped him step out of his
shoes, seemingly oblivious to the fact that he wasn't exactly
daisy fresh.

Then her hands were at his waist, dragging his pants and
undershorts down his legs in one urgent motion. She made
some little sound when his prick bounced into view, but there
was a loud buzzing in his own ears, and he couldn't quite make
it out.

Having his lovely Lily take the lead was as unexpected as
it was alluring. He'd envisioned himself gently coaxing her
into intimacy. Instead, he was being ravaged by a tigress. And
damned if he didn't love it.

When he was completely nude, she started in on her own
clothing, but he wasn't about to let her have all the fun. He bat-
ted her hands away and began to undress her. He had her buck
naked in just under a minute.

God, she was beautiful, all sleek, toned muscles and soft
skin. She was paler than when he'd seen her in that swimsuit,
but her skin still had a healthy glow. And her pretty brown
nipples were a couple of shades lighter than her eyes.

He swallowed hard. "You're a beautiful woman, Lily Langford."

Her smile warmed all the cold places inside him. She took his hand and stepped into the bathtub. It was a tight fit with both of them in there. He'd been ready for a movie-worthy bathroom fuck, but it was beginning to look doubtful. At least, for anyone not double-jointed.

Lily reached for the small knob on the faucet, and warm water hit him in the face. She giggled and picked up a bar of soap while he readjusted the showerhead. Then, before he could catch his breath, she had a soapy rag and was washing his chest with steady circular sweeps that tightened everything below his waist.

She made him turn around and tackled his back. He felt her breasts brush up against him, and his cock rose another millimeter.

His Lily was a natural nurse. She cleaned him under the arms, around the neck, behind the ears, and then she got serious. She abandoned the rag and, using only the bar of soap, took his aching boner in her hand and began to wash him with a maneuver she surely hadn't learned in nursing school. He flexed in her palm, gritting his teeth against the incredible onslaught of pleasure.

One hand soaped his balls while the other caressed him in an up-and-down motion that did terrible things to his self-control. Then she dropped to her knees, heedless of the stream of water wetting her hair. When she abandoned his dick to work her way up and down his legs, he whimpered.

She reached behind him to wash his ass, and her mouth closed without warning over his penis. He jerked like someone had dropped a hair dryer in the water. *Sweet Jesus.* His hands grasped at her wet, slick shoulders. "Lily, honey. Please. I can't . . ."

But he could and he did—climax, that was . . . She was merciless, draining him dry in the most erotic blow job he'd ever experienced.

When it was over, he was embarrassingly weak in the knees. He drew her to her feet and pulled her into his arms. The water was running cold, and little goose bumps covered her bare skin.

He cleared his throat. "Any chance we could continue this in your bedroom?" He shut off the water and waited to see what she would say.

She twined her arms around his neck, flattening her breasts against his chest. His johnson was eagerly rising to the occasion once again.

Lily pulled his head down for a kiss. "Dry me off, big guy, and we'll see what happens next."

But Lily had more patience than he did. When she realized he had nothing clean to wear, she dressed and took his keys across the street to fetch him some clothes.

While he waited, he wandered through her house, wrapped in a bedsheet, wondering how soon he could get her horizontal. When she returned he took the pile of clothing but made no move to put it on.

Lily cocked her head. "Aren't you hungry for dinner?"

He managed a tight grin. Surely she could see how the sheet tented below his waist. "Not really. I'd much rather see your bedroom, if you want to know the truth."

Her cheeks flushed, and she nibbled her lower lip. "That can be arranged," she said softly. "Let me turn off the stove and the oven."

When she reappeared seconds later, she gasped.

His clothes were in a heap in a living room chair, and he

had dropped the sheet. Lily's eyes went kind of hazy, and her pupils expanded.

She licked her lips. "You're not dressed."

He shrugged. "I didn't see any need."

Suddenly his tigress seemed shy. He took two steps in her direction, and her eyes widened in alarm.

He rubbed his prick with one hand, watching her watch him. "What's wrong, Lily?" He took two more steps, and her hand went to her throat.

She gazed past him down the hallway. "Maybe we *should* eat dinner first," she said, her voice squeaky.

He was close enough to touch her now. He traced her bare lips with a fingertip. "I'm planning on eating *you*," he said bluntly. "Until you scream and come. Over and over again. Shattering in my arms."

Now she looked faint. Her eyes were huge. "You can do that?"

"I can do anything I put my mind to, love. You wait and see."

Four

Lily stared at Ben in shock. His confident words reverberated inside her head like an X-rated audiotape. What she had done earlier in the shower was so out of character for her, it was almost as if someone had possessed her body. Lily Langford was not an erotic seductress.

But the way Ben was looking at her right now said he had no complaints.

She panicked. What if the bathroom antics had cleaned out her repertoire? What if she was too nervous to climax? The guy she'd left behind in Mississippi sure hadn't thought she was all that hot between the sheets.

She muttered something inarticulate and fled down the hall. It didn't occur to her until she heard Ben's breathing behind her that she was following Miss Matilda's directions to the letter.

The house was not all that big. And Ben was fast. He was on

her heels when she bolted into her bedroom. And he was nude. And aroused. And really, really impressive.

She swallowed hard, hovering on the opposite side of the bed. "I may have given you the wrong impression. I'm not really all that good at sex."

He grinned, leaning a naked hip against the doorjamb and crossing his arms over his chest. "What ever gave you that idea?"

She shrugged, feeling embarrassed. "My last boyfriend wasn't too impressed by my sexual skills."

He frowned. "I don't give a rat's ass about some idiot's inability to perform."

She frowned. "I never said he couldn't get it up."

"But he had trouble . . . right?"

"Sometimes."

"And he blamed you."

She glanced down at the bed, lost in thought. "He said I wasn't very talented."

"Bullshit."

Her head jerked up.

He held out his arms. "Take a good long look, sweetheart. This is all on account of you. And God knows, what happened in the bathroom should have worn me out, but as you can see . . . it didn't. You are one hot number."

She stared at his penis, really stared. It was magnificent in its raw, carnal beauty. Her gaze rose to his chest, his face. The confident grin she had grown to know and love reassured her. And suddenly she couldn't bear to wait another second. She wanted Ben inside her. Now.

She started unbuttoning her blouse.

He held up a hand. "Wait. Do it slowly."

She hesitated, but the look in his turbulent eyes convinced

her. If Ben thought she was a seductress, she couldn't disabuse him of that notion, now, could she? She played with buttons and zippers until his eyes glazed over. By the time she was wearing nothing but a pair of skimpy red bikini panties, he had abandoned his casual stance and had assumed a warrior's pose.

She slipped a hand beneath the elastic of her underwear and eased it down her legs. When she bent to step out of it, he said something she didn't quite catch.

A lock of hair had fallen over his forehead, and his hands were on his hips. His smile had disappeared.

He nodded toward the mattress. "On your back, woman."

She carefully drew the covers to the foot of the bed and crawled on the mattress, settling herself in the middle with her legs together and her arms by her sides.

Ben approached the bed and stood over her. His chest rose and fell with the urgency of his breathing, but he was very still. She wanted to close her eyes, but his hungry gaze snared hers, demanding a response.

When he put one knee on the mattress, she slid toward him. That made it entirely easy for him to straddle her with the other knee, trapping her hips between his big, muscular thighs.

Now the stiff, proud part of him that made her stomach weak bobbed over her, riveting her attention.

He sat back on his haunches and lifted her legs onto his knees. This time her eyes *did* close. She felt faint, and she wasn't even standing up.

His big hands cupped her butt and lifted her a few inches higher. His hot breath on her moist, intimate flesh gave her a half second's warning before his lips closed over her clitoris and he began to suck.

She cried out in shock. Her body was so primed and sensitive, she climaxed quickly, arching in his grasp.

Ben didn't care.

He held her gently as she rode out her orgasm, and then he bent his head and started all over again.

Ben was drunk on the smell and taste of Lily Langford. He had a photographic memory, and he knew deep in his soul that if he lived to be an old, old man, he would never forget the sight of his beautiful Lily arching in pleasure as he licked her and held her and felt her aching release deep in his gut. When he finally let her rest, he sprawled down beside her and cuddled her close.

He brushed her hair from her damp forehead. He was so horny, every muscle in his body was clenched in hunger, but he loved holding her like this, watching the hazy look in her eyes disappear as she realized what had happened.

As he leaned over her on one elbow, her face flamed bright red, and her teeth sank into her bottom lip. She wasn't able to look him right in the eyes, and he chuckled, feeling a host of emotions he couldn't bother to sort out at the moment.

He kissed her softly. "You're amazing."

She returned the kiss, her hand cupping his cheek. "Clearly you studied more than the Pythagorean theorem when you were in school. I'm almost afraid to ask."

He shrugged. "I read a lot. I absorb things."

She still seemed dazed. "Hot damn. I've found me a sex expert."

He smiled modestly. "Not an expert. But a really motivated amateur."

He eased a hand between her legs. The slight outward movement of her thighs seemed to indicate tacit approval. He slid a finger inside her, feeling the swollen tissues, the wet flesh.

His head swam, and he shook it, trying to retain some measure of conscious thought.

Without any inflection in his voice at all, he gave her fair warning. "I'm going to fuck you now."

The look on her face as he rolled on a condom she had supplied was surprise laced with definite interest. He flipped her and tucked pillows beneath her. "I love your ass," he muttered. He shaped it and squeezed it and tried to draw out the pleasure.

But he was a poor, weak bastard. He spread her legs, opened her with a gentle press of his fingers, and positioned the head of his cock at her entrance. He pulled her hair to one side of her head and bit gently at the vulnerable column of her neck. When she flinched, he thrust inside her moist sheath and groaned in shock at the almost unbearable pleasure. She was tight and hot.

With the shower incident to take the edge off, he'd intended to screw her slowly to a nice, steady finish. Be tender . . . gentle even.

But that was a crock. His whole body was tensed in anticipation despite his earlier climax. He was hot and edgy and close to desperate.

He gritted his teeth and fought for control. "Lily, are you okay?" She arched her back and squeezed down on his cock. He groaned and went deeper, trying to imprint himself in her DNA. She was his. Lily Langford was his.

He grasped her hips and entered her hard. Lily gave a keening cry, and with a mighty roar he thrust again and again until they both dissolved in blinding heat.

Lily rolled to her back and glanced at the clock. Ben lay beside her, breathing heavily. She ran a hand over his chest, marveling that she had the right to do so. "You ready for that dinner now? If it's not ruined?"

He flopped to his stomach and buried his face in his arms. "I don't think I can stand up. You'll have to carry me."

She chuckled. "Not in this lifetime. Get your fanny in gear, Mr. Reynolds. We need calories."

He lifted his head and opened one eye. "For more sex?" The hopeful note in his voice made her laugh.

"Possibly. But first things first."

She dressed quickly and headed for the kitchen, hoping her wonderful meal hadn't been ruined. Fortunately, although it might have been a tad past its prime, it was still edible. While she was setting everything out, she heard water running in the bathroom, and then Ben finally appeared, looking rumpled and gorgeous and entirely too enticing for her small dining room. Actually, "dining room" was too grand a term . . . it was more of an alcove off the kitchen.

Which meant that she and Ben sat very close. They ate in silence for a few moments, and sad to say, it wasn't a comfortable silence. Ben seemed uneasy. And his state of mind affected hers. Surely he wasn't already having regrets. She decided to wait him out.

Over dessert, mint-chocolate-chip ice cream, Ben finally got around to more than small talk. He leaned back in his chair and stared at her. His eyes were a deep cerulean at the moment, and the curve of his mouth was oddly grim.

He sighed. "I need to tell you something."

Uh-oh. She braced herself.

When she didn't say anything, he raked his hands through his hair. "I intended to lay my cards on the table before we initiated an intimate relationship."

Ouch. That sounded ominous. She waved a hand. "Feel free. The table's all yours."

He leaned his chair back on two legs, looking mighty guilty. She had a feeling this wouldn't be pleasant.

He sighed again. "I'm not husband and father material. I wouldn't have a clue how to do either. And I just needed to tell you that before we went any further."

Her heart dropped somewhere to the vicinity of her knees, but she smiled, even though the effort nearly killed her. She might despise lying, but at the moment it seemed the only viable choice if she didn't want to lose him. Maybe time would change his views on marriage and family. Even as she formulated that thought, she called herself a fool. She was asking for heartbreak.

She smiled, hoping she looked more carefree than she felt. "Lighten up, Ben. We're two young, healthy adults who share an attraction for each other. This is recreational sex. Nary an altar or an orange blossom in sight."

He blinked and looked confused. "Recreational?"

"Of course. You have your life and I have mine. But we're neighbors and we like each other, and it makes sense that we enjoy each other when it's convenient."

"Convenient?" Their conversation appeared to have reduced him to one-word responses.

She patted his hand. "No worries, Ben. I'm not after a wedding ring, truly. You're not obligated to me in any way just because we fool around."

He frowned. "I thought you were pretty traditional."

She shrugged. "Maybe. In some ways. But that doesn't mean I can't explore my sexual wants and needs with someone like you."

"Someone like me?"

"You know . . . sexy . . . hot . . . available."

He leaned forward and the legs of his chair hit the floor. "You're using me?"

"Oh, come on, Ben. Be honest. Isn't that what men want? No-strings sex?"

His frown grew blacker. "I'm not most men. And I haven't been with a woman since you moved in eighteen months ago. You're special to me, Lily."

"But not for the long haul." If there was a tinge of bitterness in her voice, she couldn't help it.

Now he didn't look mad. He looked sad. "I'll understand if you want to call it quits."

She stood up and carried their plates to the sink. "Don't be so melodramatic. People screw around all the time without benefit of a marriage license."

He stood and began to help her clear the table. "Don't be flip. It doesn't suit you. And I don't think you take sex that lightly."

She filled the sink with hot water and squirted dish soap into it. "Are you trying to talk me out of this, Ben?"

He scooped up a handful of bubbles and put some on her nose. "I should," he muttered. "For your own good."

She grabbed his hand and kissed it. "I've never been too fond of advice that was for my own good. And I'm a big girl, Ben. I can make my own decisions."

He nuzzled the back of her neck. "Then I surrender. Have your way with me. Any place. Anytime."

When he slipped his arms around her from behind and began fondling her breasts, she decided the dishes could soak. She twisted in his embrace until she faced him and flung her arms around his neck. "Here and now," she muttered. "But close the curtains."

*   *   *

Lily had discovered early on that it was impossible to sleep on a normal schedule during the weekend and still be able to go to work Monday night at eleven. So she maintained her pattern and stayed up all night Saturday night. Only this time she had a companion. An inventive, insatiable, amorous partner in crime.

She tried to convince him that they couldn't have sex all night. He was unimpressed.

"Why not?" he mumbled, his face buried between her breasts. They were in her bed again, and it was just past midnight.

She shivered when he tongued her nipple, but one of them had to show some restraint or they would screw themselves to death before morning. She shoved at his shoulders. "Come on, big guy. I had planned to go buy my Christmas tree tonight. And just because you've seduced me to the dark side doesn't mean I don't have some things I need to do. Go home. Get some work done. I'll drop by later."

He abandoned her breasts with a long-suffering sigh that she almost echoed. Was she crazy? But Miss Matilda's advice rang in her ears. Ben couldn't chase her if she didn't run. And she really did want to put up her tree.

Ben glanced at his watch that showed at least six time zones. "Nothing's open," he said with a triumphant air of superiority.

"Wrong, genius." She climbed out of bed and put on clean panties and jeans. She didn't feel safe until she had pulled an old University of Mississippi sweatshirt over her head. "The home-improvement store over on Richter Drive is a twenty-four-hour location. And they have fresh-cut trees . . . I checked."

"Then I'll come with you."

She put her hands on her hips. He was standing nude beside the bed, and it was a bit like staring directly into the

sun—blinding and not too smart. "I know your work is important, Ben. You don't have to alter your schedule because of me.
Honestly. And would you get dressed, please?"

His grin was cocky. "Am I tempting you, Lily?"

She frowned. "Not at all. I'm merely trying to tidy up the
bedroom."

"Liar."

He said it with affection, but he did get dressed, thank
goodness. She wasn't sure how much longer she could have
held out. Making love to Benjamin Reynolds was fast becoming
an obsession.

He helped her make the bed, and then he tugged her to sit
beside him. "Listen, Lily . . ."

She raised an eyebrow. "I'm all ears."

He brushed her cheek and kissed her once . . . gently. His
eyes were solemn. "My work *is* important. Not just to me, but
to a lot of people. And I do have responsibilities. But I'm not
willing to let it consume my life. At least, not anymore. I want
to be with you tonight and tomorrow night, and I deserve a
weekend off . . . don't you think?"

For some reason she felt teary-eyed. She blinked back the
surprising emotion. "Well, if you put it that way . . . I would
love to have your company."

He kissed her again . . . this time with more force. "Thank
you, Lily."

Choosing a Christmas tree was no easy task when the man and
woman involved approached it from such diametrically opposed perspectives. Ben quoted the exact dimensions of her living room and calculated branch spread. Lily wasn't concerned
with such prosaic considerations. She wanted a beautiful, fluffy,
solid tree—with lots of room for ornaments.

Ben suggested a modest five-foot spruce. Lily picked out a seven-foot monster and said they could trim. In the end they compromised. Lily paid for the tree, and they tied it to the top of Ben's car.

Back at her house, Ben wrestled the tree into the old-fashioned metal tree stand and stood by, incredulous, as Lily began opening box after box of ornaments.

He shook his head. "You moved all this from Mississippi?"

She nodded absently, searching for the angel that went on top. "My mother and both of my grandmothers gave all of us kids a special ornament every Christmas from our first birthday. Mom saved them, and when we each moved out on our own, she gave them to us. Of course, over the years, I bought additional ones here and there."

"How many siblings do you have?"

"Three brothers and two sisters."

Ben's eyebrows went up. "Whew. I'm an only child, so that's hard to imagine. Where do you fall?"

"Number five. That was one reason I moved here. I wanted to prove I could stand on my own two feet. I was always looked at as one of the babies, and I needed to separate myself from the crowd, I guess."

"But you love your family."

She grinned. "I adore them. And I've been dreadfully homesick, if you want to know the truth. But I'm going back to Mississippi on the twentieth for an entire week. I can't wait."

Ben's face darkened. "You'll be gone for Christmas?"

She paused, suddenly aware that she needed to tread carefully. "Most people go home for the holidays, Ben."

He muttered a mild curse under his breath. "Not everyone. Not me. I was hoping we might spend the time together."

She stood up and brushed glitter from her jeans. "I haven't

been home since I've lived here. It's too late to change plans now, even if I wanted to."

"And you don't."

She sighed. "I didn't say that. But Ben, we're just friends. My family is very important to me."

"I could go with you."

His stiff posture and deliberately nonchalant tone of voice put a lump in her throat. "I don't think that's a good idea. My mom is very traditional, and if I were to bring a guy home for the holidays, she'd be booking the church and ordering invitations in no time. I'll be back on the twenty-seventh. We can be together for New Year's Eve. It falls on a Saturday night, so I won't be working."

"Whatever," he said, looking suddenly bored with the conversation.

She shrugged unhappily, feeling they were on the verge of their first major disagreement. "If you're not in the mood to decorate the tree, I won't hold you to it."

He was leaning against her small mantel, staring into the fireplace and watching the flames generated by gas logs. "I'll stay. But don't expect too much. This will be my very first attempt."

He said it with a wry twist to his lips that tugged at her heart.

She gaped. "You've never decorated a tree?"

He shook his head. My mother hired a professional designer each year to decorate the house with a theme. I was never allowed to touch anything either in process or when it was done."

She couldn't help it—her heart melted. She went to him and slipped her arms around his waist, burying her head against his shoulder. "Well, in that case, we'll go whole hog."

His strong arms came around her in a reassuring hug, but his voice was wary. "I'm almost afraid to ask what that means."

She laughed softly, feeling perfectly content. "It means," she said, rubbing her cheek against his collarbone, "that we're going to re-create the Langford family tree-decorating evening. Second only to Christmas in fun and excitement."

He released her and stepped back so he could see her face. "Does that include sex?" He cupped her breast suggestively.

She slapped his wandering hand. "Certainly not. Imagine Norman Rockwell meets Andy Griffith in Mayberry. Americana at its best."

He snorted. "How great could it be without sex?"

"For a man who claims to be celibate for long periods of time, you sure seem to have sex on the brain."

He stole a kiss, his lips warm and tempting. "You've corrupted me."

She wiggled out of his grasp and handed him a stack of CDs. "Load these in the stereo. I'll get started on the popcorn and hot chocolate."

For Ben it was an evening as magical as it was unexpected. Sentimentality had never been a part of his life . . . nor had holiday rituals like trimming the tree and listening to Christmas carols. Lily didn't limit herself to listening. She sang along in a steady off-key alto that was charmingly unself-conscious.

She insisted that he handle stringing the lights. She pointed out that it was the daddy job, and laughed at him when he struggled with the tangled green plastic wires.

He frowned at one impossible Gordian knot. "I could invent something a hell of lot more practical than this junk. This is insane."

Lily giggled as she watched him yank and tug. "Be my

guest. You'll make a fortune and win the gratitude of legions of frustrated fathers worldwide."

When the lights were finally woven in and around the tree to his satisfaction, Lily made him take a break for warmed-over pizza, and then they started on the ornaments. After that it was the icicles. It was five thirty in the morning when they finished.

Lily turned off all the lights in the house and stumbled back to the living room in the dark. He felt her sidle up against him and he put an arm around her shoulders. "Now what, Mrs. Claus?"

She leaned down, fumbled on the floor, and handed him the end of the extension cord and the end of the last strand of lights. "Now you do the honors."

He tried to refuse. "It's your tree, Lily."

He felt her kiss his chest. "You're a Christmas tree virgin, Ben. This one's for you."

For some stupid reason his throat got tight, and he suddenly felt all the import that his pretty Lily infused into this one night. He felt the warmth and the caring that were so much a part of her. The ache in his chest grew to giant proportions.

He had a hard time speaking. "Okay, then. Here goes." He connected the two plugs and the tree burst into glorious life—reds and greens and blues and yellows and a host of other colors. The branches glowed and shimmered in the darkness, and despite his legendary intelligence, he couldn't for the life of him explain why such a simple experience should impact him so profoundly.

Lily stood beside him quietly. When he turned his head to look at her, her features were illuminated in stained-glass shades that lent even more beauty to her feminine features. He hugged her close, unable to articulate his feelings at the moment, even if he'd wanted to.

He kissed the top of her head. "*Now* do we get to have sex?"

His teasing question broke the mood, but Lily didn't seem to mind. She went up on tiptoe to find his mouth. "Only if we can do it in here."

"Suits me." He wasn't about to quibble over the details. Not when he could have his lovely Lily once again.

He undressed her reverently. Her skin in the soft glow of the tree lights was an artist's canvas. He stroked the curve of her hip, the slope of her breasts.

Then he dropped to his knees and found her most sensitive spot with his mouth. She cried out and fisted her hands in his hair. He loved her slowly, drawing out the pleasure until she begged for release.

And when she finally peaked and sobbed his name, he lowered her gently to the carpet, entered her carefully, and put his own personal spin on the Langford family tree-decorating evening.

Five

Lily yawned and stretched. She had always fantasized about making love in the light of the Christmas tree. And with Ben, it was everything she had imagined and more.

She poked him with an elbow. "You'd better go home and get some sleep, Mr. Reynolds."

He lifted an eyelid. "You could come with me."

The hesitation she felt had nothing to do with lack of enthusiasm for the idea. She could imagine nothing more wonderful than spending the night in Ben's arms. But she also had a strong sense of self-preservation, and she was trying desperately to convince herself she wasn't in love with him. If she could keep things light, perhaps it wouldn't hurt so much when it came to the almost inevitable time for them to part company.

She stared up at the lights on the tree until her vision blurred. "I'm not sure that's a good idea, Ben."

He propped up on an elbow. "Why the hell not?"

He looked grumpy and tired and so dear. She grimaced, wishing she'd thought to bring a robe to the living room. She felt very vulnerable at the moment. "We've agreed to enjoy each other sexually, but we also agreed that this wasn't going anywhere long-term."

He scowled. "So maybe I'm asking you to come over for more *recreational* sex."

She inhaled and released the breath. He wasn't making this easy. "I'm exhausted, Ben. I need sleep."

His face changed suddenly and he looked contrite. "Then come sleep with me, Lily. Let me hold you. No funny stuff, I swear."

Her head screamed, *No!* but her heart won out. "Okay. Let me grab a few things and we'll go."

Ben felt oddly self-conscious when Lily walked into his bedroom. She'd seen it just hours earlier when she had retrieved his clothes, but that was different. All his careful preparations paled with Lily in residence.

He took her small overnight bag to the bathroom and set it on the vanity. "Ladies first. I'll go make sure everything is locked up."

Because of the work he did, he had a state-of-the-art security system, and he was always careful to set all the alarms. Plus, at the moment it gave him an excuse to offer Lily some privacy. She seemed skittish suddenly, and he was afraid she would bolt unless he could make her feel comfortable.

When he returned, she was sitting on the far side of his king-size bed flipping through a copy of *Scientific American*. She looked up and smiled. "You have an article in here." Her thin raspberry satin robe made his mouth turn dry.

He shrugged. "Yeah." He wasn't at all interested in discussing his work.

She stood and joined him, looking up into his eyes. "Will you take me to see your lab?"

The simple request took him by surprise. In the year and a half he had known her, she had been in other parts of his house, but never the lab. It was his private place . . . his sanctuary. The spot where he felt most like himself. He swallowed uneasily. "If you want."

He led her downstairs to the main level and unlocked the door to the basement. As they descended the stairs, he noticed the surprise on her face. Most basements were dark, dank affairs.

His was quite the opposite. Bright lights and white fittings kept him alert in his modern lab. A specially designed airflow system cleaned the air constantly. There were no less than four computers, three of which were networked with national databases.

He had microscopes, scanners, even a mini X-ray machine. He was licensed to handle radioactive materials, but he seldom worked in that arena, and when he did, he preferred to go on-site.

He watched Lily wander around the thousand-square-foot facility with amazement on her face. Her peignoir was a splash of color in the stark environment. Occasionally she touched something, but for the most part she was content to look.

The countertops were bare. Unlike the stereotype, he was obsessively tidy about his work. Details could be too easily lost in a messy environment.

Finally she paused and looked at him. "This is *so* sexy."

His jaw dropped. "Really?"

She nodded slowly, looking him over from head to toe. "Do you have one of those white lab coats?"

"I'm not a medical doctor," he said, stalling for time until he could figure out what she was after.

"But do you?" She wasn't easily sidetracked.

He reached into a tall cabinet and lifted the requested item from a hook. It was spotlessly clean. He seldom bothered to protect his clothes unless he was working with something really messy.

She cocked her head. "Would you put it on . . . please?"

He slipped his arms into the sleeves and buttoned it up. Lily was staring at him raptly. The back of his neck tingled. Experiencing sexual arousal in this particular room was rare to nonexistent. But he didn't need any highly sophisticated instruments to measure it at the moment. It was off the charts.

She shed her nightwear, both the robe and the gown beneath, so quickly he was stunned. The fluorescent lights were not particularly flattering, but try as he might, he couldn't find a single flaw. She was magnificent.

She walked up to him where he stood frozen beside a file cabinet and blinked her lashes. "Are you going to do some kind of kinky sex experiments on my body?"

He gulped. "Kinky?"

Her lower lip pouted. "You know. Like a mad scientist or an alien space crew."

He tried to laugh, but her nearness and her nudity had produced a giant knot in his throat. "I did have something in mind," he muttered.

Her eyes lit up. "Oh, good. I'd hate to be down here for nothing."

His brain raced feverishly. He was a genius, for god's sake. Surely he could keep up with his playful neighbor. He produced a frown. "I'm working on a project that measures female vaginal muscle tone."

This time *her* jaw dropped, but she recovered quickly. "I'm happy to be of service," she murmured, moving even closer, close enough to feel the heat and length of his erection through his pants.

He picked her up in his arms, carried her all of six feet, and deposited her on the long stainless-steel table in the center of the room. She shrieked when the cold metal made contact with her flesh.

He stared at her impassively. "I'll need to restrain you. Any involuntary motion on your part may skew the measurements."

Color bloomed on her cheeks, and her eyes widened. "Whatever you say, Doctor."

Her submissive response flipped a switch deep inside him, and all his primitive impulses surged to the fore. The table didn't really have restraints, but he improvised. He had some two-inch-wide rubber bands that were extremely strong. He circled her wrists and one of her ankles. Then he attached the rubber bands to hooks on the side of the table that were normally used for hanging clipboards and charts.

Her nipples were standing at attention. Her lips were parted, and her breathing was quick and shallow.

He debated rapidly and then went to a sink in the corner. Occasionally if he had to run out to a meeting, he cleaned up down here rather than taking the time to go upstairs to his bathroom. He filled up a bowl with water and picked up a razor and shaving cream.

When he turned around, Lily made a little squeak. He kept his mouth in a stern line. "As you know, it's very important to conduct scientific experiments in a sterile environment. It will be necessary for me to shave you before we begin."

Lily's eyes glazed over, and his boner nearly crippled him. He approached the table, his heart punching at his chest. "Stay perfectly still."

He'd left one ankle unbound so he could maneuver her. Steadily, he coated her mound. She didn't have much hair to deal with. It was neatly trimmed in a sexy little triangle. He took the razor in his right hand and began.

If he had set out to invent a form of torture for a man to endure, this was it. He separated the pink folds of her labia and scraped carefully, pausing to rinse the razor now and then.

Lily writhed beneath his hands, her panting and murmuring nearly driving him crazy. He avoided her clitoris carefully. But the rest of her intimate area he shaved bare-baby-bottom clean.

When he was done, he wiped her with a damp cloth and ran his fingers over his handiwork to see if he had missed any spots. The slick, smooth flesh, soft and moist, was erotic and inviting.

He couldn't resist. He bent his head and nibbled her clit. She cried out and arched her back, but he deliberately didn't give her enough to satisfy.

He stepped away for a moment and rummaged in a drawer for some aluminum cylinders of varying widths. He used them occasionally when he wanted to cool liquids rapidly in the freezer. They were open on one end, but the other end was rounded. One was about an inch in diameter, another two inches, and the last three inches. They were each approximately eight inches long.

Lily gasped when he approached her, but he didn't meet her gaze. He tapped her thigh. "Make sure you move only when I tell you to." He stuck an electrode to her lower abdomen . . . the kind used for measuring an EKG. Then he connected a wire, but it hung harmlessly beneath the table out of her eyesight, unattached.

He took a notepad and wrote down some nonsense figures. "I'm going to insert these cylinders one at a time and see how well you are able to grasp them."

Lily shivered and jerked futilely at her bonds. *Holy shit, Batman.* Dr. Frankenstein was taking this pretty seriously. Was that stupid wire really hooked up to anything? She was so turned on, her body was on fire despite her nudity and the chilled air in the lab.

She saw him pick up the smallest cylinder, and her belly clenched. His face had all the impersonal demeanor of a real doctor as he separated her folds and slid the tube into her vagina.

The aluminum was cold, and she flinched.

He made a notation on that damned pad. Then he rested his palm over the electrode thingy. "Clamp down with your vaginal muscles and hold for five seconds."

Automatically she did as he commanded, feeling the metal tube warm within her sheath.

He made a notation and removed the tube.

The next tube was twice as big. And she felt the difference. *Ahhh* . . . When he gave the instruction to clamp down again, she trembled. Her body was climbing toward a spectacular orgasm, and she wasn't at all sure she could hold it off.

But her dear doctor seemed blithely unconcerned. "How am I doing?" she asked huskily.

He frowned, studying his notes. "Adequate. But we may need to explore further."

He picked up the last of the cylinders. It probed at her opening, and her body tensed. She felt him rub the end in her wetness. This time it slid in. But it stretched her. *Wow.* Her skin prickled, and she squeezed down with all her might. She was almost there.

But he withdrew it matter-of-factly and walked over to the computer, abandoning her to her aching, hungry solitude. She lay there, bereft, while he entered data in the computer . . . or so it seemed.

"Doctor?" Her voice was a breathy little sound. "Are we done?"

He turned to face her. "The results were not quite what I had hoped for. I'm debating further research."

He came back to her side and studied her nude body. He ran a hand from her throat over each breast, down her belly, to the aching juncture between her thighs. "My findings are not conclusive."

He released her rapidly and practically dragged her from the table. He urged her across the room to a chair adjacent to a table. He took her left arm and wrapped it in what looked like a blood-pressure cuff. He put some kind of large plastic clip on her finger. And then she realized what she was about to be subjected to.

"Is this what I think it is?"

He nodded, busy with wires and clips and settings. "Yep. A policeman buddy of mine got it for me. I was fascinated with how they work, and I'm working on a prototype that will be more reliable."

Her heart started to pound. He took a seat beside her. "We'll begin with baseline questions. What is your full name?"

"Lily Elizabeth Langford."

"What state are you from?"

"Mississippi."

"Are you employed?"

"Yes."

"Do you enjoy fucking your neighbor?"

She watched the telltale needle scramble over the paper. "Yes."

"Are you willing to let him perform experiments on your body?"

Another jump in the needle. "Yes."

"Do you fantasize about him?"

She paused. "No."

The needle spiked, and Ben shook his head in disappointment. "Shame on you, Lily."

She felt her face heat.

He looked at his pad of presumed questions. "Do you enjoy oral sex?"

Her throat was dry. "Yes."

"Would you ever kiss another woman?"

She grinned. "Sorry, but no."

His exaggerated sigh made her chuckle.

"Are you aroused at this moment?"

She bit her lip. "Not particularly." Might as well make him work for it. But unfortunately, the machine was damned accurate.

He reached out without warning and cupped her right breast. "Do you like it when I do this?"

Her eyes closed and her thighs clenched. "Yes."

He scooted closer and his hand dropped from her breast to the tops of her closed thighs. He nudged his fingers between them and touched her intimately. "Is your arousal higher or lower when I do this?"

She squirmed on the hard chair. "Higher." Her forehead was damp, and she was unable to breathe normally.

With one finger he stroked her clitoris. "Do you like this?"

"Yes, god, yes."

He stroked more quickly. Her thighs separated. Her teeth dug into her bottom lip. Her eyes were still squeezed shut. "Please, Ben."

He ignored her, concentrating on his hand and her body. "How about this?" Without warning, he entered her with the largest of the three cylinders. Nerve endings in her body screamed with pleasure and shock, and she came hard, clamping down on the tube and pressing wildly against his hand.

He pulled her into his arms, tossing all the *experiment* paraphernalia aside. "Lily, oh, Lily."

He swapped places with her, unzipped his pants, and pulled her down onto his cock. She peaked again, and he thrust over and over, shouting and gripping her as he rode out the wave of his own release.

In the aftermath, he could have heard a pin drop in the silent lab.

He leaned his forehead against hers. "What happened to being tired and wanting to sleep?"

She was limp in his arms, totally wiped out. "It was the lab. Don't ask me why. But it was."

"Fair enough." He stood with her in his arms, rescued her pj's, and took her upstairs.

Six

He took the shortest shower on record and exited the bathroom wearing a towel and nothing else. Lily sat primly on the edge of the bed. Dressed. Again. Her eyes widened when he dropped the damp rectangle of cotton and climbed beneath the covers.

He was hoping for buck naked, but she was wearing the above-the-knee nightgown with narrow straps. She flipped back the sheet and comforter on her side and crawled in.

He reached across the great divide and dragged her up against him. He looked down at her and winced. "Can we dispense with the nightie?"

The tip of her tongue appeared and wet her lips. "I suppose."

He helped her slither out of it, and he tossed it as far away as he could. He turned off the lights to keep himself from succumbing to temptation. But he hadn't counted on the impact of having all that soft, silky female skin curled up against him.

He lasted an hour. Lily had fallen asleep almost instantly. He rubbed a hand over her flat stomach. His fingers stroked the valley between her legs. He turned on the small lamp on the bedside table with the twenty-five-watt bulb. He wanted to see her face. "Lily," he whispered. "Are you awake?"

He skated a fingertip over her clit and felt her shiver. He kissed her navel. "Lily?"

She sighed, and it was a good sigh . . . the kind of sound a woman made when she was eating chocolate or watching the end of a romantic chick flick.

But he needed full confirmation, especially since he had rashly promised her plenty of rest. "Lily, sweetheart. I want to make love to you."

Her dark eyes opened, confused for a moment as she got her bearings, and then soft and happy. "Don't you ever get tired?"

He nudged her hip with his boner. "What can I say? He likes you."

She held up her arms. "Come here, Einstein. Show me what you've got."

He screwed her hard and fast, pumping his hips and driving deeply into her welcoming body. She met him thrust for thrust, her eager responses making him hotter and hotter . . . until they were both panting and on the edge of the cliff. His muscles quivered with the strain of holding back. "Are you with me?" He could feel her fingernails scoring his shoulders, but he had to be sure.

She bit his neck. "Now, Ben. Now."

It was a conflagration unlike anything he had ever produced in his lab. Sheer white flame bursting into an explosion that rocked him back on his heels. He'd never known its equal.

He let her rest for an hour, and then they started all over again.

*   *   *

His alarm was set for two forty-five p.m. He usually awoke minutes before and turned it off.

Sunday afternoon it buzzed annoyingly for a good two
minutes before he summoned up enough energy to slap at the
plastic button on top. The resulting silence was beautiful. He
moaned and pulled the pillow over his head. God, he ached
from head to toe.

And then he remembered why. He sat up abruptly, making
every cell in his brain scream as if he had indulged in a night of
heavy drinking. Lily. Where was Lily?

There was a damn note on the nightstand.

Dear Ben,

   *Don't panic. Nothing's wrong. But I needed some sleep,
and I needed some space to clear my head. This weekend
has been pretty intense. Plus, right before I left your house,
there was a message on my cell phone asking me to come in
to work tonight. We've got several people out sick with the
flu. So I'm going to take care of some chores, nap for a bit,
and head on over to the hospital. I'll call you when I wake
up tomorrow afternoon.*

   Love, Lily

   P.S. The tree looks beautiful. . . .

He dropped back onto the mattress and groaned. He could
go back to sleep, but what was the point? He'd just be dreaming
about sex with Lily. Unfortunately, he had given her the alarm
codes months ago; otherwise she would not have been able to
escape so easily.

So he bit the bullet and got up. After a stinging hot shower
and two cups of coffee, he felt almost human. It tormented him

to know she was just across the street, but he did his best to forget that.

He skipped his usual run. He'd had about all the exercise he could take for one day and night. Instead, he headed downstairs to the lab. It took him a full forty-five minutes to get past the visions of Lily's nude body everywhere he turned, but at last his brain clicked into gear and he got to work.

Lily drove to the hospital, hoping she could make it through the night. Sleeping in Ben's bed was a euphemism. He'd been an animal, and she had been entirely willing each and every time he had awakened her for another round, despite their earlier antics. She hadn't even known it was possible to have sex that often in one twenty-four-hour period.

She was actually sore in some very embarrassing places. Fortunately, it was a busy night in the pediatric ward. She didn't have time to slow down, much less feel sleepy. By the time she drove home and tumbled into bed the next morning, memories of Benjamin Reynolds were beginning to seem like a particularly delicious erotic dream.

Ben worked through the night with gratifying results. He shut down his computer just before dawn and waited to make sure Lily's car was in her driveway before he collapsed into his bed for some much-needed shut-eye.

When he woke up that afternoon, his first thought was of Lily. The novelty shocked him. Normally he woke up thinking about his current project. His unconscious sleep state often generated some really creative ideas, and he had to rush to get them down before they escaped him.

But today, work was the last thing on his mind. All he could remember was Lily's note saying, *I'll call you when I wake up.*

Three o'clock came and went. Four o'clock came and went. At which time he was ready to beat his head against the wall. *Damn.*

The phone rang at five after four. He snatched up the receiver. "Hello."

"It's me."

His heart staggered and then settled into a rapid beat. "Hello, me. How was work?"

"Brutal. How about you?"

"I got a lot accomplished."

An awkward silence reigned for about a minute before he gave up the effort to be an evolved, civilized man. "Can I come over?"

"I thought you'd never ask."

When she opened the door, she was wearing two of those stick-on red bows, one on each breast. And nothing else. "Look what Santa brought you, Mr. Reynolds."

He kicked the door shut and scooped her into his arms. "Nice wrapping."

She giggled, flicking the bows away and slinging an arm around his neck. "I hope it fits."

"I'll make sure of it," he muttered. The bedroom was too far. He paused in the small kitchen, approved of the bare table, and dropped his precious cargo on the clean wooden surface.

He dragged her hips to the edge of the table and unzipped his pants. He was inside her with one savage thrust. Then he froze and shook his head to clear the red haze. "God, Lily. Did I hurt you?"

She propped herself on her elbows, all bare skin and seductive beauty. Her smile was wry. "No. Unless you count freezing my butt off." She touched him where their bodies joined. "Don't get all Mr. Nice Guy on me now. We're kind of in the middle of something here."

He chuckled hoarsely, feeling himself spiraling out of control. His luscious Lily was turning him into a sex maniac. "Sorry, babe. I live to serve you." He gripped her hips and stroked deeper, withdrew, and did it again.

Her eyes were closed now, and a pretty pink flush covered her from throat to breasts. She was panting and arching her back and saying naughty little things that threatened to make the top of his head blow off.

He felt his cock swell inside her, and he reached forward to stroke her clit with his thumb. God, she was beautiful. He toyed with her, keeping his touch just off center, the pressure just too light.

But then she sat up, forcing his prick into a new and agonizingly sweet position. She plastered herself against his chest and wrapped her arms around his neck. She bit his earlobe. "Is this the best you can do?" she taunted.

He growled and lifted her off the table, turning and shoving her up against the refrigerator. He cupped her ass and pulled almost all the way out. Lily whimpered. He surged forward. *Oh, shit.* He felt it coming and was powerless. He took her again and again . . . two or three more thrusts, and then he shouted as the thread snapped and he came in a wave of pleasure that threatened to drown him.

Lily went with him, her climax milking his cock and making him so weak, he was in danger of tumbling both of them to the floor.

He managed to stumble down the hall and into her bedroom before he collapsed to the mattress with her in his arms.

*   *   *

Lily stared at the ceiling, trying to get her heart rate and her breathing back to normal. *Wow.* Benjamin Reynolds might have an incredible IQ, but his talents in other areas weren't too shabby either.

She lifted one arm and let it fall back to the bed. "I can't move. You've destroyed me."

The man beside her said something that sounded like, "hhmphh." His eyes were closed, and his chest rose and fell with each ragged breath. It struck her as extremely erotic that she was completely naked, and her handsome lover still had on all his clothes.

She closed her eyes, smiling to herself. She was becoming a slut. And darned if she didn't have an aptitude for it.

When Ben hadn't moved in at least three minutes, she summoned up her last ounce of energy and scooted on top of him, draping herself over his body and tucking her head beneath his chin.

His arms came up to hold her, but his eyes were still closed. She tapped him on the chin. "Hello. Anybody home in there?"

His hands stroked up and down her back. He opened one eyelid. "We need to date."

Okay, that was bizarre. "Come again?"

He struggled to a sitting position, no mean feat with her glued to his chest. "I need something to distract me from screwing you every five minutes. Ergo, we need to date. Movies, bowling, dinner . . . you pick."

She smiled, feeling the solid wall of his chest beneath her cheek. "Opera?"

"Oh, God, no . . ."

She laughed. "*The Nutcracker*?"

He sighed. "I suppose."

She wiggled off him and grabbed up a robe before heading

to the living room. She called the box office and scored two front-row cancellations for seven thirty that evening. "We're all set, but you still have to feed me dinner first," she yelled down the hall.

It was a memorable evening. Lily was not unaware of the glances from women envious of her tall, handsome date. Ben in a dark suit was a sight to remember. He exuded cool, masculine confidence, and he was flatteringly enamored of her simple black dress.

The performance was beautiful and the ride home in the car filled with quiet happiness. They both knew there would be no more lovemaking that night. Lily was going to have to do a quick change in order make it to work on time.

Ben groused and worried about the weather. A possible ice storm was predicted, though it was still only raining at the moment. He prowled around her house while she got ready for work and then he helped her into her coat. "Promise me you won't try to drive home in the morning if it's bad. I'll come get you."

She kissed him and smiled. "I promise."

Ben was able to split his concentration between the weather and his project with a fair amount of success. The forecasters were abandoning their early optimistic projections. The temperature had taken an unexpected tumble, and ice was already coating the bushes outside Ben's windows and bending them toward the ground.

He went upstairs for a quick bite to eat around two and flipped on the radio to catch the news. He was rinsing out his glass and loading it in the dishwasher when his cell phone rang.

It was Lily, and the frazzled note in her voice made him panic. Lily was one of the calmest females he had ever met. "Slow down," he said, his hand gripping the phone. "Tell me what's wrong."

"The ice storm is killing us," she muttered. "There are accidents everywhere, and Emergency is slammed. The power went off a little while ago, and even though the generators kicked in, it scared a lot of the kids. But the computer system crashed, and they haven't been able to get it back online. I thought you might be able to pinpoint the problem and fix it. I need you, Ben. Can you help?"

"Of course." He was already reaching for his keys.

"But be careful. I couldn't bear it if you got hurt."

"I'll be careful," he promised.

It was a horrendous drive he didn't care to repeat anytime soon. He sent several prayers to the man upstairs, and slip-sliding into a couple of near misses might have convinced him to turn around had his errand been any less important than his Lily.

He found her at the nurses' station when he arrived. She looked tired and stressed, but her face lit up when she saw him.

She was holding a tiny boy who looked as if he might have been all of three years old. Lily shoved the kid at him. "Here. Hold Eddie a minute. I'll call upstairs and tell them you're coming." She leaned close and whispered in his ear, "He doesn't have a dad. His mom's home with the other three kids."

Ben froze, feeling the odd weight of the fragile body pressed against him. Eddie had no qualms about snuggling up to a stranger. Poor little guy. He smelled of ketchup and hospital. He was mostly asleep, his little chest shuddering occasionally with hiccupping sobs.

Before Ben could fully absorb the novelty of holding a small child—or any child, for that matter—Lily was back, relieving him of his burden. She settled Eddie on her hip and used her free hand to brush a strand of hair from her face. "They're waiting for you. One flight up. The server is in two-oh-nine-B."

It took him twenty-five minutes to get the system up and running again. The techs were so glad to have the monkey off their backs, they didn't even waste any effort being resentful of his interference. He estimated it could have taken them another couple of hours to locate the problem and resolve it, so he was glad Lily had called him.

When he went back downstairs she was still holding Eddie and was trying to eat a sandwich at the same time. He frowned. "Shouldn't you have a meal break?"

She grimaced. "No breaks tonight. No time." Then she gave him a quick kiss on the cheek. "Thank you so much, Ben. I love you for coming so quickly."

He murmured a response, but her words hit him hard. She hadn't said "I love you," but it was close enough for him to realize that if he ever heard those words from Lily in earnest, it would change his life. But a smart woman didn't say things like that to a man with whom she shared hot and sweaty recreational sex, no matter how wonderful. She said them to the man who would father her children and grow old beside her.

He had a lot to think about.

For Lily, the next nine days passed in a haze of baking and wrapping and packing and any one of the other hundred and one errands and chores on her agenda. Ben offered to take her car and get it serviced, and she let him. He was always there anticipating her needs and doing his best to make her life easier.

Aside from her shifts at the hospital, she and Ben spent almost every waking and sleeping hour together. As wonderful as it was, she ached inside thinking about the time it would end. Finally, though it tore her in pieces to do so, she decided to use her vacation as an opportunity to break things off.

Ben had been very clear about his intentions, and Lily was no fool. Ben's life was heading in a far different direction from hers. It would never be normal. He had enormous responsibilities, and he was making contributions to the world community. He was a true hero.

And it didn't help that she had given up on her stupid pretense of *not* falling in love. Of course she loved him. How could she not? Her heart ached to tell him how she felt, but that would only make things worse. He would feel guilty and uncomfortable, and she couldn't live with that. It wasn't fair to him or to her.

So . . . she sparkled. And she projected happiness. She was so damned cheerful, she deserved an elf award for being the brightest, chirpiest celebrator of the holiday season in the whole darned state.

But it was all worthwhile. Ben's lovemaking turned her inside out. He was a generous lover, and at times she could swear that he wanted her for more than sex. He was so tender and so affectionate. But she was a big girl, and she kept her feet firmly planted on the ground, stomping out those fruitless pipe dreams.

Work helped. There were so many people hurting and living with terrible situations that Lily had to put her own heartache in perspective. She would count herself lucky to have known Ben and to have shared his life and his bed, even if only briefly.

He was a remarkable man. And though it would make finding another partner difficult, she couldn't regret what she had done in loving him.

After her shift ended the morning of the nineteenth, she loaded her car. Ben was at his house sleeping, she hoped. She had fudged a little bit about her plans, so she could avoid saying good-bye. She knew her course of action was inevitable, but the thought of it was killing her. She had baked him a batch of his favorite oatmeal-chocolate-chip cookies, and she planned to leave them on her kitchen table. As if cookies could make up for what she was about to do.

Once she was on the road, she would call him. He had a key so he could water her plants. They had already exchanged gifts Saturday evening. Ben had taken her out to an upscale Boston restaurant, and later he had given her a taupe cashmere robe. It was whisper soft, and the most beautiful thing she had ever owned. He said it complemented her eyes and her hair.

The robe was not making the trip to Mississippi. Lily would never be able to explain to her mother how she came to be in possession of such an expensive item.

Next to the luxurious robe, her gift to him had been embarrassingly modest. She had given Ben a small silver picture frame with a photo of the two of them from the night they went to see *The Nutcracker.* But he had seemed genuinely pleased.

She put the last box in the trunk and made one final run-through of the house to make sure she wasn't forgetting anything. She had plenty of caffeine in the car. She planned to drive until eight p.m. if she could stay awake, and then crash in a motel, and by morning be back on a normal human schedule for the rest of the holidays.

As she pulled out of the driveway and headed down the street, she didn't even glance toward Ben's house. It hurt too much. Sadly, she remembered Miss Matilda's words about letting him pursue the prize.

Unfortunately, she wasn't running at all. She was simply getting on with her life. Being a mature, rational grown-up. It sucked, but then again, so did a lot of things in this world. She had a wonderful family waiting on her in Mississippi. It would have to be enough.

Seven

Ben sat in his living room with the lights turned off and the draperies opened wide. It enabled him to look across the street at Lily's quiet, dark house. No car in the driveway. No activity of any kind.

It was dusk, and the gloomy half-light outside his window accurately reflected his mood.

He bit into a cookie and took a swallow of milk. He'd missed her phone call as she left. He'd been asleep. *Bloody fucking hell.* He glanced down at the note in his left hand. She hoped he'd have a merry Christmas.

No mention of New Year's Eve. No mention about missing him while she was gone.

The phone call had been even worse. Her voice had sounded tired and depressed. She'd apologized for not saying it to his face, but she thought it was best that they not see each other anymore. She planned to look for a house elsewhere when she got home.

He set the glass on the table and leaned his head back, feeling defeated. He hurt all over. As a teenager he'd been in a bad wreck. The seat belt had saved him from serious injury, but in the aftermath, he had ached from head to toe.

Much like now. Lily was gone. Her family was important to her, and Ben was simply a guy she screwed around with. He wasn't part of the big picture. Holidays were for loved ones, and she had probably forgotten about him before she hit the state line.

He thought about the next seven days. His parents would not expect him. The thought would never cross their minds. Ben had his work. And in past years he hadn't let a red-circled date on the calendar alter his schedule. They approved wholeheartedly. The elder Reynoldses basked in the reflected glow of their son's glory.

He groaned. Some glory. His work was personally fulfilling, and he had drawers full of accolades and awards, but glorious it wasn't.

He'd been an idiot. He'd assumed that the only thing missing from his odd life was sex. God, how wrong could a man be? He'd had sex with Lily. And it was amazing. But at the end of the day, there was still a void.

For a genius, he'd been remarkably slow to see the truth. He didn't need sex for a normal life. He needed love.

Lily arrived in her small hometown just as the streetlights were popping on up and down the sidewalks on Tuesday evening. She'd driven as if the devil were on her heels. The farther away she could get from Boston and from Ben, the safer she would be.

It was fuzzy logic, but then she never claimed to be a genius.

She pulled into her parents' driveway and shut off the

engine. She was home. It was a moment she had waited for and anticipated for the last eighteen months. So why did she feel like crying?

But when the front door flew open and her various family members tumbled down the steps to greet her, her heart lifted. It would be okay.

By Friday afternoon, it felt almost as if she had never been away. The weather was in the upper sixties every day, and she hadn't needed a coat since she arrived. Still, the weather guys were insisting that northern Mississippi might see a flake or two of snow by Christmas Eve.

Hearing nothing but southern accents every day made her realize how much she had missed her roots. Her brothers teased her. Her sisters took her shopping. Her daddy doted on her. And her mom . . . well, her mom was just Mom. There was no substitute.

It was wonderful to be home.

She fell into the family routines with ease. There were pies to bake. Gifts to deliver. Programs at church. And her family always met one evening at a local shelter to help serve a Christmas meal. It was a tradition that had expanded to include her married brothers' two wives. The three toddlers stayed with a neighbor, but her sisters and her single brother brought dates.

Later that night they all gathered around her parents' large oak dining room table and played games. Her dad made his famous peanut-butter fudge, and her siblings bickered over who was the most talented cardplayer.

She was happy. She was enjoying herself. But deep in a little corner of her soul, she grieved for Ben. Was he eating well? Was he alone?

The thought of him with another woman was like a knife to the heart, but she told herself he deserved to be happy.

On Christmas Eve morning, she ran into her old boyfriend in town at the grocery store. They exchanged awkward small talk for a couple of minutes, and then she escaped, wondering what she had ever seen in him. He was pleasant and nice-looking. But there were no sparks. If she was honest with herself, there never had been.

In fact, none of the men she had dated from high school to the present had come close to measuring up to Benjamin Reynolds. Not the IQ thing. No one could be expected to compete in that arena. But none of them had Ben's charm, his sexy smile, his compassion . . . all those things that made him the man she fell in love with.

It was tradition in her family to open gifts from each other on Christmas Eve. Then tomorrow the Santa presents would appear beneath the tree. It was a process her mother had maintained even before the grandchildren began appearing on the scene.

Lily was sitting in a pile of wrapping paper and bows, admiring the silver bracelet from her brother and sister-in-law, when her father disappeared for a moment and then reappeared with a funny look on his face.

"Lily?"

She looked up with a smile. "Yes, Daddy?" The room was abuzz with conversation underlaid with a steady stream of Christmas music from the stereo. It was hard to hear over the bedlam.

Her father crooked a finger. She stood up, brushing bits of ribbon and paper from her black slacks, and crossed the room. "What's up, Dad?" She hugged him around the waist affectionately.

He pointed down the hall toward the front door. "You have a visitor. He wouldn't come in."

Her heart began to punch against her ribs, making her feel a bit sick. Surely not the ex-boyfriend. Her daddy knew *his* name.

She swallowed hard, her throat dry. "Okay. I'll be right back."

The short hallway felt like an endless tunnel. By the time she opened the door, her hands were shaking. A swirl of surprisingly cold air made its way inside. And standing hunched against the wind was a tall, blond genius she had assumed was several hundred miles away.

She blinked as a random snowflake landed on her nose. "Ben?"

His unfathomable eyes were dark blue and his mouth was grim. "Lily."

She backed up automatically, holding the door wide. "Come in."

"No." He said it simply.

She tilted her head. "Then what?"

"May I steal you for a half hour?"

She looked back over her shoulder. They wouldn't miss her for that long. She faced him again. "Sure. Let me get my coat." She lifted it from the rack on the wall behind her, slipped it on without buttoning it, and joined him on the porch, closing the door behind her.

His head was bare. He was wearing a black overcoat, black dress slacks, and a charcoal sweater. He looked big and sexy and intimidating.

She stuffed her hands in her pockets. "I didn't expect to see you," she said quietly. "What are you doing here?"

He moved with the speed and silence of a panther, lifting

her into his embrace and capturing her mouth in a series of hungry, possessive kisses. They could have been in the midst of a blizzard, and she wouldn't have noticed. Their tongues dueled as she and Ben made panting, inarticulate little moans.

She wrapped her arms around his neck so tightly, he finally complained. "Air," he muttered.

She released him reluctantly, her head spinning. She wiped a smear of lip gloss from his cheek. "I don't know what I did to earn that, my dear Mr. Reynolds, but if you tell me, I'd be happy to do it again."

He cupped her cheek, his eyes several shades lighter than they had been before. "Smart-ass." He opened the sides of her coat and surveyed the reindeer sweater her grandmother had given her. "Does it bother you that I get turned on when you wear outlandish clothing?"

She grinned. "I think I've been insulted."

He kissed her once more. Gently. With great tenderness. And then he grabbed her hand and tugged her toward his car. "C'mon. I'm cold."

She followed him happily. "You're from Boston. I thought you came from hardy stock."

He opened the passenger door. "That's a myth we perpetuate to make ourselves feel superior."

She waited for him to round the car and slide in beside her. "And does that work?"

"On occasion." He started the engine. "I want to show you something."

It was the last thing he said for several minutes. He followed a road outside of town until they wound to the top of a low hill overlooking the river. In the distance, a white farmhouse sat forlorn, the FOR SALE sign in the yard proclaiming the building's emptiness.

Ben made no move to get out, and she was in no hurry to be cold again, so she sat patiently. The windows were fogging up from their breathing. He was staring through the windshield, his long fingers drumming on the steering wheel. He seemed unusually nervous.

Finally he let out a long sigh. "I'm an intelligent man, Lily."

She chuckled. "Thank you, Captain Obvious."

He ignored her levity. "I can read books and learn things, and you can teach me the stuff you know. People all over the world do it. I think I could master the basics and not botch them too badly."

She was totally lost, so she let him talk.

He continued with his disjointed and alarming stream-of-consciousness monologue. "I'm wealthy. I guess I haven't told you that, but maintaining two homes so you could see more of your family would be entirely feasible . . . this one, or any other place you like . . . and if you help me, we can work out some sort of system so that I wouldn't ignore you or the kids—"

She touched his arm. "Ben . . . I don't know what you're talking about."

He looked at her . . . finally. The expression on his face was an odd mix of defiance and pleading. "I love you, Lily," he said simply. "And I know I could learn how to be a good father. If you'll help me."

The edges of her vision went fuzzy and there was a humming in her ears. "You love me?" It was the one piece of information she'd been able to latch onto.

His crooked smile was whimsical. "Yes, Lily Langford. I love you. So much that it makes me sick to my stomach to think about losing you."

He leaned forward, and she met him over the gearshift.

When their lips touched, the temperature in the car seemed to go up ten degrees. His tongue played with her mouth. Wicked, wicked tongue. She whispered his name, and the kiss went from tender to tinder in one flaming heartbeat.

She clutched handfuls of his coat, trying to get closer. "Oh, God, Ben. I didn't want to leave you. It killed me. I don't ever want to leave you."

He kissed his way from her ear to her throat. "But do you?" he asked cryptically.

She shoved his hand up under her sweater. "Do I what?" she panted.

When his fingers touched her nipple, she whimpered. She wanted him naked. Now. And this car was not the ideal location for what she had in mind.

He grabbed a handful of her hair, jerking on it to get her attention. "Do you love me?"

She pulled back, staring at him in shock. "Of course I love you, Ben. Duh . . . For a supposed genius, you're really slow."

His grin lit up the car. "Hot damn." He opened his car door. "C'mon."

She followed him blindly despite the dark and the cold. He grabbed a ratty old quilt from the trunk and dragged her behind him as he strode across the field toward the house. He lost patience before they got there.

He stopped abruptly, flipping out the thick cloth and pulling her down with him. They knelt and faced each other. He crushed her shoulders between his two hands. "I need you, Lily. Please."

She was already ripping at his pants. So he helped her. They dispensed with the absolute minimum of clothing and came together with curses and rough laughter and sighs of amazement.

He paused, his hips spreading her thighs wide, and his erection buried deeply inside her. His arms supported his weight. His breath made little puffs of white in the crisp night air.

"Marry me, Lily. Have my babies."

She wiggled her hips, trying to get things started. "Yeah, sure. Can we get on with it?"

He chuckled, withdrawing and sinking to the hilt again. "God, you're romantic."

She wrapped her bare legs around his waist, feeling the gooseflesh that shivered over her skin. "If you don't give me an orgasm in the next sixty seconds, I'm pretty sure I'll be hypothermic."

"Can't have that." He grunted, changing the angle and picking up the tempo.

It was snowing harder, and they barely noticed. He reached between them and touched her in a way that made her forget all about the cold. She moaned and arched and crested the peak as tiny snowflakes melted in stinging little dots on her hot skin.

Ben was maybe fifteen seconds behind her.

When they were able to breathe again, they both started laughing helplessly. Ben tossed his coat over her legs and reached in the dark for her rumpled pants. "Lord knows what your parents will think," he muttered. "This was not my finest idea, that's for sure."

She fondled his still semierect penis while he tried to fasten his trousers. "I was on board with it," she teased. "And you're a Yankee, so there are already a few strikes against you to start with."

He finished dressing them both and dragged her to her feet. "Thanks for building my confidence, sweetheart." The wry sarcasm in his voice made her giggle.

She snuggled closer to his body. "You're welcome. I love you, Benjamin Reynolds. And so will my family. Have no fear."

While he folded up the quilt, she backed a few steps toward the car.

Ben turned around and reached for her. "Come here, woman. Where do you think you're going?"

She slapped his hand and eluded his grasp. "Tag. You're it, Benjamin."

And thus ensued a very provocative footrace with a very satisfactory ending for all concerned.

Seducing the Duke

One

Caitlyn Anderson made a notation in her BlackBerry and refocused her attention on the mayor's impassioned face. Thelma Starks, a slender, attractive black woman in her early fifties, was one of the more effective leaders in Atlanta's recent history. At the moment she was deeply involved in a massive project to reclaim some of the city's depressed and dying areas.

She had assembled a group of people with varying expertise to help her assess the feasibility of certain aspects of her initiative. Caitlyn was flattered to be included. Her company, Designing Women—named after the popular television show from the late eighties and early nineties—was seven years old and growing at a gratifying rate. But with exposure to new clients, she could take her dreams to the next level.

This morning's meeting had been a fascinating give and take, and Caitlyn was excited to be a part of it. There was only one fly in the ointment . . . Duke Yancey.

He sat across the conference table from her, and although she had done her best to ignore him for the last two hours, Duke Yancey was not a man to be easily overlooked. At six feet three inches and two hundred and ten pounds, Duke was a walking, talking ad for testosterone.

These days he kept his wavy brown hair cut short. His eyes were hazel, but she happened to know that with the right shirt and in the right light, those devilish peepers could turn as green as the money he piled up in his bank account minute by minute.

Duke owned a string of males-only workout facilities. He'd positioned them purposely in run-down parts of the city, thus giving those areas a boost. His insight, savvy business sense, and entrepreneurship were precisely the reasons the mayor had included him in her plans. Plus, his father owned a highly successful construction business, and Duke had grown up learning everything there was to know about the building industry.

Caitlyn hated him. Well, okay, that was a bit over the top. The truth was, he needled her. He had a way of looking at a woman like he might have just enough X-ray vision to see straight through her clothes to a pretty set of underwear . . . or worse.

It outraged her. And she would die before admitting that it intrigued her maybe the tiniest bit.

Duke was a legend in Georgia. From the day his parents christened him after John Wayne's famous nickname, Duke had done everything a little bit larger than life. His college football exploits were still fodder for the sports mill, and when the man walked into a room, he commanded attention. He knew how to make an impression.

And then there were the women, scads of women, a veritable harem of women. And what ticked Caitlyn off the most was the fact that not one of Duke's ex-girlfriends ever had a bad word to say against him. Seriously. It was like he did some Middle Eastern snake charmer thing and brought everyone within a ten-mile radius under his spell.

But not this girl. Not Caitlyn. She was born and bred in the south alongside four brothers, and she was made of sterner stuff. She was immune to the good-old-boy routine. She could make a potato salad that would melt in your mouth, she knew how to bring a man to his knees with a single flirtatious glance, and she sure as heck knew how to recognize a pile of you-know-what when she saw it.

No one could possibly be as suavely perfect as the image Duke showed to the world.

They had known each other forever. His father and her dad had been fraternity brothers at the University of Georgia. His mom and her mom had cochaired the United Way campaign a few years back. But Duke was four years older than Caitlyn, so it had been easy for her to keep her distance.

Her brothers practically worshiped the guy. It made her sick. He was nothing more than a conceited, arrogant, pompous—

"Will that work for you, Ms. Anderson?"

She felt her face heat as the mayor's polite question penetrated her mental fog. Caitlyn gave herself a figurative shake, embarrassed and caught off guard. "Yes, ma'am. No problem."

From across the table there was a quickly suppressed snort of laughter, but she ignored it. She hoped the mayor had not noticed her distraction.

After a couple of general announcements and some last-minute directions, the meeting broke up. Caitlyn's stomach churned. Somehow she had to figure out what the mayor had asked her to do without revealing her total zone-out at the time.

A large presence appeared behind her right shoulder, heralded by a whiff of really fabulous aftershave. Pheromones, she told herself stubbornly. That was all.

She swallowed hard.

Duke brushed a strand of hair from her cheek with a careless gesture. "Nice to see you again, Caitlyn."

She bit her lip, gathering up her things and stuffing them into a briefcase. The room was emptying, and she had to grab somebody quickly and beg for information.

But Duke was effectively blocking her exit. He propped a hip on the conference table, bringing their eyes level. Her knees trembled. She told herself it was because she had skipped breakfast.

She took a deep breath. "You'll have to excuse me," she said, her voice cool. "I have to run."

"The mayor wants us to start today."

She looked directly at him for the first time. The mischief in his long-lashed eyes was not at all reassuring. "I'm aware of the timetable," she said primly.

His large thigh, covered respectably in dark suit fabric, was practically touching her hip, so she inched away from the table.

He picked up her BlackBerry, and it was all she could do not to snatch it back. "I really am in a hurry," she said with as much politeness as she could muster.

He cocked his head. "Don't you think we should program some dates into this little electronic thingy of yours?" He poked at a button and the screen went blank.

"Give me that," she hissed. "And no. I'm all booked up in the date department. Thanks anyway."

Now the devilment spread across his face, and his straight white teeth flashed in a grin of blinding proportions. "Well, Miss

Caitlyn . . . you may be willing to offend the mayor, but I'm not. Turn this thing back on and let's get down to business."

Her mouth gaped. "What the hell are you talking about?"

He brushed her lips with a fingertip. "Tut-tut. Such language from a lady. I know your mama wouldn't approve."

Temper threatened to blow the top of her head sky-high. Her pale skin blotched with color when she got angry, and she knew from experience that it wasn't a good look on her. But god, he made her mad.

She pursed her lips. "My vocabulary is none of your concern. I'm out of here."

She grabbed up her things and scooted around him, but he was not so easily defeated. He caught hold of the end of the pretty braided raffia belt she wore and reeled her back in, tucking her firmly between his thighs. It would have been a highly inappropriate position had the room not been empty. Even so, she deemed it insulting.

She narrowed her eyes. "Swear to god, Duke Yancey. I'll knock the crap out of you with my purse if you don't let me go right this instant."

Duke studied the face of the woman who defied him nose-to-nose and sighed inwardly. He had as much chance of moving Stone Mountain as he did of calming the pretty termagant in his semiembrace.

It was odd really. Everyone else he knew thought Caitlyn Anderson was the perfect lady. Refined. Well educated. Poised and even tempered. Apparently he was the only one who brought out her inner shrew.

Which was a damned shame, because Caitlyn was the most beautiful woman he had ever met. Silky blond hair, gray eyes that could reflect a hint of blue on occasion. High patrician forehead, pert nose, eminently kissable lips. And a body that could stop traffic.

Despite the fact that she regarded him with all the enthusiasm of a cat faced with bathwater, it had just about killed him to read the announcement of her engagement six months ago.

Fortunately for his peace of mind, the official entanglement was short-lived, and in his fantasy world, there was still the possibility that he might one day convince his pretty Caitlyn to give him a chance.

Today was not that day.

He sighed, shoving his hands in his pockets to keep from doing something really stupid. "The mayor assigned us to work together," he said simply.

That stopped her in her tracks. She stared at him blankly for at least fifteen seconds, the color drained from her face, and she dropped into the nearest chair, leaning forward to beat her head gently against the table.

He allowed her self-flagellation for only a moment before he took her briefcase and purse from her lap and set them aside. In doing so, he brushed the side of her breast. It was an honest accident, but that one brief touch sent his pulse skittering.

He cleared his throat. "Did you really not hear her?"

Caitlyn lifted her head, her face rueful. "I was woolgathering. What can I say? I'm an idiot."

He chuckled. "Not hardly." He paused and studied her genuine mortification. What could have dragged her attention away from such an important meeting? He stared out the window for a moment, studying the Atlanta skyline as if he had never seen it before.

Then he turned back to his reluctant partner. "I hate to rush you, but I have a couple of late-afternoon meetings, so if we're going to get a jump on this thing, we'd better head out. I'll even buy you lunch."

Caitlyn stood up, her face resigned. "Fine. Whatever. Where are we going?"

"Briley Park."

Caitlyn had at least been listening when the mayor did a run-through of the various neighborhoods she was targeting. Briley Park was a small, forlorn area close to Downtown that had suffered a series of blows in recent years. The once-thriving Catholic church had closed its doors, and the diocese had looked in vain for a buyer. Unfortunately, fire code issues and asbestos problems complicated things. When no one came forward to purchase the building, the entire block was bulldozed.

Now developers were squabbling over who got to build what. The mayor was hoping to see low-income condos go up. In the adjacent blocks, a number of empty structures offered possibilities as well. Duke and Caitlyn were charged with studying the available space, assessing the area as a whole, and making recommendations.

Duke made good on his promise to feed her lunch. He pulled into the parking lot of Atlanta's famous Varsity restaurant and ushered her inside. It was plain and crowded and a bit seedy, but it was beloved by locals and tourists alike.

As they climbed the steps, he took her arm. "I hope you're not one of those women who lives on bean sprouts and tofu."

She sniffed in disdain. "Out of my way, Yancey." She stepped up to the counter and ordered a naked steak (translation—plain hamburger) and onion rings with a Coca-Cola. Duke went for two chili dogs, French fries, and an orange shake.

As she smothered her burger in ketchup and bit into a

greasy onion ring, she sighed inwardly. Any man who dined at the Varsity couldn't be all bad.

They didn't talk much over their meal, other than the most superficial chitchat. The place was loud, and she was content to eat and enjoy the food.

Back outside they climbed into Duke's large black truck. She sniffed again, but he didn't appear to notice. Once she was seated, he closed her door. She refused to be impressed by his manners. What a cliché; a Georgia boy and his truck. Was there a real man inside all that posturing?

She would much rather have been driving her own little Saturn, but somehow Duke had convinced her to leave her vehicle at the mayor's office. Something about gas prices and saving the environment.

She was darned glad she was wearing slacks. Duke's truck and a skirt wouldn't have mixed.

After a brief ten-minute drive, he pulled into the parking lot of a two-story strip mall. It was about four businesses wide, and only the bottom right unit appeared to be still occupied.

Duke, ever the gentleman, helped her out of the truck, and then they both stood and surveyed the dismal structure. As they walked forward, Caitlyn picked her way gingerly through beer cans and discarded condom wrappers.

Duke had keys. They entered the unit on the bottom left. Fortunately the electricity was still connected. Or maybe not so fortunately. The light merely pointed out glaring faults such as large holes in the Sheetrock, and scurrying roaches. The smell of rotten food hung in the air.

Her nose twitched. "Yikes. Is this the best we can expect?"

Duke wandered the edge of the room, checking outlets and whipping out a retractable ruler to do a quick measure of square footage. "It's mostly cosmetic," he murmured, clearly deep in thought as he made calculations.

When he was finished, they went upstairs. These units weren't quite so bad. But some appeared to have been abandoned at the last minute, the prior tenants leaving stacks of odd boxes and paper garbage and a smattering of dilapidated furniture.

Duke flipped open the lid of one box and grinned. Caitlyn stepped closer. "What is it?"

He held up a purple monstrosity, still in its original plastic packaging, thank God. He tilted it back and forth. "The Purple Pounder," he said with a straight face. "Batteries included."

She refused to blush. She wouldn't give him the satisfaction. She took it from his hand and pretended to study it. "Low-end. Not even lifelike. No wonder they couldn't sell them."

Duke chuckled as he watched Caitlyn lift her nose and exit the room with all the grace of a queen. She was some piece of work. And she made him hotter than a firecracker. He adjusted his pants with a rueful grin and followed her like a well-trained hound.

They met up downstairs. He glanced at the watch. "Sorry to cut things short, but I'm out of time. We can come back on Monday and scout out some more of the neighborhood."

She smiled, a genuine smile that hit him somewhere in the gut. "No problem. I've just bought a new apartment, and I'm closing on it this afternoon."

"An apartment or a condo?"

She followed him out to the truck. "Well, actually a whole building. Daddy's purchasing it and I'm going to buy it back from him bit by bit. I know that's not exactly standing on my own two feet, but it's such an amazing place, I couldn't bear to pass it up."

He shook his head. "I've seen you stand on your own two feet plenty, Caitlyn. And I happen to know that your parents are damned proud of you." He helped her into the vehicle. "Tell me about your new digs."

She pulled her seat belt across her lap, making her thin silk shirt mold to her breasts for a moment. And he noticed; how could he not? He glanced in the rearview mirror, his mouth dry, and backed out into traffic.

Her face was alight with pleasure as she gave him the details. "It's a two-story, late-1940s design, one previous owner. I believe it was a small residential hotel at one period in time, but it's been standing empty for several years. I'm going to convert the second floor bit by bit for my living space, and I hope to rent out the downstairs to a lawyer or some other professional person."

He sneaked a sideways glance. Her profile made him ache. "So when do you move?"

She practically bounced in her seat. "Starting tomorrow. I'll do it a little at a time, no rush. I've been living in my grandma's garage apartment, so I don't have to be out by any certain date."

He slammed on his brakes and cursed when an idiot on a side street cut in front of him. It was an instinctive movement on his part to fling his right arm in front of Catilyn and keep her from flying forward. The near miss shook them both, and silence reigned in the cab of the truck for several seconds.

He took a deep breath. "You okay?"

She nodded. "Yes. Thank you. You're a very good driver."

Her lips were puckered as if she'd eaten a sour pickle, and it amused him to realize that she was honest with her praise, even for a man she didn't like.

"So . . . back to the moving," he said lightly. "Take it from me, honey—you'll drive yourself nuts doing it that way. Why don't you let me line up a couple of my buddies? We can all bring trucks and have you relocated in an afternoon. We'll even set up your bed and computer and television and anything else. We've done this drill dozens of times, and I promise, we're careful. Our only fee is beer and pizza when it's done."

A slight frown creased the skin between her eyebrows. "I don't want to take advantage of your kindness," she said, her stilted sentence straight out of Miss Manners. "I know you're a busy man. Don't you have to be at some gym on Saturdays?" She said the word "gym" as if it were a loathsome and disgusting place.

He grinned. "I'm my own boss. I think they can live without me."

She hedged. "I'm not entirely packed."

"Just point us in the right direction. We can load and tape with the best of them."

Still she hesitated.

"What's wrong?" he said, finally getting irritated. "It's a perfectly reasonable offer, Caitlyn. Why don't you get off your prissy high horse and accept some help, for god's sake."

Storm clouds gathered on her face. "Well, if you want to know the truth," she said, "I don't want to be beholden to you."

"Beholden?"

"You know what the word means," she snapped.

He pulled into a parking space at their destination and turned in his seat to stare at her with narrowed eyes. "What you mean is, you think I'll expect something in return."

She unfastened her seat belt, but he had the child lock on, so he wasn't too worried about her escaping. She wet her soft lips and damn near distracted him from the conversation. But not quite. She shrugged. "You have a reputation."

"For what?" he demanded, not willing to let her off so easily.

"For philandering."

He hit his forehead with the heel of his hand. "Oh, my god. What happened to you, crazy lady? Did you get amnesia and wake up thinking it's the nineteenth century? I date. A lot. So what? I'm single. It's a free country. And I can assure you that accepting my help with a few boxes and sticks of furniture is not going to endanger your precious virtue." By the end of that speech, he was practically yelling.

Not that she appeared in any way cowed by his bluster. She was looking out the window at a school group that had just toured the mayor's office. Her hands were folded in her lap. "Well, all right then . . ."

Her voice was subdued, but he didn't trust her sudden capitulation. The little witch was turning him inside out. He unbuttoned an extra button on his dress shirt, inwardly cursing the earlier meeting that had required him to don a suit and tie.

He glanced at his watch and sighed. He was going to be late. "What time would you like us to be there?"

Her teeth were nibbling on her bottom lip, a job he'd gladly have offered to do if she'd allowed it. "Nine o'clock?"

He smiled at her, his quick temper fading as rapidly as it had flared. "Put on the coffee and make it strong."

She nodded, her eyes big in her perfectly oval face.

He ran his finger from her elbow down her arm with a featherlight touch. "We're going to be working together on this city project for several weeks. Don't you think you should call me Duke?"

She looked uneasy. "Well, to tell you the truth . . ."

He groaned. "Now what?"

She stared at him in a long, pregnant pause. "It seems like a silly and pretentious name for a man your age. Aren't you almost forty?"

He nearly choked. "You know damn well how old I am, you little wiseass. I'm thirty-three."

She ignored his remark and plowed full steam ahead. "And besides, I never thought John Wayne was all that sexy *or* attractive."

He rubbed his finger over the inside of her wrist, feeling her rapid pulse. "So you're saying the name doesn't fit because I'm *both* of those things?"

She gawked at him, clearly shocked that her words could have been construed in that way. "That's not what I meant at all," she stammered, her face turning red.

He grinned, enjoying himself enormously. "I suppose you could use my first name. Duke is my middle name."

She jerked her arm away from his grasp. "Okay, what is it?"

"Lover."

She shook her head. "You're such a liar. There's no such name."

"I promise you there is. There are a number of my fellow Lovers in the old US of A. It was my maternal great-great-grandmother's maiden name. English, I believe. Or maybe Irish."

She jerked on the door handle, unable to budge it. "I can't call you that and you know it."

"What?"

"Lover."

He leaned his head back and smiled blissfully. "I like how you say it."

More jerking on the door handle. "Let me out."

"Not until you decide what to call me. And in all fairness, you can't use Duke. It would be hypocritical after your little speech."

Her chest was rising and falling with mesmerizing effect on his libido. "You're insane."

"Say it," he coaxed. He had approximately thirty seconds before he absolutely had to leave.

The standoff was erotic. At least in his mind. Caitlyn looked like she might faint. Or smack him.

Without warning, she curled a hand around his neck, took his lips in a sizzling kiss, and before he could do more than open and close his mouth like a landed fish, she whispered in his ear, "Lover. Now open the damn door."

Two

Caitlyn wondered if twenty-nine was too young to become senile. Had she lost her mind? Kissing Duke Yancey? Clearly she had been under too much stress lately. She had snapped, that was all. It had nothing to do with sexual attraction or sudden lust or even her dead-in-the-water sex life.

She had momentarily gone off the deep end. People made mistakes every day. She was entitled to her own quota. And perhaps her sudden penchant for watery metaphors was because, in Duke Yancey's presence, she felt as if she were drowning. She tried to keep her feet on solid ground, but something about his deep, gravelly voice and his sexy smile made her knees weak and her breathing fractured.

He made her sweat. And she hated sweating. At least on some cardio machine or during an aerobics class. She much preferred long walks in her grandma's neighborhood enjoying the changing scenery and feeling the sun on her face. Or skiing on the lake, or riding the horse she kept stabled at her cousin's farm in the country.

It galled her to admit it, but spending time with Duke Yancey was as exhilarating as any of those activities. When they were together, her heart pumped faster, her blood tingled as though it were full of little champagne bubbles, and she felt alive . . . frustrated maybe . . . but alive.

The closing on her building went without a hitch. Her dad offered to take her out for dinner, but she declined. Instead, she got a sandwich and a drink from Subway and took it to her new home-sweet-home.

It felt good to slide the unfamiliar key into the lock and wander around the quiet, empty space. When she headed upstairs, she really got excited as she imagined what it might look like when the remodeling was finished. There was a basic bathroom and a small antiquated kitchen that would serve her needs in the meantime.

She sat down on the floor near a window and propped her back against the wall. She could see trees and other buildings, some residential, some commercial. It was the kind of neighborhood she loved, and it was much closer to her work than where she had been living.

Staying rent-free in her grandma's garage apartment had been a godsend for the last few years. It had enabled her to put all her available cash into Designing Women. The name of her company was ambitious. Right now it was only one woman—her—and a college intern who helped out twenty hours a week. But things were beginning to happen, and the mayor's invitation couldn't have come at a more perfect time.

She finished her sandwich and sipped her drink, wondering how she would face Duke in the morning. He hadn't asked for directions, of course. He knew her grandmother, and her grandma thought the world of Duke. Which gave Caitlyn something to chew on, because her grandma was generally a shrewd judge of character.

Caitlyn planned to give her beloved Gran a weekend package at a luxurious spa as a thank-you for her support in recent years, both financial and emotional.

The light was beginning to fade, and she still had some chores to do before morning. She took her trash into the kitchen and noticed that one of the drawers below the counter was sticking out an inch or so. Someone could catch a hip on that and get a nasty bruise. Probably the many layers of paint over the years had caused it to stick.

She tried to shove it closed to no avail. Finally she jerked the whole thing out, set the drawer on the counter, and bent to peer into the cabinet. Something was back there. Hoping it was nothing sinister, she stuck her arm in, fished around, and extracted a small and definitely mangled leather book. Part of one corner had been ripped off, and the spine and cover were too faded to read.

She turned to the title page. *Miss Matilda's Guide to Love and Romance for the Proper Young Lady,* copyright 1949. She laughed out loud, the sound echoing in the empty rooms. What fun. The book had been published only ten years after the Atlanta premiere of *Gone with the Wind*. No telling what kind of advice Miss Matilda might have offered to all those Scarlett O'Hara wannabes.

She tucked it in her pocket to read later. Enough lollygagging. Tomorrow was moving day.

Duke stopped by the gym nearest his house and ran through an abbreviated version of his usual workout. He'd be getting plenty of exercise tomorrow, but he needed something to take the edge off of his sexual hunger.

Ever since the moment Caitlyn had pressed her lips to his in the cab of his truck, he'd been cursed off and on with a most inconvenient boner. And try as he might, he couldn't help reliving that surprising kiss over and over.

He was embarrassed to admit it, even to himself, but he'd been so damned shocked, he hadn't even had a chance to respond before it ended. And with the look on Caitlyn's face and the sure knowledge that he was perilously close to being late for a very important meeting, he had released the child lock instantly and watched her walk away from him without a backward glance.

He'd contacted four of his best buds already, and all but one were planning on meeting him at Caitlyn's tomorrow morning. Duke was damned glad to be seeing her again so soon, but he had a feeling Caitlyn would use his friends as a human shield. Knowing his prickly new partner, she would try to pretend the kiss had never happened.

She could try, but she would fail. Duke wasn't about to let the tiny piece of ground he'd claimed be lost. His Caitlyn was about to see the Duke in action.

Caitlyn sat propped up in bed, feeling nostalgic and a bit sad. This was her last night in the cozy place that had served her so well. She'd already walked over and said good night to Gran. And it wasn't like she was moving to the other side of the country. She would be only six or seven miles away. Still . . . it was a significant change in her life. Moving on. Growing older.

She picked up the battered little book she'd rescued from the drawer. As she flipped through the brittle pages, some of the suggestions made her smile . . . some raised an eyebrow.

Old Miss Matilda wasn't squeamish about digging into the tough stuff.

She stopped reading when she hit suggestion number thirty-nine:

> All's fair in love and war. We women are strong and confident, but allowing the man to be the boss is important. Let your man call the shots. Defer to him as much as possible. Ask him to balance your checkbook. Seek his help in purchasing a car or an appliance. Allow him to run your life, in theory only, of course. The pretense will feed his sense of masculine superiority and will make him feel like a chest-thumping Tarzan, complete with deliciously hard appendage and virile dominance.

She giggled. She couldn't help it. It was so weird to think of some old lady giving advice about how to get a man hard. And then she sobered. Was what she felt toward Duke Yancey war? Or love? The first, surely. She couldn't stand the guy.

So why did you plant one on his delicious, gorgeous, sensual lips? Her snarky little inner voice refused to be silent.

Well, hell. She winced guiltily. Duke was right. Her mother hated to hear profanity from any female, much less her only daughter. But strong language seemed appropriate at the moment. She was so screwed.

What if all the righteous indignation she'd indulged in regarding the irritating, macho, overly confident Duke Yancey was merely a disguise for something else far more alarming? What if she had feelings for the big lug?

Her stomach flip-flopped once—hard—and then dropped to her knees. *Oh, lord.* She faced the fear head-on, and bowed her head in defeat. *Freakin' unbelievable*. She had the hots for Duke Yancey.

Like a hundred other women in the Peach State. She was simply one claim ticket in a whole pile of them.

She frowned. Not this girl. Not in a million years. She had too much self-respect to be one more peach on the tree. Her uncooperative libido might be yearning after the man, but her brain was a lot smarter.

Sexual attraction burned brightly, but in time always faded. When she got really serious about a guy, it would be someone who was interested in home and hearth. Duke probably couldn't even spell the words.

He might be temptation in the flesh, but she could be strong. So what if her big soft bed was lonely at night? She wasn't up for a wild fling, and Duke wouldn't be interested in anything else.

So . . . stupid, impulsive kisses were definitely out. She would be cool and elusive. Pleasant but firm. This was neither love nor war. And Miss Matilda could take her seductive advice and shove it where the sun didn't shine. Caitlyn Anderson could handle Duke Yancey.

Duke intentionally arrived twenty minutes early on Saturday morning. *Catch your opponent off guard*. It was solid advice he'd used in any number of sporting and business situations, and he had a hunch it might help him with the thorny, touchy Caitlyn.

She opened the door wearing a thin terry robe that stopped several inches above the knee and with her hair still damp. Round one to Caitlyn.

He managed to find his voice, but it came out sounding like sandpaper. "Mornin'," he muttered, trying not to notice that her nipples poked through the fabric. Was she wearing panties?

He was thankful that she seemed equally flustered. Her expression was guarded. "There's coffee over there. Help yourself." And then she disappeared. The scent of her shower gel lingered in the air. For about two seconds he contemplated following her. Grabbing her. Ripping off that flimsy excuse for a robe and covering all that damp, creamy, fabulous skin with kisses.

It was a little late for a morning erection, but apparently his body didn't have a watch. He ground his teeth together as his cock swelled and hardened. The urgent ache almost made him forget the one in his head. He hadn't slept worth a damn last night.

He prowled her tiny apartment, noticing that despite her equivocation yesterday afternoon, she really was in good shape. There wasn't much left to pack.

When she reappeared moments later, she was wearing a white T-shirt with pink lettering that said, *Designers do it in every room,* and a pair of hot-pink knit shorts that hugged her ass and revealed a mouthwatering length of toned, tanned legs.

He frowned. "I'm not sure that T-shirt is appropriate to wear in front of the guys."

Caitlyn rolled her eyes. "It's a joke. They're grown men. I'm sure they can handle it."

He dropped his mug of coffee on the table with a thud. "This isn't doing it for me."

She slipped small gold hoops in her ears and checked them in a small mirror on the wall. "Not the right brand?"

He shook his head. "Not strong enough."

Before she could respond, he went to her and slid his fingers into her hair, cupping her neck in his palms. The cool, almost but not quite dry strands felt like silk against his skin.

He gave her every opportunity to say no. And then he

kissed her. It was like getting kicked in the chest by a mule. His heart took the hit even as the rest of his overheated body reveled in the feel of her in his arms.

It took everything he had to keep his hands in their chaste position when all he wanted to do was stroke every inch of her, from her lush, curvy breasts to her narrow waist and flared hips.

He slid his tongue inside her mouth, almost groaning aloud when he felt her respond. Even as her tongue licked delicately at his, her small, cool hands settled at his waist, gripping handfuls of his cotton polo shirt. He backed her against a table, letting her feel the press of his erection. He was burning up from the inside out.

He had fully intended a quick, teasing kiss. Nothing more. But he was in way over his head, and his out-of-control mouth ravaged hers, taking and taking and drinking in her sweetness . . . her tart, spicy flavor.

He heard an odd sound and realized that he was gulping in great lungfuls of air, trying to breathe amidst the incredible pleasure.

A hammering at the door ended the erotic interlude with all the courtesy of a faceful of cold water. He jerked back, stunned, feeling like a horny adolescent. He ran his hands through his hair. *Shit. That was kick-ass stupid.*

Caitlyn fled to the bedroom, leaving Duke to open the door and greet his buddies. By the time Caitlyn joined them a couple of minutes later, she had pulled her smooth fall of hair into a high ponytail and tied it with a pink bandanna. The boys had their tongues dragging the floor, and she didn't even seem to notice.

She introduced herself to each of them, smiling and laughing and snaring them from the get-go. The whole lot of them would have a crush on her by day's end, Duke predicted sourly.

And so it began. . . .

Caitlyn was amazed by how quickly the guys worked. It took four loads, but by two p.m. everything was at her new place. The men had consumed a staggering amount of pizza and a couple of beers each, and then headed for home, leaving her and Duke to collapse into chairs in her new living room. If anyone could call it that.

Mentally she bumped up the timetable for getting started on her renovations. She was not a fan of living in chaos.

Duke wasn't seated for more than a minute. He was already up, prowling through stacks and boxes, looking for another job.

He held up a picture she wanted hung beside the phone table. "Do you have any tools?"

She ran a hand over her face, yawning. "In my purse. Out in the hall."

When he returned, he had the hammer and screwdriver and he was also holding an invitation she had stuffed in the top of her pocketbook.

He scanned it quickly. "Are you going to the High Museum benefit tonight?"

She waved an arm. "With all this to do? I don't think so. I'll send a check."

He waved the rectangle of heavy cream-colored card stock in front of her face. "The mayor will be there. She'll be impressed with your commitment to community causes."

She groaned and closed her eyes, dropping her head to rest on the chair back. She knew he was right. "Oh, heck. Don't play the guilt card, please."

He bumped her knees. "I'll take you. And I won't even bring the truck."

She opened one eyelid. "No truck?"

He grinned. "How about a Mercedes convertible?"

Now he had her attention. "You wouldn't lead a girl astray, would you?"

"Not about cars."

Whew. Nothing like a little sexual innuendo to give a woman hot flashes. She manufactured a bored glance. "I guess I could go . . . for a little while. But you have to wear a tux."

His eyes flashed hot and full of mischief. "I guess I could wear a tux . . . for a little while."

The statement hung there between them. Ambiguous. Loaded with possible interpretations. She had a sudden vision of Duke Yancey slipping off a tux jacket and everything else. Her thighs clenched. Her nipples tightened.

Sweet holy heck. What had she just agreed to?

Duke showed up on Caitlyn's doorstep at seven o'clock. They had agreed to skip dinner, because the reception and dance included heavy hors d'oeuvres.

He rang the buzzer and waited impatiently for her to answer. Her head appeared from an upstairs window as she called down to him, "I unlocked the door two minutes ago. Come on up. I'm almost ready."

He let himself in and wandered upstairs. The fragrance of perfume wafted faintly down the hall. Beguiling. Seductive. He ran a finger beneath his collar and went to the kitchen for a glass of water.

He was sprawled in her comfy armchair in the cluttered living room when she came through the doorway and cut him off at the knees. *Jesus.* He staggered to his feet. "Where in the hell did you get that dress?"

She twirled a slow pirouette. "A new little designer boutique at Phipps Plaza. Do you like it?"

"Like" didn't begin to describe it. The full-length frock was smoke gray and was slit from the hip to the floor, exposing tantalizing flashes of a single shapely leg.

But the skirt was practically tame compared to the top. It was one of those engineering marvels modeled on the red carpet at the Academy Awards. Sleeveless. Backless. Cut deeply enough in front to show off more than a hint of cleavage. He shoved his hands in his pockets, his fists clenched.

"Everybody in town will like it," he muttered. "Should I be concerned about sudden gusts of wind?" he asked, only half kidding.

Her smile was mysterious. "Have no fear. I won't embarrass you."

He cocked his head, studying the dazzling display. Her hair was up in some sort or tousled little knot on her head, but it simply gave him ideas for undoing it later. "Are you wearing anything at all underneath that?" He knew he croaked out the words, but he had to find out.

"Not much," she admitted softly.

Her smile made him weak. Apparently they were at war, and he hadn't even had time to pick up a weapon. The first skirmish went to the lovely lady in gray. Whether or not he would be able to recoup his losses was a question that would have to wait.

Caitlyn was having a wonderful time. Why had she ever worried about Duke Yancey? He was the perfect gentleman. They were dancing. Again. Perhaps for the fifth or sixth time. And he was wonderful. She didn't know many men who even knew *how* to dance, much less enjoyed it.

Duke could twirl and dip with the best of them. At the moment they were swaying to a slow, dreamy melody. His strong arm was at her back and hers was curved around his neck. In four inch heels it was comfortable, natural. Their other hands were clasped, fingers twined, and Duke had them tucked close to his chest.

She rested her head on his shoulder. He smelled delicious. She could get drunk on his scent alone, all woodsy and crisp and masculine. In his arms she felt fragile and cosseted, and she decided she liked it.

As the evening passed, they chatted with friends and acquaintances, including the mayor and her distinguished husband. They laughed and teased and joked over shrimp and Brie and skewers of veggies. Duke fed her cheesecake from his fork. Their eyes met and held as her lips closed over the sweet, chilled dessert.

She dabbed her mouth with a napkin and sat back. "I'm glad you persuaded me to come," she said simply. "I needed the break. Much more fun than unpacking boxes."

His eyes were dark tonight, the line of his mouth unusually serious. "I can help you tomorrow."

For a moment Miss Matilda's words echoed in Caitlyn's head. But she didn't want a man running her life. "You've done enough," she said gently. "Really."

His sternness was sending shivers down her spine. She was accustomed to a laughing, teasing Duke. This silent, intense male was slightly intimidating.

He groused good-naturedly when one of the men Caitlyn had met just that morning demanded a dance. She glanced at

Duke from time to time as she and her partner moved across the dance floor. His gaze, fixed on her, never faltered, his jaw firm, his posture not quite relaxed.

At ten thirty she called it quits. "I know it's early, but I'm exhausted. And you must be sore. Or maybe not. I forget you're a fitness guru."

He pressed a hand to her lower back as they threaded their way through the crowd and slipped outside. The spring evening was balmy and pleasant. He seated her in the car, carefully tucked in her skirt and closed her door, and took his place behind the wheel.

He slanted her a glance. "Top up or down?"

"Down, by all means," she said. There would never be a more perfect night for such an activity.

On the interstate Duke pushed it up to eighty. Caitlyn shrieked and laughed when the wind snatched at her carefully styled do and sent pins flying. She grasped at her wildly billowing hair and tried to capture it in her fist.

Duke drove with one hand on the wheel and the other arm resting on the door. He was smiling, and when he looked at her from time to time, his expression was a dizzying mix of amusement, lust, and something else she couldn't pin a name to.

When they parked in front of her building, he put the top up and locked the car. Apparently he was coming in.

She tossed her little purse on the kitchen counter and put some decaf on to brew. Grabbing a brush from the bathroom, she returned to the living room and tried to restore her hair to some kind of order. Duke took the brush from her without a word and began working the tangles free.

The feel of his long, strong fingers on her head and ears and neck made her long to lean back against him. But she kept her spine straight. She was not so easily seduced.

When her hair was smooth, he pressed a kiss to her crown. "Let's have that coffee," he said gruffly.

She poured them each a cup and they carried it into the living room. Her small sofa was covered with boxes. Duke dispensed with them in short order. He tugged her down beside him. She used her cup as a shield, savoring the ounces of fragrant brew as slowly as possible.

But eventually the cup was empty.

He took it from her hand and set it on the floor beside his.

He played absently with a lock of her hair. "I want you, Caitlyn." He said it simply, didn't dress it up with extra words.

She should have been insulted, perhaps. But those four simple words set her on fire. She wanted him also. But could she live with the consequences?

It was difficult to make logical decisions when all her brain cells were fried. He was looking at her as if she held the key to every one of his fantasies. As she watched, he loosened his bow tie and tossed it aside. He had kicked off his shoes earlier, and his sock-clad feet were propped on a box.

She swallowed, feeling hot and edgy. So what if Duke Yancey was not a long-term investment? She hadn't been with a man since she broke off her engagement. And she had needs. Any man would do, she told herself with blatant dishonesty. But Duke was here . . . and available. What harm could there be in enjoying him? Just once. They had to work together, sure. But not for long. And Duke was a man of the world. Surely with all his experience, he knew how to defuse awkward situations.

She wasn't in any danger. She had a good head on her shoulders and she knew the score. Duke enjoyed women. And Caitlyn herself was on the dessert menu for tonight. He wouldn't be taking advantage of her. If anything, just the opposite.

She would be using him for sexual release, because he was

confident, sexy, and good in bed, if the rumors were true. She might be strongly attracted to him, but it was ridiculous to think she might actually be in danger of losing her heart to him.

She was too smart for that. When it came to the future, she wanted a man who would put her first. A man who could commit to one woman. But in the meantime, she had every right to indulge in casual sex.

Again, Miss Matilda's words rang in her ears, but she pushed them aside. She wasn't interested in snagging this man for the long term. And he wasn't bossing her around or coercing her. She *wanted* to have sex with Duke Yancey—something a single, respectable woman from 1949 would never have admitted or dared to do, in all probability.

Duke sat quietly, his eyes focused intently on her face. She wondered if he could read her mind. With his wealth of experience, possibly so. The top three buttons of his shirt were undone, and she could see a sprinkling of hair on his chest. He was big and rumpled and dangerous to her equilibrium.

She smoothed the skirt of her dress and summoned her best "come and get me" smile. "What did you have in mind?"

Three

Duke blinked once. He'd been ninety-five percent sure she was going to boot him out of her apartment. Even now her body language wasn't quite in sync with her words. She looked nervous, and he hated it. He didn't want her to be afraid of him. Of them.

He slid an arm behind her back and scooted closer on the small sofa. He captured the hand that was making tiny wrinkled pleats in her skirt and brought it up to his mouth. He teased the tip of her forefinger with his tongue, then bit down on it gently. "I have lots of ideas, sweetheart. Give me a minute to triage them."

That won him a smile, a genuine one this time. One that lit up her eyes.

He abandoned her hand and tipped up her chin. "A kiss first," he murmured.

Her head fell back, resting against his arm, and her eyes fluttered shut.

He tapped her nose gently. "No hiding, Caitlyn. Look at me."

Long lashes darkened with mascara lifted. Her eyes were the color of rain on a cloudy afternoon. In her gaze he saw uncertainty. It made him ache that she wasn't sure of him. He looked his fill, seeing the vulnerable woman behind the sharp wit and razor-edged tongue.

Her throat was bare, but from her small, perfect earlobes dangled tiny crystal earrings that sparkled and caught the light. He played with them absently, enjoying the way they moved against her slender neck.

Finally he bent his head and captured her lips. It was like sinking into a warm, sweet dream. His hands were shaking, and it was all he could do not to crush her to him. An odd sort of fear crouched on his back, making him dread what might come after.

He would please her in bed. He knew that. But what if he couldn't be the man she wanted?

Her slender arms circled his neck, and he half lifted her into his lap. She tasted like sin and redemption, and the lure of the unknown drew him deeper. Her rounded ass pressed against his crotch and made him harder and hungrier. He felt the outline of narrow panties, but he dared not explore further. Not yet.

He swept a hand over the bodice of her dress, testing the thinness of the fabric. It revealed every curve and slope to his questing hand. He mapped them all, feeling the slight roughness of his fingers catch on the fragile silk.

Caitlyn murmured and arched her back, urging him on with silent permission. His fingers slipped beneath the soft fabric and found skin impossibly softer. His thumb stroked a tight nipple. They each groaned.

He cupped her breast fully, squeezing and shaping it with reverence. Suddenly impatient, he found the tiny fastener at her nape and released the top, baring her to the waist. Her skin was alabaster with blush pink highlights. Where his fingers trespassed. Where her arousal bloomed in her hot throat.

He laid her back as best he could, mentally cursing the cramped conditions. But he was afraid to choose an alternative. Afraid to break the mood.

He bent and suckled one raspberry pink nipple. The taste made him dizzy. Her eyes were dark and huge, her lips parted with her ragged breathing.

When tasting wasn't enough, he stood and scooped her into his arms. He would have to take his chances. The sofa would never do for what he had in mind. He didn't have to ask for directions to the bedroom. He had assembled her sleigh bed himself hours earlier, and even then he had fantasized about sharing it with her.

Down the hall and around the corner—an easy walk any time but now. Piles of *stuff* hindered his progress. In her bedroom, he stubbed his toe on a box and cursed as Caitlyn giggled.

He pinched her bottom. "Brat."

He pulled back the covers and deposited her gently on the bed. "Don't move a muscle," he said roughly. "I want to see you."

She lay as he had commanded, her face turned to one side, her chin on her hand. Her lush seminudity taunted him and made his hands clumsy.

He stripped off his shirt, scattering the remaining studs without remorse. Socks, pants. When he was down to his silk boxers, Caitlyn sat up, seemingly unself-conscious about her bare breasts. She was looking at him intently, and every blink of her long, beautiful lashes sent his hunger one notch higher.

She held out a hand. "Come here."

Refusal was never an option. He stepped close to the bed, looking down at her. She reached out a hand and cupped his balls through the silk. He sucked in a raw breath and clenched his fists at his sides.

Her fingers stroked his testicles, testing their weight, roving up and over and behind until he thought he would lose it. He was staring past her at a bare wall. If he looked at her, he might embarrass himself.

Then she brought her second hand into play and grasped his cock. His mind went blank for about three seconds, and then heat gripped his spine in a vise and settled in his scrotum and his cock. He clenched his jaw, feeling her fingers slide up and down his rock-hard shaft.

The damp spot on the front of his boxers grew. She tested it with a fingertip, licked it, pushed the fabric round and round the head of his aching erection. Then with deliberate slowness, she peeled his boxers down to his knees and waited for him to step out of them.

Seconds later, her warm, wet mouth closed over the head of his penis.

Duke enjoyed sex. A lot. Always had. But what he was experiencing at the moment skated perilously close to the line between pleasure and pain. He was trembling from head to toe. His breathing was labored. He felt himself throb between her lips and felt the gentle rake of her teeth on his prick. His eyes were squeezed shut.

And in the darkness, every sensation was magnified a hundredfold. His hands slid into her hair, his fingers clenching her skull. His hips surged forward. *God in heaven.* He couldn't bear it.

And then she released him and sat back on her haunches.

He blinked in shock, taking in the sight of her once again. She was covered in gray silk from the waist down, and she was bare-ass naked above that.

He took a step backward, searching fruitlessly for control. "Is that dress expensive?" he asked. His voice was almost unrecognizable.

She nodded.

He exhaled. "Then you'd better be the one to take it off."

She stood on the mattress and shimmied out of it, losing her balance at the last second. He grabbed for her arm and steadied her. Then he picked up the dress and laid it carefully on the closest clean surface he could find, which happened to be a stack of linens.

He turned back to face her. Only a minuscule strip of black lace protected her secrets. Such a vision had turned many a mythological man to stone. Duke had the stone part down pat, in his dick. And he was standing before her like a kid in a candy store, trying to decide where to start first. He held out a hand. "My turn."

She stepped to the edge of the mattress. His mouth was on a level with her pretty navel, so he stopped there to explore. Apparently she was ticklish. No problem. He had plenty of territory left to navigate. He ripped the pretty underwear without a qualm and tossed it aside.

Then he gave her a little nudge and she tumbled to the mattress. Before she could recover, he had buried his face between her legs and was gorging himself on the taste and smell of warm, aroused woman. His woman. The little caveman blip on his radar didn't faze him.

He was too busy hooking her thighs over his shoulders and testing her heat and wetness with his tongue. She was ready. *Damn.* He'd wanted to draw this out. To show her that he could be the lover she deserved. But his own raging hunger and her body's unmistakable signals did him in.

With two last passes of his tongue, he shot her to a quick, sharp orgasm, and before she could come down he repositioned their bodies. "Condoms?" He choked out the question at the last minute.

She shook her head, her voice nothing but a thread. "Don't need them." She trusted his good sense, and she was on the pill.

"Thank God." With a groan and a mighty thrust, he entered her.

For several heartbeats he froze. He felt lost suddenly, standing on unfamiliar ground. Something about this was different. He felt a yawning chasm at his feet and didn't understand what was happening to him.

He was in Caitlyn's bed between Caitlyn's legs. It was what he wanted. But the other stuff, the tight throat, the pressure in his chest, the swamping wave of tenderness . . . What the hell was that?

He shook off the odd and unsettling feelings and moved inside her. Her eyes were closed, and this time he didn't challenge her. It was better if he couldn't look into them. He was afraid of what she might see in his.

He ran a hand over her flat belly, tugged gently at her nipples. She was panting, her chest rising and falling with her rapid breaths.

And then suddenly he was no longer able to assess his partner's state of mind or body. Sharp, aching pleasure snaked through him, seized his brain, and exploded in shards of white-hot light behind his eyelids as he emptied himself in a draining orgasm that left him spent and gasping and raw with doubts.

*   *   *

Caitlyn woke up as the pearly light of dawn peeked through the uncovered window. The large weight holding her down was Duke's arm. He was sleeping on his stomach with his face turned away from her. She allowed the brief, sharp burst of joy one moment to swell and fill her heart before she shut it down.

She lay perfectly still, wondering how she would survive the next couple of hours. She hadn't a clue what she would say to him. In fact, she hadn't expected him to stay. But after they made love he had fallen into a deep, exhausted sleep, and she hadn't had the courage or the inclination to wake him up and demand he leave.

She slipped from beneath his arm and went down the hall to the bathroom. At the moment she was glad it wasn't adjacent to the bedroom. After a quick shower, she rummaged in a box for some clean clothes. Often she joined her parents for church and brunch on Sundays, but today she wanted to get at least a room or two unpacked.

She put coffee on to brew and opened a small box of last-minute items she had scooped up on the way to the truck yesterday. Her birth control pills, checkbook, a jewelry box. An address book. And there amongst all of that was Miss Matilda's guide.

She opened it at random and flipped toward the back. She winced when she saw the chapter near the end entitled simply, "Disappointments." *Uh-oh.* The old gal could be blunt when necessary.

> You cannot make a man love you. Either he will or he won't. And never fall into the trap of believing you can change a man. Many a male will adapt his behavior in the short term. He can be very accommodating dur-

ing the courtship phase. But in the end, his true colors will show. If you believe he loves you, congratulations. But if it is clear that his feelings are less involved than yours, don't torment yourself by dragging things out. You will lose your self-respect and break your heart on the reef of his indifference.

You must also be wary of the man who seeks to manipulate you with truly great sex. The male of the species knows that we are vulnerable in those situations . . . and savvy men are also aware that we women tend to equate sexual compatibility with an intimate connection. Our emotional guard is down when we are in the aftermath of strong physical pleasure. We make assumptions that are not always true. Beware of the incredible orgasm. If it is all a man has to offer you, it will never be enough.

There is a man out there for you, my dears. But you must never settle for less than you deserve. Be strong. And don't give up on love.

She closed the book and tucked it away. She didn't want anyone to stumble upon it and make fun of her, especially Duke. Her stomach felt queasy, and she almost regretted what had happened last night.

But how could she regret something so beautiful? As a lover, Duke was beyond anything she had ever experienced. In his arms she had felt cherished, adored. He was passionate and eager and talented. He made her body sing with pleasure. And when he held her close afterward, gently stroking her hair, her eyes had stung with tears.

Because she knew the truth now, and it was painful and hard to swallow. She was in love with Duke Yancey. The man who went through pretty southern blossoms like Sherman on his famed march.

Duke liked variety. And he loved sex. But as charming and sexy as he was, she couldn't see him ever settling down with one woman. At least, not anytime in the near future. He had plenty of wild oats left to sow.

So it was up to her to be strong.

When he entered the kitchen moments later, she was able to greet him with a natural smile. "Hey, there, sleepyhead. I made coffee. I hope you're not a breakfast person, because the cupboard is bare."

He pulled her close for a quick kiss and then yawned. "Coffee's fine."

While he poured a cup, she studied him. He had pulled on his boxers, thank heavens, but the rest of his lean, bronzed body was mouthwateringly bare. He was all smooth, fit muscle, broad through the shoulders and narrow through the hips. Big hands and feet. Big everything, as she now well knew. The quintessential male animal.

He leaned against the counter, his eyes heavy-lidded and his hair sleep-tousled. Like one of those sexy French ads for aftershave or jeans or fast cars.

When he drained the cup and set it aside, he scraped his hands through his hair and yawned again. "Let me go home and change, and I'll be back to help you get started on all this." And then he smiled, turning her knees to jelly. "Unless, honey, you have a hankering to pick up where we left off last night. And then I'm your man."

She felt herself blush and couldn't help it. But she kept her smile steady. "Don't tempt me." She couldn't hold that wicked gaze, so she turned to the sink and began rinsing out their cups. "I played hooky to go to the party. I really have to get busy today."

He sighed with mock disappointment. "Okay, slave driver."

She touched him on the arm, realizing that she was acting in direct opposition to Miss Matilda's advice. "Please don't take this the wrong way, but I would like to be here on my own today. This is a new start for me. I want to get organized and think about things and get used to my new place."

He frowned. "Without me."

She smiled placatingly. "Without anybody."

The disgruntled expression on his face finally lifted and he shrugged, his body language visibly relaxing. "Whatever you say, honey. You're the boss."

Every internal red flag she possessed waved at once. Had Duke somehow read a portion of Miss Matilda's book? Surely not. It was safely hidden away. Her eyes narrowed. "What do you mean by that?"

He looked confused. "Nothing. It was just a statement. You *are* the boss in your own home . . . right?"

She wasn't buying it. First the spectacular orgasms and now this? He was trying to play her . . . to make her think he was sensitive and able to let a woman make decisions without his input. *Not bloody likely.*

Duke Yancey was a take-charge kind of guy. He'd boss her around till the cows came home if she let him walk all over her. Was there a masculine version of Miss Matilda's tome floating around out there somewhere . . . a naughty guide that advised guys how to get women in the sack? Or was his behavior sheer coincidence?

Well, two could play at this game. He didn't know who he was dealing with. Bravely, she went up on tiptoe and kissed him, leaning into him as though she needed his support. "Thanks for understanding."

Duke dressed and left, his brain working overtime to figure out what had happened between last night and this morning. The sex had been earth-moving. And something like that couldn't have been one-sided. Caitlyn's honest, sexual responsiveness had blown him out of the water. He was still reeling.

He'd been more than a little disappointed to find himself alone in her bed. Even then, he'd hoped that after a rejuvenating jolt of caffeine, they would find themselves ready for another round.

But it wasn't to be.

On the surface, she had seemed perfectly normal—cheerful, even affectionate there at the end with that last kiss. So why was his gut twisting in a knot? He had a bad feeling about this, but he couldn't pinpoint the cause of his unease.

He had plenty of stuff at his own place to take care of. Grass to mow. Mulch to spread. A shed that needed a coat of paint. All day he worked himself to death trying to outrun the questions that buzzed in his brain.

At four o'clock he called her and suggested dinner and a movie. Her familiar voice was breezy and teasing. She was making great progress. She didn't really want to stop. She would see him tomorrow.

They both had full schedules on Monday, but they had agreed to meet and go back to Briley Park at four. He picked her up at work, admiring the colorful, eye-catching window of Designing Women. Caitlyn had a natural gift for creating harmony in her surroundings, and he was sure her new place would bear her mark in no time.

He leaned over and kissed her when they were seated in the car. Her lips moved under his, soft . . . giving. He was so hungry for her, he could have pulled her beneath him in the backseat and taken her then and there.

But his civilized side won out. Barely. He released her and put the car in drive.

They visited another building this time, one a bit more aesthetically pleasing. While he checked out structural details, Caitlyn jotted notes about possible inexpensive window treatments and floor coverings. The mayor was hoping that the condos, wherever they ended up being located, would be outfitted and sold using the Habitat for Humanity model . . . involving the prospective homeowners at every level. Duke thought it was a brilliant plan, and he was determined to provide as thorough an assessment as possible.

It took them an hour and a half. This building had no electricity, and it was hot, sticky work. He and Caitlyn were both dressed in business clothes, and he had hoped to take her to a nice restaurant afterward. But by the time they were finished, they were a bit worse for wear. So instead, he suggested Mary Mac's. Home-cooked food. Attire not important.

It wasn't the ambience he had hoped for to ease the conversation around to his plans for later in the evening, but he went ahead anyway.

She was eating half of his pecan pie when he leaned back in his chair and made his pitch. "Saturday night was amazing, Caitlyn. *You* were amazing. I've had a damn hard time concentrating on anything else since then."

She paused with the fork halfway to her mouth. And then she set down the bite uneaten. A half smile tilted her lips. "Yes, it was," she said quietly.

He reached across the table for her hand and stroked his

thumb across the back of it. "I was hoping you might like to re-create the magic. Tonight. With me."

A swift flash of *something* in her expressive eyes let him know instantly that she wasn't on the same page. His stomach clenched, but he kept his smile with difficulty. "What do you say, honey?"

She tugged her hand away and fussed with the napkin in her lap, placed her cutlery precisely on her plate. Her lips twisted in a cross between a grimace and an apologetic smile. "I need to talk to you about that."

Shit. Here it came. He braced himself. "I'm listening, Caitlyn."

She sighed. "I'd be lying if I said I didn't enjoy Saturday night. You really are a great guy and a wonderful lover, with or without the capital L. The sex was . . ." She trailed off, looking flustered. "Well, you know. You were there."

He managed a smile. "I hear a 'but' coming."

She nodded slowly. "The thing is, I think we're each heading in different directions. We both want different things out of life."

He frowned. "I can't say that I've ever had to give a happily-ever-after guarantee before beginning a relationship with a woman."

"And I'm not asking you to," she said earnestly. "Truly I'm not."

He wished he had a roll of antacids in his pocket, because the dinner he had just consumed was sitting like lead in his stomach. "Then what?"

She took a sip of water and sat back in silence as the waitress refilled Duke's iced tea. Then she spoke again, but it wasn't a direct answer to his question. "I suppose you know I was engaged last year."

He nodded slowly. "Yeah."

She lifted a shoulder, the movement evocative of regret and disappointment. "Then you obviously also know I ended it. I found out he was cheating on me with another woman."

He met her gaze steadily. "I'm sorry, Caitlyn. He was a fool."

She looked away briefly and then grimanced. "When I found out, he insisted it meant nothing. That I was the one he loved. I was hurt, of course, but not completely devastated. It was a salutary lesson in the long run. I think I was in love with the idea of love. I was looking forward to marriage. To being a wife. Nesting. It's what we interior designers live for." Her attempt at levity didn't erase the somber mood at the table.

He was listening intently, searching for the points in the story that applied to him.

Caitlyn went on. "I learned, though, something I had maybe known at a gut level. A lot of men simply aren't cut out to be with one woman. They want the opportunity to enjoy multiple partners. And in all fairness, I suppose there are females with the same attitude, though I don't think as many. It's not right or wrong. It's just a basic difference in the sexes."

"And you think I fall into that category?"

"You said it yourself," she said simply. "You date a lot. And you enjoy it."

"That doesn't mean I'll be doing so forever," he said stubbornly, sensing that he had lost the war without ever having a chance to fire the first shot.

Her smile was wistful. "I'm not criticizing you. I understand. I really do. Variety is fun and interesting and stimulating. But I've reached a point in my life where I'm ready to be settled. I want children and stability. Not in a dull, boring way. But in a growing, flourishing, looking-toward-the-future kind of way.

That was really my only true regret in breaking off my engagement . . . that I had lost that chance."

Her lower lip trembled for a half second, making him feel like a heel. But she went on. "And I think I wouldn't be doing myself any favors by continuing a sexual relationship with you. No matter how incredible the sex is."

He was torn between deep hurt and anger. But he clung to the anger because it was safer. "So how do you expect to find this paragon of ready-to-commit-right-now male? I haven't seen too many standing around."

His overt sarcasm made her flinch, but she recovered quickly. "I don't know. But I'll carry on with my life, and trust that he's out there somewhere. I hope you'll respect my decision with no hard feelings."

His fists were clenched beneath the table, and he wished to hell he and Caitlyn weren't in a public place. "So that's it?"

"We have to work together a little while longer," she said quietly. "I don't want there to be awkwardness between us."

He snorted. "You ask a hell of a lot."

Her eyes glistened with tears, and he wanted to break something. "Please."

His jaw clenched. "I'll respect your decision on one condition."

Her brow furrowed in confusion. "One condition?"

He nodded grimly. "You agree to give me one last night."

Four

Caitlyn glanced wildly around the restaurant, suddenly real-izing the folly of having this conversation in a public venue. The noisy chatter from nearby diners ensured privacy, since she and Duke had kept their voices lowered, but now she felt the need to flee, and she was momentarily trapped by her reluctance to create a scene. She cleared her throat. "One more night?"

His eyes were hot, his jaw granite. "Something to remem-ber me by," he said silkily.

She swallowed, caught between the proverbial rock and hard place. She wanted Duke Yancey more than she had ever wanted anything in her life. But she was trying to be strong. To be sensible. Yet here she was . . . a beginning dieter . . . ready to trash it all on the first day with a cheeseburger and a hot-fudge sundae.

Ack. Bad idea thinking of hot fudge and Duke Yancey in the same breath. She prayed fervently for a vision from heaven, a deus ex machina, a blinding light. Apparently guidance, heavenly or otherwise, was not available at the moment.

Even thinking about his proposition made her panties damp and sent her good sense on a vacation. One more night with Duke. And then cold turkey.

Was this what happened to smokers when they tried to quit? Maybe she needed the patch. A sex patch. Something with a slow release that could control her hunger for Atlanta's hot and horny bachelor. Anyone who could invent that would make millions.

Suddenly she remembered Miss Matilda's matter-of-fact advice. *Let the man be the boss.* Maybe Caitlyn owed Duke that much. She was dumping him before they'd even had a chance to get started, really. He was demanding recompense. Perhaps it would save his pride to end it this way. With him in control.

Or was this merely a ploy on his part to manipulate her with amazing sex? And if it was . . . did she care?

Despite her frantic mental gyrations, it was no contest. With a superhuman effort, she slowed her breathing, calmed her pulse, and feigned a matter-of-fact, pleasant smile. "Well, all right then. One more night."

He flatly refused to let her pick up her car where they had left it at Designing Women. Probably because he thought she might try to escape. Smart man.

He made one quick stop at a corner pharmacy/grocery. When he came back out, she didn't ask him what was in the bag, and he didn't offer.

The drive to her apartment was far too short. When the vehicle came to a halt in front of her building, she was still trying to come up with a plan to keep her heart safe while her body played Russian roulette.

Duke came around and helped her out. They hadn't said a word since they left the restaurant.

Upstairs, she hesitated in the foyer. Would he expect them to go straight to the bedroom?

He reached out a hand and brushed her cheek. "Quit looking so panicked. Let's clean up first."

She gaped at him. "You know we'd never fit in that shower. No way."

He chuckled. "I like how you're thinking, darlin'. But I was talking about the bathtub. One at a time. Go fill it up with some froufrou bubble bath stuff and get in. I'll be there in a minute."

She searched his face, seeing nothing to alarm her. But she distrusted his sudden good humor. At the restaurant she was sure she had pissed him off. Now he was all smiles and congeniality. And yet beneath the surface she sensed another man entirely.

With a sigh, she did as he asked. The porcelain tub was the old-fashioned claw-footed kind. It was stained with rust spots and age, but she planned to keep it if at all possible, because it had character, and it was far longer and roomier than the prefab tub/shower units that builders installed nowadays.

When the water was at the appropriate level and the bubbles threatened to spill out, she turned off the faucet, pulled her hair up and secured it with a rubber band, and stepped in.

She was barely decent beneath the frothy surface when Duke appeared wearing snug navy cotton briefs. She had thought the silk boxers were sexy. They didn't hold a candle to what he had on at the moment. And the cotton knit was pretty damn revealing.

Duke was hard. Really hard. And big. And long.

She swallowed a mouthful of water and choked. "Well, hey, there. Long time no see."

He chuckled, looking relaxed and about as tame as a mountain lion. "At your service, ma'am." He held a folded piece of plastic in his hand. He bent his head and put his mouth on a small valve.

Her eyebrows rose. "A blow-up doll? Really, Yancey. When I said you liked variety, I was talking about living, breathing women."

He stopped puffing long enough to give her a wry grin. "Very funny. Did anybody ever tell you you have a smart mouth?"

She blew bubbles at him. "Maybe once or twice." Now she could see that he held one of those neck pillows for lounging in the tub.

He tucked it behind her head. "Relax, honey. Let the Duke take care of you."

His words slid down her spine and settled deep inside her. If this was her last night with him, she planned to enjoy it to the final good-bye.

He knelt on the terry bath mat and soaped up a washrag. "Close your eyes, Caitlyn."

She flinched when she felt his first touch on her thigh. And then she melted into a puddle of longing when he lifted her legs one at a time and washed them thoroughly from above the knee to the ankle. He urged her forward long enough to scrub her back, moving up and down her spine until every kink was gone. When he was finished there, he slid the rag beneath the water and went to work on her breasts.

Her bones went limp, and she shuddered as his fingers, shielded by the washcloth, brushed roughly over her nipples, then skated down her cleavage and came back to soap each aching breast.

"Yancey?" Her voice was slurred.

"Hmmm?"

"I think my boobs are clean."

"Okay," he said calmly, his voice agreeable. And then he headed south.

Somewhere between her navel and the swollen folds of supersensitive flesh between her legs, he lost the washrag. When he arrived at his final destination, there was nothing but the soap and his hand.

He rubbed the bar of Ivory over her mound and trespassed a bit below. She sucked in a breath and choked on a bubble. He must have assumed she could recover on her own, because he never faltered. He soaped up every crevice, fore and aft, and then he entered her with two strong fingers.

She went rigid and lost her breath entirely. Her muscles gripped him eagerly.

But he abandoned the hot spot for a moment and soaped her belly and the curls below. "Relax, honey."

She shivered, so close to climax she wanted to beg. "How would you suggest I do that?" she panted.

The bar of soap found her clitoris and circled it lazily. "Think about your happy place."

"Oh, I'm thinking about it," she muttered. "But you're the one dancing all over it."

He laughed softly and soaped the crease where her thigh met her torso. "Have I told you how beautiful you are, Ms. Caitlyn Anderson?"

She wiggled her hips, trying to force him back to the game plan. "I can't remember at the moment."

He was leaning over the tub with both arms in the water now. "Well, it bears repeating." He gently pinched a nipple with his left hand while his right hand cupped her and then slid lower, three fingers deep.

She cried out as her release slammed into her. She felt like he possessed her everywhere at once, his magical touch playing her body like a maestro. "Yancey," she whispered his name in a plea.

He kissed her hard as he massaged the hidden spot inside her vagina. "Call me by my first name, angel, and I'll let you come again."

She couldn't think . . . couldn't breathe. She was balanced precariously on a terrifying precipice. Drugging, addictive pleasure beckoned. But if she fell, she might never recover. This was a one-shot deal. A swan song for her and the man who touched her so wickedly.

"Say it," he whispered, his lips brushing the shell of her ear.

She bit her lip, straining to fly. "Lover," she cried. "My lover."

And with one last tender caress, he sent her soaring.

She hardly remembered him scooping her out of the tub and drying her off. Her limbs felt weak and shaky, like the aftermath of the flu.

He tucked her into her robe, then held her close. She could feel the thunder of his heartbeats. He urged her toward the door. "Go wait for me in bed. I'll clean up and be with you in a second."

She shook her head stubbornly. "Not a chance." As much as she wanted to lie down and absorb what had just happened, she wanted to return the favor even more.

His gaze held hers, eroticism filling the air like steam. "Really?"

She nodded. "Of course."

He shed his underwear without ceremony and stepped into the tub. He was heavier than she was, and water slopped over the side. She threw down some towels and knelt beside him. "Put your head back and close your eyes."

He obeyed without question, and something about his silent compliance resurrected the ache between her legs. She took a breath and wet the rag without soap. Gently she washed his forehead, his nose, his cheeks. The shadow of a late-day stubble made his chin rough.

With his eyes closed, he looked younger, sweeter. And then she wanted to laugh at herself. Duke Yancey was an alpha male. Any perceived vulnerability was an illusion. He was impervious to the doubts that plagued her. If he saw something or someone he wanted, he went for it, never giving a thought to the consequences.

She admired his "damn the torpedos, full speed ahead" outlook on life, but it didn't work for her.

She wet the rag again, with soap this time, and began to clean him bit by bit. His strong neck, wide shoulders, taut collarbones. She followed the arrow of hair that led below the water, but she stopped short.

She wasn't able to lift his legs completely out of the water, but she managed to soap and rinse them well enough. She spent time on his feet, the arches and ankles and between his toes, until his jerks and protests convinced her he was ticklish.

As she slid the soapy rag over his healthy, tanned flesh, she noticed an anomaly. Instead of being relaxed and at peace, he became tighter the more she washed him. He was rigid, tensed as though resisting torture.

She soaped the rag one last time and found his penis. She couldn't see it. The water was too deep, the remaining bubbles too opaque. But she felt it, all hard, hot steel, covered in slick, velvety skin.

He cursed and struggled beneath her hands, but she

scrubbed him mercilessly, from balls to tip and back again. The sensitive skin behind his scrotum. The little slit at the head of his erection.

He trembled and jerked and flexed in her hands. In the end he resorted to begging. She liked that. She liked having the big, bad Duke Yancey at her mercy.

But a man could bear only so much. He almost flooded the bathroom when he came out of the tub with a subdued roar. Dripping wet, he snatched her to his chest and crushed her lips beneath his. His tongue fucked her mouth repeatedly. His hands grabbed her hips and plastered their bodies together, soaking her robe until it was useless.

She peeled it off frantically, needing to be closer. Before she could toss it aside, he snagged the narrow belt and without warning tied her hands at her back. She sucked in a breath, shocked and aroused.

He sat on the edge of the tub and dragged her with him to his lap. Helpless, she watched him align their bodies, and then he pulled her steadily, inexorably downward onto his bobbing erection.

The sensation of being filled was excruciating. She cried out, feeling her body stretch to accommodate him. He tipped her backward and bent to suckle her breasts, biting gently at the nipples. She clenched her legs around his thighs, trying to push him deeper still.

He took the hint. With a smile that sent little chills down her spine, he gripped her ass and shoved upward. The shock was instantaneous. She came . . . again and again . . . peak after peak of blinding sensation.

In some far corner of her mind she heard his hoarse shout and felt the rush of hot fluid deep in her body, but then her world went blank and she slumped in his arms.

She was vaguely aware of being carried back to her own bed and dried with a towel. She might have dozed for a moment. Now Duke was threading his fingers through her hair with lazy motions. The lamp in the corner, the one with the red Victorian shade, cast a modicum of illumination over their nude bodies.

She turned her head to look at him, feeling shattered and dangerously without armor. "We might have broken several laws on the books in the state of Georgia."

He touched her hip lightly. "Want to make a citizen's arrest?" His face was solemn, but little sparks danced in his eyes like lightning bugs on a hot summer night.

She sighed. "I'm thirsty." When she went to sit up, she discovered that her hands were tied to the headboard. "Yancey?" There was incredulity in her voice. "Have you always had a bondage fetish? And shouldn't that come with a warning label?"

He leaned over her on one elbow, a lock of hair falling onto his forehead. He toyed with her nipple. "I can honestly say, Ms. Anderson, that until this night, I have never before tied up a woman."

"Liar." She said it without heat.

"Honest to god. Something about you brings out my caveman instincts."

She wet her lips. "Should I be flattered?"

He pursed his lips. "Hard to say."

He grabbed a bottle of water and lifted her head so she could drink. Then he lowered her to the pillow, put the plastic container aside, and knelt beside her. "Do you object?"

She let his question roll around in her brain. "I suppose not. Unless you think I'm into pain. Which I'm not," she added hastily.

He nodded. "I think I knew that."

He reached down beside the bed and picked up a can of whipped cream.

Her eyes widened.

He chuckled. "I know. It's a cliché. But I've always wanted to try this."

She tugged uselessly at her wrists. "Don't tell me you're a whipped-topping virgin, too."

He squirted a blob of fluffy white cream into his palm, dropped the can, and rubbed his hands together. When they were coated, he massaged her breasts.

She jerked harder on her wrists. She wasn't sure she could stand this. While she was playing Houdini to no avail, he bent over her and licked away the unconventional massage lotion. His tongue was rough, and he ate at her breasts as if he were starving.

Yearning coiled in her belly, spread to her thighs, and settled low and deep in her feminine passage. Her legs moved restlessly.

He was silent now, apparently ignoring her. He went for all the usual targets . . . her navel, the hollow at the base of her throat, her begging-to-be-decorated nipples. When he raked her puckered buds with the serrated nozzle, she had her second orgasm.

And then he licked her clean from stem to stern and started all over again.

She worried about calories and sugar shock. On his behalf, of course. The shock she was experiencing was of another origin entirely.

Finally, when the wheezing aerosol sounded as if her torment might finally be coming to an end, he grasped her chin and tugged. "Open up."

When her lips separated to voice a protest, he filled her mouth with sweet, light cream. And then he proceeded to lick and suck it out.

It was amazingly carnal. Her tongue curled with his, tasting the delicious combination of sweet dessert and spicy man. He reached behind them to flick her clit. Orgasm number three.

She felt his erection bump her hip. When she could catch her breath, she pleaded with him. "Aren't we ready for the main event?"

"Not yet," he muttered. He retrieved the can and squeezed out the final tiny bit of the contents . . . right onto the end of his penis. Then he straddled her chest, lifted her head with two hands, and thrust against her lips. "One last serving."

She lapped at him with urgent strokes. Her arms were starting to ache, and she didn't care. She sucked him deep into her mouth and heard him curse. Even when he was clean, she didn't stop.

But he was onto her little plan to sabotage him. Just when things were reaching a critical stage, he withdrew and wiped a dollop of cream from the edge of her lips. His eyes were dark, his gaze so hot it threatened to incinerate her. "Well-done, my little captive."

"Do I qualify for early release?" she whispered. "I do my best work when my hands are free."

He untied her with a rough, unsteady laugh. "Then by all means . . ."

He rolled over her, supporting himself on his arms. He let the weight of his hips settle between her legs, spreading her thighs until she lay open at his mercy. "I'm going to fuck you slowly this time."

She couldn't decide if it was a warning or a promise, but it stole the air from her lungs.

He didn't allow her to look away as he entered her. Her breath caught in her throat. Their eyes locked. She had no idea what he read in hers. In his she saw hunger and determination, and although it might be wishful thinking . . . tenderness.

He moved in and out smoothly, stimulating swollen tissues that were already weeping with arousal. Her head tossed from side to side as the tide gathered. She wanted to beg for something, but the thoughts were all jumbled in her brain. Every thrust of his thick, hard penis sent shock waves battering against her overstimulated nerve endings. She couldn't breathe, much less think.

It was such a conventional position to produce such shockingly erotic responses. She felt sexual tension spiral higher and higher and higher. Her skin was tight and supersensitive. Her fingernails clawed at his back. Their bodies were hot and damp.

Deep inside her, the vulnerable woman was sobbing, recognizing even in the midst of the firestorm that no amount of strength or good sense could countermand this assault. She was lost, abandoned to the forces buffeting her.

She loved him.

Almost as if he could hear her inner voice, he dragged in a breath and pleaded with her. "Say my name, Caitlyn."

It was a demand that brooked no opposition. "Lover," she whispered, lost to reality, bound in the moment. "Lover, my lover."

Those three tiny words made him snap. He lost his steady, gentle rhythm and pounded into her, pressing against her womb, imprinting her with his essence permanently.

They came in the same instant, crying out and grasping each other to ride out the wave, falling at last, around one a.m., into a tangle of arms and legs and the welcoming embrace of sleep.

At three o'clock he took her from behind.

At five he lifted her leg over his hip and took her spoon fashion.

At seven, when the alarm went off, he was gone.

Five

Caitlyn rolled over, dry-eyed, and surveyed the room. Every last trace of Duke Yancey's presence was gone. No billfold. No cell phone. No keys.

So that was it.

She couldn't even think about what had happened. Every time her mind drew close to the events of the night before, it skittered away, as though avoiding a hot stove.

She hobbled to the bathroom and took a long shower. She didn't look at the tub because the memory conjured was too painful. Perhaps she could sell it to an antiques dealer.

By the time she got to work, her stomach had quit heaving and her hands were barely shaking anymore.

The cheerful, barely twenty-year-old college girl who helped her was bubbling with the possibility of a trip to France next month. A chance to tour the design houses in Paris.

Caitlyn responded to her enthusiasm as best she could, but she felt about eighty years old.

The knowledge that she had wrecked her life mocked her at every turn. Not only had her engagement combusted, but she'd managed to ruin anything she'd had with Duke Yancey. So what if he was short-term? What if she had indulged in a naughty, hedonistic affair with the man, and he had then moved on? Could it possibly have hurt any worse than this?

Was that the lesson he meant to teach her the night before? That women enjoyed the ride for however long it lasted, and she was a fool to give it up? Perhaps that explained why there were never any disgruntled ex-girlfriends. They were all too grateful for the experience to whine when it was over.

They were all a hell of a lot smarter than Caitlyn Anderson.

Tuesday and Wednesday she met with clients, worked on sketches and portfolios, ordered fabrics and paint. She smiled and chatted and planned and dreamed . . . for other people. Her future lay in ashes.

Even if she went crawling back, there was no guarantee he would be interested. Not after her self-righteous speech about marriage and children and picket fences. She had insulted him and hurt his pride. She was pretty sure no woman ever rejected the Duke.

They were due to meet Thursday afternoon to walk through one last building before assembling their written reports and giving them to the mayor. Caitlyn dreaded it, but her stupid heart threatened to jump out of her chest every time she thought about seeing him again.

Even Miss Matilda didn't have an answer for this one.

When Duke left Caitlyn's apartment in the wee hours of Tuesday morning, he jogged to her place of business. It was several miles.

He didn't have running shoes. He was wearing rumpled business clothes. He didn't care. He was trying to outrun his demons.

He had swiped her keys from her purse, so he drove her car back to her place, parked it in front on the street, and locked her keys inside. He knew she had an extra set. Caitlyn was organized to a fault.

Back at his own home, he showered and dressed for work, trying to keep his mind a blank. There was a great, yawning hole in his chest, and he was afraid to acknowledge its presence.

He was confused and angry, and for the life of him he couldn't think of a way he might have handled the situation any differently. Caitlyn wasn't interested in having a relationship with him. She'd spelled it out pretty clearly. She seemed to think he was some kind of Peter Pan.

Her assessment was unfair, and Duke had a feeling he was getting a bad rap based on her ex-fiancé's behavior. *Asshole.* What kind of man cheated on Caitlyn Anderson?

The thing about dating a lot of women, as Duke had, was that a guy began to figure out the qualities that made a female special. Intelligence. Humor. Caring. And when they came wrapped in a package as appealing as Caitlyn's, they were damn near irresistible.

Hell, if he'd had a little time to get used to the idea, he might have been able to sort out his feelings. But Caitlyn had cut him loose before anything deeper had been able to bloom.

He wasn't sure what he wanted. Well, that wasn't true. He wanted Caitlyn. He ached for her already. But he was still trying to bring the big picture into focus.

She was wrong to bail on him . . . on them . . . so quickly. That much he knew. He'd agreed to respect her decision, but he didn't like it. And he wasn't above using dirty tactics to win her back.

That was precisely what Monday night had been about. He wanted her to know, to feel, to remember how it was between them. That kind of heat was so rare as to be priceless. Things weren't over. Not by a long shot. But he would have to lie low and see what developed.

He wanted Caitlyn in his bed. And in some nebulous, not-quite-ready-to-hatch way, he knew he wanted more. He'd beg for another chance if he thought it would do any good. But he didn't have any particular screwup he could do penance for. Caitlyn was protesting his lifestyle in general. Who he was. What he represented. It hurt. A lot.

Curiously, the same speech from another woman wouldn't have fazed him. He'd have brushed it off, assuming they simply weren't compatible.

But he and Caitlyn had something special. He knew it in his gut. He just hoped she realized it and came back to him before he went crazy.

Thursday afternoon they met in Briley Park. He had e-mailed her and offered to pick her up. He'd received a politely worded refusal in return. Not surprising, but depressing nevertheless.

When they rendezvoused on the sad, narrow side street that was their destination, he watched her get out of her car. She was wearing a slim black skirt with a sleeveless, pale blue cotton blouse. It was another hot Atlanta afternoon, but Caitlyn looked crisp and cool.

She was wearing solid black designer sunglasses that matched her briefcase and shoes. There was nothing overtly sexy about her outfit, but he got hard at first glance and stayed that way.

There was something about her posture as she approached him that shouted her unease, but her hesitant smile was genuine. "Hello."

He bent and kissed her cheek. "Hello, yourself." He removed her sunglasses without permission and studied her face for a long minute, making her blush. "I've missed you," he said quietly.

Her hands gripped the handle of her bag. She reached for the sunglasses and replaced them, perhaps intentionally blocking out the flash of vulnerability he was sure he had seen in her eyes. She ignored his muttered sentence. He hadn't really meant to say it, but the words just popped out of his mouth.

When she didn't say anything, he sighed. "I guess we'd better get started."

The building was the most promising of the ones they had seen so far. It had actually held apartments in the not-too-distant past, and the infrastructure was intact. It was only a block and a half away from the nearby elementary school, and the units had large windows.

In the back, a smallish section of grass still remained, shaded by a couple of big trees. It wasn't difficult to imagine a few picnic tables, a basketball goal, maybe even a sandbox.

Caitlyn had her laptop with her, so when they finished, they walked a couple of blocks to a nearby Starbucks and sat down to put their ideas and numbers on paper.

He sipped his black coffee and smiled inwardly. It was a small, silly thing, but it pleased him to see how well they worked together. Their thoughts were in sync, their recommendations aligned.

Which shouldn't have surprised him, given the intuitive way her body responded to his and vice versa.

It was on the tip of his tongue to ask if he could see her again, but he resisted. It had been only three days. And he had promised. But he sure as hell was regretting that promise right now. He wanted to kidnap her and take her back to his place and spend the evening making love to her.

The thought of it made him ache. He ground his teeth together and scanned the room while Caitlyn made a few last tweaks to the document they were working on.

She looked up finally and smiled. "I'm e-mailing this to you right now. We can each look it over one last time this weekend, and then I'll print out a finished copy and take it to the mayor's office first thing Monday morning."

He nodded, still not looking at her. He was so hard, he wasn't sure he could stand up, and every second in her presence was making it worse.

The two-block walk to their cars felt like a condemned man's last stroll to the gallows. Without this project to bring them together, he had no hold on her at all.

When they were almost back to the building, Caitlyn began rummaging in her bag for something, and then frowned. "Oh, shoot. I think I left my favorite pen out back on a ledge when we were looking at the yard."

She handed him her keys. "Would you mind starting my car so it can cool off? I'll run get the pen and be right back."

She was maybe ten steps away from him when disaster struck. Without warning, a green Ford Fairlane with rusted fenders jumped the curb and headed straight for Caitlyn.

He yelled. At least, he was pretty sure the shocked cry made it out of his throat. But Caitlyn never even had time to turn her head before the car clipped her and sent her airborne.

It was the worst fear he had ever known in his life. People came out of nowhere. He felt like his legs were moving in slow motion as he ran to where she lay in a crumpled heap on the sidewalk.

Someone tapped him on the shoulder and said they were calling 911. He didn't answer. Couldn't answer.

She had landed on her side. He was terrified to touch her, but he put a finger to her wrist and checked her pulse. When he felt it, faint but unmistakable, he was light-headed with relief.

But the relief didn't last long. She had a nasty knot on the left side of her forehead, and a raw, bloody scrape went from there over her left cheekbone. Her face was deathly pale, despite the heat, and her chest rose and fell only slightly with her breathing.

He chanted her name over and over in an agonized whisper as he slid his hands gently over her body. Her arms and legs didn't appear to be broken, but the head injury could be serious. And God knew, he couldn't bear to imagine the possible internal damage.

He lifted her neck the bare minimum to slide his jacket beneath her cheek. It hurt him to see her face in contact with the rough, dirty sidewalk.

He held her hands and rubbed them gently, talking to her in a soft voice. Begging her to open her eyes and look at him. There was a loud roar in his head, and his stomach pitched and heaved.

Behind him, he was only vaguely aware of people removing the idiot driver from his car where it had tangled with a light pole. The man was drunk, and he lurched from the driver's seat with profanity and angry oaths.

Duke didn't turn around. If he had, he might have strangled the man with his bare hands.

It seemed like an eternity, but according to his watch, it was only eight minutes before the paramedics arrived. They eased him aside with professional sympathy and began examining Caitlyn. Oxygen. An IV. A careful hoist onto a board with her arms and legs immobilized, and then in seconds she was inside the ambulance roaring away from him.

How he made it to the hospital, he never knew. In the

emergency room, all his bluster made not one whit of difference. He wasn't allowed to see her. He paced, helpless. It was a crappy feeling.

She couldn't die. Not Caitlyn. Not now. Not when he had just figured out that he loved her. Fate wouldn't be so cruel. And if she didn't want him, he would live with that . . . somehow. As long as he knew she was okay. As long as he knew her quick smile and sassy tongue were back to normal.

It was forty-five minutes before a doctor appeared to speak to him. The man's face was grim.

Caitlyn was dreaming, more of a nightmare, really. She saw flashes of images . . . heard the screeching of tires, and beneath that the sound of Duke's voice.

She hurt . . . everywhere. People kept moving her and poking her and cajoling her to do things she wasn't capable of, even if she had wanted to. Which she didn't. She wanted to sleep. To forget this awful pain.

She wanted Duke. But she couldn't find him in all the confusion inside her head. . . .

When she opened her eyes some time later, the room was dim. Her body felt heavy, and she knew from the fog in her head that she was drugged.

Breathing hurt. So she tried not to do it. But apparently living meant breathing, so she was out of luck. She attempted to take stock of the situation. She knew she was in a hospital. The decorator in her winced at the unimaginative color scheme and the antiseptic odor.

She turned her head slowly. Duke sat in a chair beside her, staring straight ahead. His eyes were open, so she didn't think he was asleep.

She tried to force moisture into her dry mouth. "Duke?" It came out as a cracked whisper.

His head snapped around so quickly, she thought his neck might break.

She frowned. "You look terrible."

His face went blank for a half second, and then a rusty laugh emerged. "It's about time you came back to me." He touched her hair gently. "How do you feel?"

"Truthfully? Not so hot." She moved fretfully, gasping when pain shot through her chest. "I'm thirsty."

He put a hand on her shoulder. "Be still, honey." He picked up a cup and held it to her lips so she could drink from the bent straw. The ice water was so delicious, she whimpered. He made her stop after a few sips. "Not too much. We don't want you to get sick."

She carefully moved her arm from beneath the sheet and looked at the IV taped firmly to her hand. "Can I get rid of this?"

He smiled, but his face was gaunt and shadowed with whiskers. "Not yet." The dark smudges beneath his eyes emphasized his pallor.

She frowned. "What happened to you?"

He ran a hand through his hair, ruffling it into even worse disarray. "You don't remember?"

She squeezed her eyes shut. "We were walking. I was going to get my pen."

He shuddered. "Yeah. A drunk jumped the curb with his car and hit you."

Her mouth opened in a little O of shock. "Are you all right? Were you hurt?"

He shook his head, looking a bit sick, a trace of remembered horror in his eyes. "I was behind you. He didn't touch me. I saw it happen."

"Oh, Duke." She reached for his hand. "I'm so sorry. That must have been awful."

If he hadn't already been in love with her, he would have fallen hard in that moment. She was the one battered and bruised, and she was worrying about his well-being.

He scooted his chair closer and brought her hand to his lips. "Do you realize that today is the first time you've ever called me by my name? Duke, that is."

Her eyes widened and she blushed. "I'm sure it was the drugs talking," she said primly.

He grinned, feeling shaky and so damned grateful.

She bit her lip. "What time is it? How long have I been here?"

He rubbed her arm with a soothing motion. "It's Saturday morning. You were in a lot of pain, so they've kept you lightly sedated. Your parents have been here, but they finally took your grandmother home. She was exhausted. They're all worried about you."

She seemed to absorb that for a moment. "And you? It seems like you were wearing that shirt on Thursday."

He shrugged. "I couldn't leave." He didn't tell her that he had informed her family he would be marrying her. It might give her blood pressure a boost. And some things could wait until later.

Tears filled her eyes, and his heart clenched. "What is it, angel? What's wrong?" Seeing her upset scared the shit out of him.

Her lower lip trembled. "I was so hateful to you, but you stayed with me."

He kissed her then—he couldn't help it. A gentle brush of the lips. "You weren't hateful, honey. And where else would I be? You're my best girl." He caught her tear on his finger and wiped her cheeks. "You need to rest."

Her expression was petulant. "I've *been* resting. What's wrong with me?"

He closed his eyes for a moment, remembering how the doctor's words had put his heart in a vise. He eyed her carefully, not wanting to upset her. "You have a couple of broken ribs and a punctured lung. All of that is healing nicely, but it takes a while. Plus, you're covered with bruises and scrapes. No skimpy bikini for a few weeks, I'm afraid."

She asked for more water and a mirror. He gave her the first, but not the second. "You look beautiful, as always. Quit worrying." The contusions on her cheek and forehead would fade in a few days, but right now her beautiful face looked pretty rough.

The nurse came in to deal with several things, so he stepped outside into the hall. When he went back in, Caitlyn was asleep again.

They let her go home on Tuesday afternoon. Caitlyn was more than ready. She was tired of the noise and being awakened at night and eating bland food.

She had begged Duke to bring her a pizza or even a hamburger. But despite his careful consideration of her every need, he had held firm on that point. He refused to give her junk food. Not while her body was healing.

For some unfathomable reason, she was going home to Duke's house. And stranger still, no one in her family seemed to think that was odd. She had assumed her mom would want to deposit her in her old childhood bedroom and nurse her back to health. But both her parents showed up at the hospital prior to her release, brought her presents, kissed her, and promised they would check on her regularly.

Through it all, Duke was a quiet, steady, comforting presence. And since she didn't really want to protest the arrangement, she held her peace.

He lived in a tree-lined neighborhood just outside of the Buckhead area . . . older homes, lovingly maintained. His brick colonial was two stories, and he insisted on carrying her upstairs. Which was a good thing, because the trip home from the hospital had depleted her tiny store of energy.

Her eyes were closed before he deposited her beneath the covers of his big king-size bed.

For two days he waited on her hand and foot—meals, antibiotics, trips to the bathroom, movies to entertain her. And every night they shared his bed. Time and again she awoke to feel his big, strong arms holding her carefully as she curled into his embrace. He kissed her from time to time, but they were gentle, affectionate kisses with not a hint of passion.

It was all she could handle, but she missed his sensual caresses. And she wondered if he was caring for her out of duty, or pity, or something else.

By Thursday, a week from the accident, she was beginning to need a bit of independence. Tops on her list was a shower . . . on her own.

Duke was grumpy and concerned, but he acquiesced grudgingly. He insisted she keep the door open, and he sat in the hall the entire time. When she was finished and dried off, she capitulated and buried her pride to ask for help. Her ribs still hurt, and she was light-headed from the modest expenditure of effort.

He scooped her up and carried her back to the bedroom. Without asking, he retrieved her large-toothed comb, removed all the tangles from her hair, and used the blow dryer with rapid efficiency. She felt as though she should protest. He had done so much for her already. But she was so tired.

After yet another nap she gave herself a firm lecture. This evening they needed to talk.

Duke brought dinner up to her room on a tray every evening. Sometimes he cooked. Sometimes it was carryout. She finally got her burger . . . and her pizza. And in between he made her eat all kinds of healthy stuff.

That night after they had finished their grilled chicken and squash, prepared on the grill by Duke himself, she broached the subject of going home to her own place.

Storm clouds gathered on his face. "Don't be ridiculous. "You're weak as a baby."

She smiled gently. "Actually, I'm not. And I think having you around to pamper me is not really a great incentive to get back on my feet. Why don't we see what the doctor says tomorrow?"

They left it at that, but she could tell from his face that he didn't like it.

She had misjudged Duke Yancey badly. He was neither selfish nor immature. And at the first opportunity she was going to burn that stupid etiquette book. Men were far more complex than Miss Matilda gave them credit for.

The next morning she dressed carefully and insisted on walking down the stairs under her own steam. She had hoped to have lunch out at one of her favorite restaurants, but by the time her doctor's appointment was concluded, she was flagging. Duke took her to his house and fixed them each a Reuben sandwich.

She ate half of hers and picked at the rest. Duke seemed restless, and she wondered if she was the cause. She shoved her plate aside and stared at him. "You haven't been to work in over a week."

He shrugged, his expression guarded. "I have good people on my payroll. They're taking care of things."

"The doctor said it's perfectly fine for me to stay by myself. I'm not taking pain medication anymore. It's time, Duke. I don't know how I'll ever be able to repay you for all you've done for me."

His eyes narrowed. "Do you really want to know?"

She cocked her head in confusion. "Of course."

"Don't leave my house." He said it flatly, without inflection. But something in his eyes seemed to be saying far more than his terse words.

She tried to smile. "I'm not your responsibility."

"No, you're not. You're the woman I'm in love with."

The room spun dizzily, and she felt herself slide off the stool.

He caught her with a curse before she hit the ground. He strode to the living room, settled into an overstuffed leather chair, and cuddled her in his lap.

When her vision cleared and she could think again, she stared up at his grim face. "What did you say?" she asked faintly.

He grimaced. "I'm not sure I should repeat it. I seem to have an adverse effect on your recovery."

"Please."

He played with her hair absently, his gaze hungry on her face. It was the first time since her accident that he had allowed her to see his passion. His need. And it took her breath away.

She touched his chin, stroked his neck. "Please, Duke." She waited impatiently.

He sighed. "I love you, Caitlyn. With all the bells and whistles. I was pretty much there already, but when you decided to scare the hell out of me by getting hit by a car, there was no question."

"It wasn't exactly my fault."

"Doesn't matter. My life flashed before my eyes."

"I thought that was only when you were dying."

"Not my past life. My future. With you. And those two-point-five kids."

Her jaw went slack, and that shuddery, faint feeling assaulted her again.

He shook her gently. "Goddamn it, Caitlyn. Don't you dare pass out on me again."

She sucked in several breaths of much-needed air and tried to focus. "Are you sure?"

He laughed roughly. "Oh, yeah. You hit me right between the eyes. I'm a goner."

"And you're okay with that?" God, it hurt to ask that question.

This time his smile was blinding. He touched her mouth with his fingertips. "I wouldn't have it any other way." Then a wry grin tilted his lips. "The thing is, honey, all those women you were so concerned about served a very important purpose."

"What do you mean?" she asked sulkily, incredulous that he was bringing up his past harem at this particularly sensitive moment.

He bent to kiss her, sliding his tongue gently into her mouth and making her breathless again. "They made it possible for me to know the real thing when it showed up on my doorstep. I love you, Caitlyn, heart and soul. I love your amazing body and your sharp wit and your kindness. I love your stubbornness and your ambition. And I love your eye for beauty."

He teased her nipple through her blouse. "I need you, honey. Don't leave. Please."

She was crying, and she hated emotional tears. She was a damned watering pot these days. She sniffed and wiped her face with the back of her hand. "I love you, too, you big, bossy man. I thought I had you all figured out, but you were someone else entirely. You're the man of my dreams, and I don't deserve you."

He feigned shock. "Who is this sweet, agreeable woman? And what have you done with my Caitlyn?"

She punched his arm. "Very funny. Do you think you could make love to me now?"

Something beneath her bottom flexed, and she giggled.

But Duke looked torn. "We shouldn't. I might hurt you."

"We'll be very careful," she whispered. "I promise."

"You'll have to be on top," he muttered, his cheekbones flushed and his eyes glazed with heat.

He eased them both to the soft carpet and undressed her carefully. She wanted to return the favor, but he brushed her hands away. When they were both nude, he sprawled on his back. The sight of him like that threatened to make her feel faint again, but she wasn't about to miss this.

Carefully, wincing only slightly when her ribs reminded her to be gentle with them, she lowered herself onto his erection.

Duke supported her with his hands at her waist. He searched her face. "Are you okay? Does it hurt?"

She exhaled. "It feels wonderful."

She tried to ride him, but she didn't have the strength. So he took over, pumping his hips and thrusting upward until she groaned.

He froze. "Caitlyn?"

"Don't stop," she commanded raggedly.

He moved again, slowly, gauging her reaction. She squeezed him with her inner muscles and heard him gasp. He increased the tempo, feeling her come apart in his arms, and then finding his own release.

She couldn't lie forward on his chest, so he disengaged their bodies and picked her up gently to carry her upstairs. When they were cuddled in each other's arms in his big, soft bed, he kissed the top of her head. "Did I remember to propose?"

She snorted. "I wondered when you were going to get around to that."

"Well, the occasion demands a ring, or so I've been told. And I haven't had much time for shopping."

"I'm free this afternoon."

"Patience, my love. I'd prefer you not pass out in the middle of the jewelry store."

"Oh, wow. Is it going to be *that* big?"

He slapped her butt lightly, laughing softly. "Brat."

She licked his nearest nipple. "Stud."

And as they settled in for a nap, Miss Matilda smiled and crossed another one off her list.

About the Author

Janice Maynard came to writing early in life. When her short story "The Princess and the Robbers" won a red ribbon in her third-grade school arts fair, Janice was hooked. Since then, she has sold numerous books and novellas. She holds a BA from Emory & Henry College and an MA from East Tennessee State University. In 2002, Janice left a fifteen-year career as an elementary teacher to pursue writing full-time. *Suite Fantasy*, her first release for NAL, hit number eight on the Barnes & Noble trade romance list.

Janice lives with her husband of thirty-one years in beautiful East Tennessee, and they have two grown daughters who make them proud. She can be reached via e-mail at JESM13@ aol.com.